The House Beautiful

ALSO BY ALLISON BURNETT

Christopher

The House Beautiful

A NOVEL OF HIGH IDEALS, LOW MORALS, AND LOWER RENT

ALLISON BURNETT

CARROLL & GRAF PUBLISHERS
NEW YORK

THE HOUSE BEAUTIFUL
A Novel of High Ideals, Low Morals, and Lower Rent

Carroll & Graf Publishers
An Imprint of Avalon Publishing Group, Inc.
245 West 17th Street, 11th Floor
New York, NY 10011

AVALON
publishing group incorporated

Copyright © 2006 by Allison Burnett

All rights reserved. No part of this book may be reproduced in whole or in part without written permission from the publisher, except by reviewers who may quote brief excerpts in connection with a review in a newspaper, magazine, or electronic publication; nor may any part of this book be reproduced, stored in a retrieval system, or transmitted in any form or by any means electronic, mechanical, photocopying, recording, or other, without written permission from the publisher.

ISBN-13: 978-0-7394-7825-7

Book design by Bettina Wilhelm

Printed in the United States of America
Distributed by Publishers Group West

For Allison Lee Burnett

The greenhorn is the ultimate victor in everything; it is he that gets the most out of life. . . . All doors will fly open to him who has a mildness more defiant than mere courage. The whole is unerringly expressed in one fortunate phrase—he will be always "taken in." To be taken in everywhere is to see the inside of everything. It is the hospitality of circumstance. With torches and trumpets, like a guest, the greenhorn is taken in by Life. And the sceptic is cast out by it.

—G. K. Chesterton

Thus, great with child to speak, and helpless in my throes,
Biting my truant pen, beating myself for spite—
"Fool," said my Muse to me, "look in thy heart and write."

—Sir Philip Sidney

Greeting

.

It is, indeed, a rare gift that, at the age when most men are welcoming retirement with open, flabby arms, I have at last found my true calling: I am a novelist. Sadly, some would disagree. I know this because within moments of the publication of my debut novel, *Christopher,* they attacked me with ruthless vigor. Now, I am well aware that the longevity of one's fame depends as much on abuse as it does on praise (Fame is a shuttlecock, which to stay aloft must be struck at both ends), but it seemed that the entire critical community of Manhattan—a hideous assortment of bawling and blowing swellheads, hopeless waste-goods, unctuous award-seekers, fallow fancy boys, illiterate drones, crawling freelancers, Ivy League anti-sexers, righteous marplots, coy, cringing compro-misers, suicidal bookworms, blind men, pimpled men, fat men, stinky men, the lousy combings and born idol-smashers of the world—hurled at me every sort of nasty criticism.

I was called a "plagiarist," a "lunatic," a "homeless man's Rabelais," and "Nabokov on poppers." A local East Side giveaway newspaper, a favorite among dying pensioners, called my Prose of

Fire "fatuous and overripe." They claimed I was "Wilde without the wit" and that my eponymous hero was not worth a sane man's devotion or even the common reader's attention. They despised my particularity in times and dates. A librarian's fishwrapper, with a circulation upward of seven, even had the gall to accuse me of unreliability, claiming that I had simply "made it all up." My groundbreaking use of the virtually omniscient first-person narrator they labeled "arrogant monkeyshine." Another blabsheet, printed on pink toilet tissue, clearly catering to the homosexualists who cluster like Dickens fans of yore along the docks of the West Side, labeled me a "self-loathing grotesque." They charged that I, like some great lump of undigested cheddar, had "set back the Movement." The other prigs who deigned to review my book dwelled mostly on how dull it was.

I would love to report that I hovered above the fray, secure in my knowledge that it was not for the critics of this generation that I had written my life-affirming tale but for the schoolboys of the next, yet, truth be told, I was wounded. Although I knew these criticisms were quite simply wrong, born of envy more than anything else, and while on the surface I bore them stoically enough, inwardly I mewled like a nettled kitten. Here I had given all of which I was capable, consuming myself like a very meteor to light the earth, and this was how my epoch had repaid me? It was enough to make a proud man set down his ballpoint and fags and turn on the TV. And I almost did—especially when sales of *Christopher* stalled in the high four figures.

Then the tide turned.

I began to receive letters, almost three dozen in all, mostly from old bachelors, thanking me for the golden light my novel had shed on their dismal, untenable lives. These communications came from every corner of the city. I read them again and again, struggling to make out the words through a scrim of my own grateful tears. It would be immodest for me to repeat what they said, but their outpourings of praise were as lavish as they were sincere. My intuition had been confirmed! My labor had *not* been in vain. The love that I felt for my protagonist and the value that I had placed on his struggle were not aberrations. I was not a freak. I was not alone. I enjoyed a readership.

Renewed! Recreated! I rose from my queen, threw on my best tweed, and trotted off to the local stationers, where I picked up a brand-new three-pack of legal pads and a carton of generic cigarettes. Then I hurried home and plopped down at my desk. The window admitted a cool, fresh breeze. From the next room could be heard the cozy clicking of computer keys, and from the basement the muffled glissando of a trombone. Gazing down at the street, I freed my fancy. Like a wind-blessed balloon, it drifted up and away, gliding over our recent troubles with our Cousins of the Sands, to more innocent times. I was in search of a second tale to make deathless in prose—one to instruct the young, delight the old, correct the town, and castigate the age. An hour passed. My hips and buttocks were numb in the hard chair. An open bottle of too-new Chianti wheezed at my side. I felt dizzy and afraid. Just as I was about to give up, it came to me, like a descending angel: I would tell of a single summer in The House Beautiful. Not just any summer, but the sweet, sweltering season that brought me Adrian—a lad every bit as pretty and slim-hipped as Christopher, but even more sympathetic. A boy whose anguish reaffirmed for me the eternal truth that the life of the artist is the only life worth living.

— B. K. Troop

We Spend More Money
on Toilet Seats

It was June 16, 1989, the third anniversary of the death of my ex-landlady and dearest pal, Sasha Buchwitz. Sasha had gone to her reward as the result of a stroke suffered during a much-needed round of electro-convulsive therapy. While in the hours following the vascular accident the prognosis had been hopeful, by morning it had all turned grim. Sasha, ever on the plump side, began to shed girth at an alarming rate, dipping for the first time since her salad days at New York University below 200 pounds. Her prodigious powers of speech did not return. Her left arm and left leg remained as lank as poached string.

As she had no surviving family and no other friends, it fell on me alone to give comfort. Day after day, I squatted at her bedside, stroking, humming, swabbing, adoring. My saintly ministrations recalled those of Mr. Walt Whitman at the cot-sides of his beloved soldier-boys. Although Sasha rarely moved a muscle, I entertained her with spirited readings from her vast trove of detective fiction, many of whose volumes still carried midcentury library slips on their inflaps. For a while it seemed that I had the healing touch. Her color deepened, and one afternoon, in reply to one of my count-less *bons mots*, she even managed something terrible that resembled a smile. Then, on Bloomsday morning, 1986, her breathing became labored and I heard (or imagined I did) the tap-tap-tap of the Deathwatch. A few hours later as, reading aloud, I hastened toward the predictable climax of an Agatha Christie, she gasped, coughed, and heaped. I screamed for the bearded Bengali nurse. Because I had screamed for her so often, it was a full eight minutes before she ambled in, carrying a pineapple Popsicle, and by that time Sasha's great, pure heart was still. Three days later, she was laid to rest in a discount bone orchard in Queens. A stooped rabbi and I were the only witnesses. Before the unfinished pine box was lowered into the earth, I managed (in the manner of the pagans) to jam a silver dollar inside, so that she might pay her fare.

In the weeks of mourning that followed, the last thing on my mind was whether or not I would be named in her will. In fact, there was absolutely nothing on my mind, for I had come apart at the threads, shedding a Nile of tears, not only for the death of my friend but for every other loss I had sustained during my half-century on earth. The most recent was the passing, six months earlier, of dear, old Wolf Zeller, my mentor, who met his maker on the corner of Fifty-fifth Street and Eighth Avenue, felled by a tardy bicycle messenger. Imagine, then, my surprise, when Sasha's attorney called to inform me that I had been named sole beneficiary of her estate, which, after all her debts had been paid, came to more than three thousand dollars in cash and sole ownership of her exquisite turn-of-the-century brownstone and all of its contents.

At first I was overjoyed, because there were few places on earth where I would rather have lived, but then, late one night, reviewing all relevant documents and crunching every vital number, I realized that the tax and utility bills alone were far more than my subsistence trust and meager government check could manage. And this was not even taking into account the hefty mortgage payment. Alas, it was true. Although this was Sasha's ancestral home, purchased decades before by her grandparents when they arrived on our shores after fleeing a less-than-efficient *pogrom,* Sasha had, at some point in the 1970s, following a demented spending spree, borrowed on the place. It was in hock up to its eaves. I would have to sell. There were no two ways about it, and it broke my heart. It would have broken Sasha's as well.

The rising sun found me on the red vinyl of my beloved Parnassus Diner, rocking anxiously, like an unchosen orphan. My sole surviving friend, Ms. Cassandra Apopardoumenos, an expert waitress and amateur sorceress, strolled over to condole.

"Boy trouble?" she croaked, pulling her pencil from behind her fuzzy ear.

It was a reasonable assumption. Since the disappearance of Christopher from my life, I had embarked on a series of ill-advised erotic adventures, each surpassing the last in futility and devastation. I shook my head, choked back my snot, and told her all. I ended by comparing the selling of Sasha's cherished home to the selling of her very carcass to a glue-and-wig factory.

Cassandra was not only well versed in signs, charms, divinations, and other quaint prospects of love, but she was also pretty shrewd with a drachma. Her witchy eyes twirled like pinwheels as she pondered the fiscal matter, then she snapped her fingers.

"Rent out rooms!" she said.

By God, she was right.

In no time at all, I had dismantled my *Bloomsbury Aesthetic* and sold it on the sidewalk outside my building. (It did not bring in a tenth of what it was worth.) Then I set to prowling the neighborhood for cardboard boxes in which to transport my vast antiquarian library. The morning probate closed, I vaulted from my bed, astir with cockeyed optimism. I brewed some coffee for the removalists and taped shut the last few boxes. By day's end, I was settled into my new digs. Rather, my *old* digs. I had, after all, lived in Sasha's brownstone for twenty-three years. But I was no longer the base-ment dweller; now I ruled the master suite. After using my own two mitts to apply to the most important rooms a fresh coat of paint (canary on the walls and ceilings; parchment on the trim), I tore apart a brown paper bag. I scrawled in majuscules the words, "ROOMS FOR RENT," and, beneath that, the word "CHEAP!" and, beneath that, my new phone number. I taped it to the front window, and in no time the phone began to ring.

The rooms I had to let (five in all), I priced at a mere $200 a month. I did this not because I am foolish, but because, ever devoted to Apollo, I had made up my mind to rent them only to artists. The thought of living with anyone else depressed me to no end. What on earth would there be to talk about? Plus, my experience with Christopher had taught me that my chief calling was to serve as mentor, if not muse, to those artists most in need: the young, struggling, and unhappy. I knew the word "cheap" would draw that particular demographic like fleas to the Irish, and I was right. From the large pool of young, strug-gling, and unhappy applicants, I chose the lucky few based on a long list of other more narrow qualifications: charm, beauty, talent, and, most important, cultural and religious similarity to myself.

Before I am accused of bigotry (another slander hurled at my head by a knee-jerk-Judy after the publication of my first novel), let me remind you that I have always been politically liberal to the extreme. I was, until his death, a lifelong supporter of Mr. Gus Hall, a fire-breathing Commie, and every year I dig deep in sup-port of a charity that feeds hot lunches to bloated foreign infants. Furthermore, in the bedroom, my tastes have always tended toward the exotic; my sexual résumé reads like a Red Cross drop sheet. But cohabitation is a different thing altogether. If I am forced into close quarters with my own species, I am most com-fortable with those who most closely resemble myself. For this reason, I admit into my home only English-speaking pagans. I'm sorry, but that's just the way it is.

In terms of sexual preference, I naturally favor young, pretty male homosexualists, but I have learned from bitter experience that they are hard to come by and even harder to keep. Lesbians, on the other hand, are easy to find and keep, but for some reason they do not like me. I do not know why. Perhaps it has something to do with their bitter natures.

But I digress.

It was June 16, 1989, the third anniversary of Sasha's death. As though in her honor, the city was enjoying a rare day of cool breezes, and the smell of trash and urine was unusually slight. At the precise moment that I dropped my feet to the parquet floor, a mere twenty blocks away the hero of our tale, young Adrian, was dropping his heavy suitcase to the marble floor of the Grand Central Terminal. In his other hand, he carried a loaded trash bag. He had heard about the station's ceiling, but he saw it now for the first time and his face softened with reverence. It was not only the spidery beauty of its constellations that touched him; it was also what it told him: at last he was in New York City. The Big Apple. It didn't matter anymore that his suit was old and ill-fitting or that he carried a bulging trash bag; what mattered was that he was alone. After the swarm of relatives and guests at his father's funeral, after the days spent with his grandmother, comforting her, solitude was what he craved most. And where better to be alone than Manhattan? He had no friends here. No one even knew his name. No one pitied him. He tottered past an information booth, listing toward the weight of his suitcase, and turned for a last, fond look at the ceiling's stars, as though they were the back of a departing friend. His shoulders already ached when he reached the top of the ramp. Ahead, the glare of Forty-second Street was visible through a row of filmy glass doors. To his right lay the men's room. He stopped. His bladder wailed for relief.

(To those critics, rank literalists all, who are already objecting to my use, once again, of the first-person virtually omniscient voice, let me remind you that I am not only highly intuitive, often able to glean with little more than a glance the innermost thoughts and feelings of others, but also extremely curious. There is very little that goes on in the hearts and souls and beds of my lodgers that I do not eventually ferret out. I achieve this not only through direct interrogation but by every other available means, including, but not limited to, eavesdropping, rummaging, pinching, and peeping. While such behavior is certainly unethical, I justify it in two ways: first, ethics are a luxury of the secure, and, second, I am a novelist.)

At the instant that Adrian made his way into the men's room of the Grand Central Terminal, a floor above me in The House Beautiful, Carl Alan Dealey lay on his stomach, a cigarette hanging from his thin Protestant lips. His freckled arms lazed out the window. Below him was my backyard garden—the Vale of Health, I call it—a chaos of crumbling walkways sunk into clusters of rare wildflowers. Across the way stood the rear of a tenement apartment building from whose windows shot an occasional wink of midday sun.

Carl, thirty now, losing, daily, both muscle tone and hair, dreaded another summer in the city: baking garbage, human stink, subways like speeding coffins, midnight sirens, damp, dirty morning sheets wrung tight as tourniquets. Worst of all was the telephone. It slept at his side now. The only person who knew its secret number was his talent agent. The last time it had jangled, a month before, it had brought him news of an audition—for a honey commercial in which, had he not overslept, he might very well have been cast as a bumblebee. Sadly, this ebony abomination was the center of his existence. There was not a moment when his conscious or unconscious mind was not on bended knee, praying that it would ring. During the year it rarely did; during the summer, it *never* did. How on earth would he distract himself until fall? His answer came when his eyes landed on a window across the way. It was wide-open and bore no blind. For a long time now the flat inside had been empty, but now he spied a television, a hanging plant, a Renoir print, a frilly lamp, and a fancy antique vanity. His reverie was abruptly struck by the sound of footsteps outside his door. Who could it be? Was it some new lodger?

(A logical assumption. After all, the room down the hall from his had been empty for weeks—ever since Alexander Kecalek, a film director from suburban Chicago, had suffered a *grand mal* seizure during a cocaine binge and been whisked home to the tough-loving embrace of his blue-collar parents.)

The door opened before Carl could yell, "Go away!" and the face of a young woman appeared. She was tiny, with owlish blue eyes, and blond hair yanked into pigtails. Her long johns were Pollocked with paint.

"You're up," she said, her voice soft and shy.

"Ever heard of knocking?" Carl snapped. "Can't you see I'm busy?"

Immune to sarcasm, Miranda Buchner scanned the filthy disarray of Carl's room to see what he was busy with. Nothing suggested itself. Maybe it was his acting. Maybe that's how actors did it—they memorized all those lines while looking out the window.

"An audition?" she asked hopefully.

"Yeah, I'm workin' on a monologue for the unemployment people. What the hell do you want?"

"I'm out of Goldenrod. My dad's check is late. Can I borrow ten bucks?"

The thespian turned away and sucked smoke. Miranda never popped in unless she wanted something. And it was never sex. Not that he would have wanted it, anyway. It would be like defiling a broom. Maybe worse.

"It's on the dresser," he sighed wearily.

As she made for his wallet, Carl grumbled, "By the way, I'm quittin' show business. I'm gonna have a real life. You oughta follow my lead. Quit the paintin' business."

She chuckled, snatched the cash, and shut the door. Carl did not care that she thought he was ridiculous; he had more important things to worry about—like the window across the way. Who was this new tenant? When would she return? And was she pretty enough to warrant such a fancy vanity? He took in the last, best smoke from his cigarette and flicked the tawny filter into the Vale of Health. What would he do until she got home? He stared at the telephone. It did not ring. He stared longer. Piece of shit. Maybe he ought to practice his art. Act. Kill time acting. Like a dog yearning to be scratched, he jutted his chin onto the sill. He parted his dry lips and whispered, "O that this too too sullied flesh would melt, thaw and resolve itself into a dew!" It was a heartfelt reading, but, as usual, nothing. No applause.

In the corner of the men's room, a scabby hoochhound stood next to a plastic pail, wailing in the minor key about a woman who had left him. One by one, local commuters, inured to such aesthetic insults, walked to and fro without so much as a glance in his direction, but Adrian winced with disgust. Back home in Iowa, such a fellow would never be allowed to walk the streets. Adrian quickly chose a urinal and planted his brown work boots on the sticky floor. To his right, a bald man, unable to urinate, gently teased his manhood, as though coaxing petrol from a siphon. Adrian stared straight ahead into the grimy tile where some clever urchin had scrawled the words, "Pee Here Now." Yes, that was the goal, but first he needed to take his mind off the stink of ammonia and the vagrant's ugly singing.

Thoughts of water might help. Adrian pictured the St. John River in northern Maine. He had swum there just a week before, the morning of his father's funeral. The current was so strong that had he wanted to swim straight across to Canada he would have had to dive in a quarter-mile upstream. The water was clear and numbing-cold. An island of shrubs bent in the breeze in front of him. His father had claimed that Indian treasure was buried at its southern tip. Adrian's little buttocks tensed. The vagrant was not singing anymore, just growling and whooping. A door slammed behind him. A toilet seat fell. Someone emptied a pound of giblets into a deep well—at least that's what it sounded like. Adrian exhaled heavily and looked down. Nothing.

Different water. His grandmother's house in the Hudson Valley. The brook in back swirled, calmed, and trickled between green rocks—a demi-paradise for wheeling bugs and darting flies. That very morning, he had stood on its shady brink, listening to the dunking call of bullfrogs lying camouflaged in the cool moss, and told his grandmother for the tenth time about the funeral of her son. She was nursing a broken hip and a crumbling mind and had not made the trip.

Success! A fast, happy stream of gold. When Adrian was finished peeing, he glanced away and was surprised to see that the bald man was still at his side, only he was jerking frantically now. Adrian jumped away, as though the man were clutching a hamster or a rat. He stifled a cry of fear and turned to see who else had noticed. No one. Red-faced and sweating, Adrian hauled his bags to the exit and wondered if this sort of thing was an everyday occurrence in New York City. Could life here actually be so foul and depraved?

(The answer, of course, was yes.)

Twenty minutes later, Adrian emerged from a taxicab, dragging his bags. The place was not at all what he had expected. Its reddish facade was badly weathered. Shutters tilted off their hinges. The windows were dirty. A hand-painted wooden placard nailed to the peeling front door read "The House Beautiful." What did it mean? Was it a joke? The place seemed desperate more than anything else. Maybe he shouldn't have come. Then he saw, scrawled on a piece of paper in the window, the words "ROOM FOR RENT! CHEAP!" and he smiled for the first time since the funeral.

Because I was busy in the kitchen unscrewing a bottle of stormy Chablis (hail of raw fennel, drizzle of butterscotch) I did not hear Adrian's first shy knock, but I did hear the second. I strode angrily through the front room, certain that it was a door-to-door solicitor to whom I would be more than happy to give a heaping helping of my outraged mind. Imagine my delight when I peeked out and saw instead a tiny lad with delicate bones, a candid nose, a wide mouth, and gorgeous rust-colored hair (rare on one unfreckled). His big hazel eyes were dreamy with depression and intelligence. He looked like someone, but I wasn't sure whom. I flung open the door and flashed a smile, which, now that I paid regular visits to a Pakistani sadist, was no longer oyster-gray, but the color of the spring's first daffodils.

"Well, hello," I said.

"Mr. Troop?" he asked cautiously, his voice soft, gentle, and low—an excellent thing in a boy.

I was suddenly breathless. It hit me whom he resembled. He was the spitting image of Johnny Keats, my favorite Romantic poet. How marvelous.

"Yes?" I replied.

"You rent rooms?" He gestured with his little head toward the sign.

"I most certainly do. Please come in."

I stepped aside and the little lad slithered past, grazing my knees with his trash bag. I heaved a deep sniff of him. As I had suspected, his hair was scented with innocence. I leaned out for a quick look up and down the street. No, this was not a practical joke. The Gods had actually sent me a gift. And what an improvement! While Alexander Kecalek had been a model lodger and a gifted film-maker (à la Lubitsch), toward the end of his stay, he had been rendered, by his coke habit, sweaty and chubby.

I laid a hand on the boy's shoulder. "Come this way, boy. Who told you about me?"

"Pardon?"

"I doubt you were merely passing by with your suitcase and trash bag. Who referred you?" My tone was brusque, all business. There would be plenty of time for fun and games later. "Who told you about my colony?"

"Ummm . . . Jim. Jim did."

"Jim who?" I dropped into the leather armchair that had been Sasha's throne. In her honor, I refused to replace it, even though the seat was cracked and required taping.

The lad settled on the sofa, from whose tired springs rose a puff of Edwardian dust. "I'm not sure what his last name was. I met him at a party. He used to live here. Or . . . or maybe his friend did."

My brow furrowed for an instant, then I pointed. "Jim Fuchs!"

He nervously cracked a knuckle. "That's right. He gave me your address. He said you might have a room to rent."

"A talented boy, Jim was, but so sloppy. He had a tail and everywhere he went it trailed clay."

"A tail?"

"Are you a sculptor, too?" I asked with sudden worry.

"Oh, no. No, I'm—"

"Thank God. The way they mix their mud is like an infant playing with its own diaper-dirt. *Nostalgie de la boue,* the frogs call it. Some enterprising young Freudian ought to write a thesis." He smiled warmly. Good start. I demand that all my lodgers appreciate my wit, or at least pretend to. I crossed one knee over the other and fumbled for a cigarette. "I only rent to artists, you know. Jim must have told you. And they must be young, struggling, and desperately unhappy."

Adrian's eyes ricocheted away. He was about to crack the knuckles of his other hand, but I threw him a warning look, and he thought better of it.

15

"Artists are treated dreadfully in this country," I resumed. (This was not the first time I had delivered the speech, but you would never have known it. It seemed plucked from the very air.) "We spend more money on toilet seats for our submarines than we do on the arts. That's why artists are all I allow to take refuge here." I snapped open Sasha's trim gold lighter and spoke as I torched up. "And I don't just admit anyone who happens to own a tuba or a paintbrush. My tenants are all exceptional. No dilettantes, no *poseurs,* and definitely no nihilists—if you can't say 'yea' in your work, don't say anything at all." I exhaled a plume of smoke. "Don't you agree?"

He smiled and nodded wholeheartedly. Lord, he was a swooner, his teeth straight and white. I imagined him kissing me. Then I remembered with a start that I was already spoken for. I had recently met a young man to whom I had pledged sexual fidelity—a first for me. So far, the experiment had been in progress a full six days and I had never felt more relaxed. Why jeopardize it now? It struck me that perhaps the Gods had sent me Adrian not as a gift but as a test. They have a tendency to do that, sly buggers. No sooner do you feel the crisp click of your heel on the moral high ground than they send down a distraction, some smooth-skinned dryad standing nude in a distant olive grove, waving a floppy hand, crying out, "Yoo-hoo, handsome! Over here!"

"Excellent." I patted both arms of my chair and jumped to my feet. "I'll be right back." I thundered up the steps, which seemed to crack as I hit them. My guts seized. I lost breath as I lunged for the toilet.

Left alone, Adrian ventured a look around. But for the paint job, the room was just the way Sasha had left it. The antique furniture was stout, squat, dark. Oil paintings of the Ashcan School hung too low on the walls. The air was dusty, as though years had passed since sunlight had been allowed to enter. Adrian noticed on my mantel, amidst a slew of quaint doodads, gewgaws, and whatnots, a dozen snapshots, each housed in a sterling frame. He was holding one of the photographs when I burst back in.

"So sorry," I said, out of breath, having just voided my bowels. Recently this had become necessary at the most inopportune times; the embarrassment it caused me was the cardinal reason I had pledged loyalty to my new boyfriend after just a few nights together.

"Oh, you enjoy photography?" I asked.

He smiled a bit sadly. "Yeah."

"In my old digs, I had no room for them, but now that I own a mantel I display them proudly. There they are, boy. The visual record of a rich and varied life." I walked over and prodded Adrian's garbage bag with my foot. "Where are you coming from, if you don't mind my asking?"

"Maine."

"What a small world. The man in that picture you're holding is from Maine."

"Really? That's weird. Who is he?"

"I'd rather not say. Here. Let me dust that off." I dragged a sleeve across the top of the frame.

He took a closer look at the man's sensitive face. "I'm not from Maine myself. My father was. I just got back from his funeral."

"Oh, I'm sorry to hear that," I said. "My father died, too."

"I know."

"You do?"

"Well, you've got so many pictures of him."

"You could tell this was my father? How?"

"You have the same smile."

"That's odd. I was adopted. He molested me until I was nine."

Adrian gulped. I had revealed too much. I plopped back in my chair and asked about his mother.

"She's dead, too," he said. "Of cancer. My senior year in high school."

So the lad was an orphan. Just like Keats. The ants multiplied in my pants, but I stayed on point.

"And what, boy, is your name?" I asked.

"Adrian," he said. "Adrian Malloy." He cracked another knuckle.

"Stop doing that!" I screamed. He looked as though he might burst into tears, so I fell friendly: "Boy, let me be frank. I'd like you to live here. The rent is only two hundred dollars a month. All I ask is that you give away or put to sleep any pets you might have, keep your room free of dust mites, and work very, very hard. I expect all my lodgers to produce." He could barely conceal his relief. "But I do have two final questions. Do you believe in many gods?"

Surprised, he thought for a long time.

"I'm not sure," he said, finally.

"Good enough. Second, what is your art? I like to keep a balance." He began to answer, but I stupidly cut him off. "No, let me guess. You're an actor." He looked surprised, even a bit flattered. "No? Well, you could be. You're pretty enough. Oh, I know. You're a painter." He began to answer, but I cut him off again. "No, no, your fingernails are too clean. I've got it. You're a poet. A lyric poet!"

He smiled and nodded.

Why hadn't I trusted the obvious? I nearly levitated. The modest lad looked down, his face prickling with self-consciousness.

On the second floor there was a room so tiny that it was all but unusable. A few days after I had filled my home with its first batch of lodgers, I answered the bell to find standing in the pouring rain a young woman of about twenty-eight, with fiery red hair. She shivered under a soaked parasol, her cotton dress pasted indecently to every curve of her tall, well-formed body. Her face was homely in a striking, gorgeous way. Her name was Louise D'Aprix and she was a lady novelist, she said, speaking very quickly, her eyes a bit bugged. I immediately diagnosed her as suffering from an acute manic disorder. Like all pure products of America, the girl had gone mad. I plucked her from the deluge, handed her a tea towel, and assured her that although there was nothing I loved more than helping young, hopeless artists in distress, I really had nothing available at the moment, only a virtual closet.

"I'll take it," she said, toweling her sturdy legs.

"But you'll feel like you've been put in storage," I said. "Like an old trunk."

"That's what I want. I just went off my medication. I want to be *stored.*"

As one who had long ago set aside all pharmaceuticals in favor of "letting it all hang out," I was impressed.

"Anyway, I *prefer* small rooms," she explained. "They make my ideas seem large."

"But you won't even have space for a desk."

"I write in bed."

Against my better judgment, I showed her the closet.

When she saw it, she cried, "Home, sweet home!"

A deal was struck, and since that day almost three years before, hardly a minute had passed when Louise's manual typewriter could not be heard clicking and clacking behind her door—except, of course, during the hours she slept, which, due to her unipolar afflic-tion, were alarmingly few. Louise was the only one of that first batch of lodgers who remained today. The rest had fled within just a few weeks or months, unable to live up to the exacting standards I had set for them, both as artists and as human beings.

As Adrian and I neared Louise's door that day, she knew without opening it that a new tenant was moving in and that he was male and pretty. She knew because my voice was bright and musical and I walked on the balls of my feet like a Park Avenue hostess. She set aside her typewriter and pillow and crawled close to the door. She smiled as I declared, "Louise D'Aprix sleeps in the closet here. She is a great novelist. In the mold of Ms. Willa Cather. But her prose is far less precious and her head is smaller than a bowling ball."

After we passed by, Louise cracked open the door for a peek. She would have called out and introduced herself, but she was wearing only underwear. (I forbid air conditioners, and her little window could not be lifted above halfway due to a sloppy paint job during the Coolidge administration.) Her keen, crazy eyes fed on us, gobbling every detail.

I pointed to Miranda's door. "Miranda Buchner. A painter. Gorgeous abstracts. Her use of color recalls Matisse, but her subject matter is strictly . . . oh, what's the word? Gynecological. This is the last flight," I said, laying a hand on my stomach as it endured a sharp spasm. "In the good old days, Sasha and I would do jigsaw puzzles up here. I'd run up these stairs. Nay, *gallop!*"

"Who's Sasha?" he asked.

As we disappeared around the mahogany banister, Louise pulled in her head and reached for her typewriter. Incredible, she thought. She had been having trouble finding a hero for her new novel and now he had been delivered to her doorstep. This is exactly what she typed about Adrian: *"His hair is the color of dead leaves and his jacket hangs from his frail shoulders like a cape. He is a fairy tale prince, banished from the kingdom."*

(Later that week, reading over these words, I was skeptical about the "tale" and the "prince," but I had a pretty good feeling about the "fairy." If my intuition was correct, young Adrian was teetering on the fence and it was my job to give him a hearty shove into the fertile compost of the homosexual way of life. Not for myself, of course, but for him. I would not be his first lover [my frail monogamy dared not even entertain such a prospect]; I would merely guide him toward a suitable candidate and be there when it was over to help him make sense of it.)

Everything on the top floor was smaller than in the rest of the house—the ceilings, the doors, the windows.

"And now, unveiled, the Toilet stands displayed!" I flung open the door to the tiny, vile bathroom. "Your floor mate is a pig, you see." I pointed to a door across the way. "But he's brilliant, so I don't nag. He's an actor. Born to privilege. A young Franchot Tone by the name of Carl Alan Dealey."

I tapped on Carl's door. When I got no answer, I opened it. Adrian peeked under my armpit. Carl lay sound asleep on his back, his paltry hair tickled by a breeze. His boxers were, unfortunately, wrapped around his ankles and his T-shirt was hiked. Fused to his sparse stomach hair was a mangled duckling of crusty tissue. In one hand, he limply held a bottle of baby oil.

"He's rehearsing," I lied, slamming the door.

Adrian's smile was queasy.

"And here is your Cave of Quietude!" I proclaimed, opening the next door to reveal a clean, square room, graced with a dresser, a desk, a single bed, and a stretch of dun-colored carpeting. "You'll have plenty of privacy. Nothing to come between you and your muse." I tossed him a twinkle. "Keats, too, slept in an attic."

Wearing a look of confusion and wonder, the lad stepped in.

He Reads Dante and Stinks to High Heaven

In these United States, during the 1980s, lyric poets, especially toothsome ones, were particularly hard to come by. (Even today, they hardly grow on trees.) The moment Adrian confessed his vocation, I knew that he was exactly what our little colony needed and that his presence would make for a most diverting summer. The very next night, lying in the smooth arms of my boyfriend, Pip, I could barely contain my excitement. Unfortunately, Pip was unable to share in it. I deduced this because, although possessed of only the most tenuous grasp of English, Pip was usually quite chatty, especially when drunk or stoned, but that night he simply lay there, staring up at his mirrored ceiling like a corpse. Like most Vietnamese men born before the armistice, Pip had a jealous streak a click wide. Even though I already knew the answer, I asked him what was wrong. He replied with a grunt. I sat up and studied his face. He had slipped into an Asiatic fugue state. What awful suspicions churned behind those lifeless, narrow eyes?

Suddenly, he snapped to. "I no cale about Adlian! Shut up!"

My first impulse was to return fire, emptying both barrels, for I am not one to be bullied, even by a young lover, but instead I kept my cool, laying a gentle palm on his chest and explaining that while Adrian was certainly a most delectable morsel, my plate was already full, thank you very much. I bestowed a loving peck on his almost indiscernible nose. From the way he scowled, I knew he was not convinced. I was tempted to go further, "lay it on thick" as the old men at the Carnegie Deli say, but I reminded myself that one of my chronic errors of the boudoir has been to give too much too soon. I remained strategically silent.

It backfired.

Pip jumped up, pushing me away. "You love Adlian mole than you love me!"

I laughed—a full-bodied Falstaffian roar.

"You no cale!" he cried out. "You no cale about Pip!" He flipped onto his flat tummy and wept.

It must be noted that there was more to this ghastly display than the mere introduction of Adrian into my home. First, Pip was creeped up on hashish. Second, Pip and I, although new lovers, had already known our share of discord. Not forty-eight hours after our first kiss amidst the shadows of the Fifty-ninth Street Bridge, he had expressed a desire to move in with me. I found this absurd and inexplicable. His Park Avenue apartment was gigantic and filled with the trendiest of chrome furnishings. (His bed was a king.) Why on earth would he want to give it up for *my* dusty digs, which, although brimming with soul, crawled with lodgers who would present a continual encroachment on our lovemaking? But when I tried to talk sense to him, suggesting that it would be far more practical for me to move in with *him,* he became alternately teary and mute. On the fourth night of our acquaintance, he had actually crawled out of bed and slammed the door in my face. In the morning, I found him passed out on the living room rug, clutching, like a stuffed Teddy, a bottle of expensive Danish schnapps.

Needless to say, my delight at Adrian's arrival was only making things worse. In the end, that night, we fell asleep without so much as a cuddle or smooch, and the next morning, after sharing a silent omelet (Pip was a fabulous chef), we parted like strangers. While it tore at my heartstrings, I knew that to relent would be folly. We had been dating for only eight days. If I fell prey to his manipulations so quickly, where would that leave me? He must not think me his marionette. As I plodded home, my guts enduring the first of the day's many bouts of monstrous upheaval, I told myself that I had acted shrewdly, holding firm in the most manly fashion, letting Pip know who was boss. Soon, he would realize that he had nothing to fear—my feelings for him were deep and true—and that there was no need for us to rush pell-mell or willy-nilly toward the merging of our households.

Because the day proved seasonably muggy, after emerging from the toilet, I retired to my bedroom, where, fan awhirl, I lost myself in quiet hobbying. Since last year's lucky flea-market acquisition of a *carte-de-visite* of Mr. Edward Bulwer-Lytton (the least talented of all the Victorians), I had declared my collection of photography complete and had moved on to caring for Sasha's cache of sterling pillboxes. (I clean them with Q-tips dipped in vinegar and salt.) I worked for hours, interrupted only by frequent flights to the loo. If the condition of my bowels did not improve, I told myself, I would have no choice but to visit a doctor.

Since opening my home to lodgers, a half-dozen philosophers had appeared on my doorstep, but Michael Shannon was the only one I had ever admitted. I don't care for modern philosophy. To my mind, the last great philosopher was Mr. Marcus Aurelius. (Strangely, he was enjoying a sudden revival among the yellow-tied Visigoths of Wall Street.) But Michael Shannon looked the part entirely and that weighed heavily in his favor. He was a darksome house of flesh, a sturdily built lad from Flushing with stippled scars from boyhood acne and thick hair that swept back from his tense brow in an oily midnight wave. He rarely shaved or bathed. Like me, he was a crawling slave to Lady Nicotine.

Early that afternoon, I found Michael sitting on a wicker chair in the backyard, shirtless, sucking an unfiltered cancer stick, reading, I kid you not, *Death on the Installment Plan*.

"Have you heard?" I thrummed, as I sat down across the table from him. "I finally found someone for Alexander's room." Michael looked over, straight into the hard glare of the sun, but said nothing. "His name is Adrian Malloy. Irish-American like you. I love the name Adrian, don't you? It's androgynous. All the best names are."

Michael removed a speck of tobacco from his tongue and flicked it away. "Is *he* a fag, too?"

"Go to hell!" I snapped, with an uncharacteristic lack of imagination. "That's no business of yours. And don't you dare talk that way in front of him."

"Why, is he in the closet?"

"He's a lyric poet and he's exquisitely sensitive. In fact, I haven't had a lodger so thin-skinned since—" I shielded my eyes and looked up at a line of pigeons making a lavatory of a neighbor's fire escape. "Since Adam Schechter. Poor Adam. He wrote odes and elegies. His fine Semitic spirit was no match for the grinding gears of modern life. I always knew one day he'd destroy himself."

"What happened?"

"He moved to Long Island and married for money. But that won't happen to Adrian. He's not only enormously talented but passionately devoted to his work."

"How do you know that?"

"He brought with him an entire trash bag of odes and sonnets."

"Well, that proves it."

"Indeed, it does."

Two stories above us, Miranda Buchner, the little Expressionist, stood naked in the bathtub, looking down from the window like a highborn maiden from a palace tower. Her wet, golden crucifix lay on the sill. Lines showed on either sides of her mouth as she tried to think of something funny to call out to Michael. When nothing came, she spit instead. Her saliva fluttered in the wind. When it hit him, he jerked back and reached for his chest as though he had been struck by an arrow.

"God damn it!" he shouted, looking up in time to see a flash of yellow.

I pulled a handkerchief from my pocket. "No need to get hysterical. It's only a bit of pigeon-dirt."

"No, it's not! It's that little weirdo! She spit on me!"

Suddenly, a haunting feminist melody rose from the basement, and Mary Pilango's sweet soprano voice, supported by a nylon-stringed guitar, began to sing of high tide and unicorns and sagging bosoms and of the chronic selfishness of men.

"Great," Michael growled, slapping shut his book. "Lesbian folk songs—just what I need!"

He stormed inside.

Love inspires, even in the most sane of us, behavior more befitting beast than Man. Within moments of spitting like a baby camel on her beloved's chest, Miranda was balled up on Louise's cot, wrapped in a damp towel, banging a fist on her pretty knee.

"What's the matter with me?" she cried.

Louise towered above her in maniacal grandeur, her red hair electric and formidable. "You're in love. Big deal. I saw it coming. Everybody falls for Michael sooner or later."

"Even you?" Miranda asked, surprised.

"And how. He reads Dante and stinks to high heaven. He's irresistible." Louise rifled through a stack of typed pages on a high shelf. "I've got two hundred pages on the guy. He's all I thought about for weeks."

"But you guys never even talk. You don't even know him."

"I know the way he looks, don't I? The way he walks? And scowls? I don't need much." She gestured frantically. "I mean, love comes and goes. I've loved a million guys. I love half the guys I meet. I even love the new kid upstairs and we haven't even been introduced yet. So what if I get nothing back? So what if men find me overbearing. If it weren't for love, I'd know nothing about pain. I'd write big books about little things. Bestsellers. I'd be rich. I'd be happy."

Miranda shook her head at this loony improv (the bilge water of a brain devoid of ballast) and moaned, "I don't know what to do. I get so nervous around him." She punched her knee again. "Why did I have to *spit?*"

"Guys love being spit on. You don't, they take you for granted."

"Does he have a girlfriend?"

"How would I know?"

"What do you think?"

"No."

"How come?"

"'Cause he's solipsistic."

Before Miranda could ask what that meant, there was a knock and she gasped.

"Jesus, relax." Louise threw open the door. There was no one there, until she looked down and saw Adrian.

"Excuse me," he said, breathlessly. "I'm on my way to Greenwich Village. I was wondering if you could tell me which bus—"

"Greenwich Village?" Louise laughed. "No one calls it that." She studied him from head to toe: polyester short-sleeve shirt, khaki shorts, black socks, dirty work boots. "What are you, a tourist? You need help, kid." She grabbed him by the lapel and hauled him in.

Adrian's cheeks rouged when he saw Miranda. Not only was she the most adorable creature he had ever laid eyes on, but her towel had slipped, revealing a sliver of pink nipple. Miranda, seeing him stare, quickly scootched up the towel.

Louise decided to have some fun. "Look, if you need a tour guide, take Miranda here. She knows the Village like you know the cornfields of Nebraska."

"Iowa," Adrian corrected.

"But handle her with kid gloves, okay? She's in love with a guy who can't stand her."

"Louise!" Miranda whined. She looked at Adrian. "I'll take you. Just let me get dressed."

Miranda skittered out the door but was stopped by my bulk. "What? What is it now?!" she shrieked defensively, her hands on her hips.

I dragged her (perhaps a bit too violently) into my bedroom, where I explained that this was an artists' colony, not a brothel. I forbade her to abandon her creative work or to encourage Adrian to abandon his, in the name of some capricious weekday-afternoon jaunt. I strode back to Louise's closet and announced to Adrian that Miranda would not be joining him after all. The boy was gutted. Before I could cheer him with the news that I had an even better idea as to how he might pass his day (lunching with me at the Parnassus Diner), he scampered upstairs as though fleeing a deadly enemy.

Why?

It was a mystery slow to unravel.

I shut the door and questioned Louise until she spilled every last bean of what had just transpired. By way of thanks, I invited *her* to lunch with me instead. My treat. She declined. She was too busy with her new novel, she explained. It was an excuse with which, as her mentor, I could hardly argue.

Carl Alan Dealey lay on his stomach, a pillow jammed under his chin, observing for the very first time, through a three-inch gap at the bottom of his shade, the new tenant in the building across the way. She sat at her glamorous vanity, back turned, slim, unaware, and entirely naked. Strong and delicately ribbed, her torso began with wings of muscle just beneath the shoulder, then curved down to a tidy little waist. She arched her back, brushing her short margarine hair with languid self-enthrallment as though it were thick and shoulder-length. When she switched sides with her brush, her profile became visible. Something aristocratic reigned in the sweep of her long neck. Suddenly, she shifted and her pretty bosoms exploded cubistically in the vanity's triplicate mirrors—a crazy collage of swells, curves, and clam-foot nipples. She marked her eyelids with a liner. She rubbed her underarms with a deodorant stick. She mumbled a few smiling words. Was she singing to herself? She reached for a white blouse. She stepped shakily into black slacks. A minute later, she was gone.

Carl rolled over and looked at the floor. Take-out containers lay everywhere. Headshots littered the carpet amid a strewn archive of *Backstage* and *Variety*. His eyes lifted. A toupee lay crooked over Siberia on a child's globe. The telephone was resoundingly silent. He was the loneliest man alive. He reached to the floor for his bottle of oil. How many more times would he be forced to find his only relief this way? His new neighbor across the way had brought him momentary distraction, yes, but she was gone now. Maybe forever. She would probably install blinds. He slithered his boxers to his ankles. He flexed his oversized calves. Suddenly, a knock. He had left his door ajar. A niblet-nose poked in. Carl let out a yowl and yanked up his undershorts.

Alarmed by the yowl, Adrian barged in. "Are you okay? What's wrong?"

"Who are *you?* Get out!"

"I-I-I live down the hall!"

"Get out!" Carl screamed. Adrian looked so afraid that even Carl felt a pang of compassion. "Wait! Sorry, sorry!" Carl leaned off the bed and offered his hand. "Carl Dealey. Nice to meet you."

They hastily shook. Adrian's face changed. He looked down at his palm. He sniffed it. It smelled like a baby's bottom. Carl, stricken by his *faux pas*, jumped up and shoved the boy into the hallway.

Descending the stairs, wiping his hand on his shorts, Adrian thought maybe it would be best if, in the future, he left his house-mates alone. He walked to the corner, asked for directions, and a few minutes later boarded a city bus. Unfortunately, he jumped off a bit shy of Greenwich Village. For hours he walked Fourteenth Street from river to river, browsing noisy markets that sold poorly made goods at comically low prices. While he suspected that this could not be the seat of bohemian culture he had heard and read so much about, he was too embarrassed to ask anyone where it actually was. As the sun dwindled, he purchased three postcards of the Statue of Liberty and a bottle of Guatemalan shampoo and made for home.

Bartending had once seemed to Michael Shannon the ideal job for a young philosopher, one that would bring him closer to those at the bottom with few pretensions or illusions. It was, after all, on their voiceless behalf that he had become a writer in the first place. But in the five years since he had taken the job, he had seen the seedy barrelhouse where he worked transformed into a popular watering hole for the sorts of predators who every day, it seemed, were threatening to destroy the city. Nightly, he was surrounded by them: pot-bellied corporate attorneys with polka-dotted ties and shiny chins; reptilian hedge fund managers partial to yoga, wheat-grass, and statutory rape; smug stockbrokers with fat wallets and recurrent herpes about which they habitually lied. And the women who loved them were just as vile: fatuous shrills with fake tits, bobbed noses, gigantic hair, and scrawny arms. They laughed too loudly and misery lingered in their eyes like mustard gas. Every night, Michael worked the stick, dispensing ale to these atrocities as they screamed their orders and waved their money in his face. He did not talk back, but when he got off at two, his eyes burned and hatchets of pain lay buried in both sides of his neck.

Why didn't he just find another job? He wondered this himself. He had no answer, except that he felt that somehow he *deserved* to suffer, to pay dearly for the fact that he was a failure. Such a failure, in fact, that he had never even failed—for the simple reason that he had never shown his writing to a living soul. After work, to restore himself, he walked until he vanished—sometimes into the verdurous gloom of Central Park, at others into the lowest circles of Hell's Kitchen. Occasionally, he disappeared into crumbling neighborhoods where very few white men understood that they were perfectly safe. It was only when he was free of privileged society that he felt remotely alive.

Returning that night from his exploration of Fourteenth Street, Adrian glanced into a bar window a few blocks from home and spotted Michael shaking a cocktail. It was only the second time that Adrian had ever seen him. (On his first night in town, Adrian had watched from his bedroom window as Michael trudged out after midnight.) Although Adrian had come to the city to be alone, he already craved companionship, so he pushed his way through the mob of scoundrels and harpies and mounted a stool. Michael asked him what it would be.

"A ginger ale," he said.

Michael stared blankly, as though he had just ordered a shot of pus.

For a full quarter-hour, the fretling sat there, jabbing at his ice cubes, gathering the nerve to speak. Finally, he cried above the din, "I live with you!"

"*What?*" Michael replied, dipping an ear close.

"I live with you! I took Alexander's room!"

Michael gave him a second look. He sure didn't *look* like a lyric poet. He looked more like the president of a high school glee club. Michael smirked and walked away. It wasn't that he was unfriendly; he was simply laying down the law. He was ashamed of his job. The other lodgers had already learned that they were not welcome here. Now the boy would learn. And he did. A few minutes later, Adrian hopped off his stool and slid into the night, never to return.

Thus it was, Dearest Gossips, that two lonely souls, who might have had plenty to talk about, avoided meaningful intercourse. Although our hero did not know it yet, it was an everyday occurrence here in the cruel city.

Adrian heard outside his cave the distant-ocean sound of traffic. The curtains by his bed, browned by years of car exhaust, billowed in the meager breeze. He lifted the shade and looked down to where strangers moved through the cool night. Among them was a pair of teenagers, wrapped in each other's arms, laughing as though there were no such thing as heartbreak. He would have liked to be so carefree, but it was impossible. He had work to do. He lifted his trash bag onto the bed.

Just days before, Adrian had stood before an open casket, staring down at the remains of his father. Rosary beads were enlaced in the man's waxy fingers, whose nails were yellow from thirty years of cigarettes. Adrian studied his father's shrunken face and repeated to himself, "I loved you, I loved you, I loved you." Abruptly, he noticed that his father was *breathing,* his chest rising and falling in a steady cadence. It was just an illusion, of course, the imposition of his own breathing onto the incomprehensible stillness of the corpse, but he liked the trick and let it continue. He smiled at the help he was lending him. If only it were real.

Later, Adrian found himself sitting in a one-bedroom trailer with his father's second wife, Lillian. Not yet forty, she had grieved for years when his father was alive and drinking; now that he was dead she was enjoying a faintly hysterical mirth.

"Guess I'll hit the road again," she said, clapping her hands. "Back on the road!"

"Do you know where?"

"Nope." She crossed to the counter and opened a quart of domestic beer. "Probably Florida. I've got some pals down there. Want some?"

"No, thanks."

"A splash?"

"Nope."

As she filled a big glass with the cheap lager, she stretched out her other arm like a waking cat. "Boy, it feels good to be able to have a drink again and not feel guilty." She moved to the couch and sat, one leg under the other. "It's good to see you, kid. Your dad and I missed you an awful lot. If you weren't so darned scared of flying, you could have come up sooner, stayed a while, seen him before he died."

Adrian reminded himself that he had not been invited and that if he had been he would have flown the plane himself.

"By the way, you want something?" she asked suddenly. "Of your dad's? I'll be selling most of it, so you'd better grab it now."

"I know he kept a lot of papers. His scientific stuff."

"You want that? It's yours." She pointed with her beer to a closet. "It's in there."

Under a stack of clothes, Adrian found the bulging trash bag.

"Might as well take these, too," Lillian said, grabbing some lab books from a high shelf and dropping them in. "Nobody else'll want 'em."

Standing in his cave now, Adrian watched as his inheritance fell in a flurry onto his single bed. It was pounds and pounds of paper: two published books, reprints of articles, photos from electron microscopes, old lectures and press clippings, and the lab books. It was more and less than he had expected—more in its bulk, less in its tie to the living reality of his father—but it was all he had now. He would have to make do.

Adrian stared at the papers for a long time. He began to cry— not in the purging way that he had seen Lillian weep at the funeral, but in the only way he knew how: in dry, wrenching bursts torn from his throat, as though against his will. Although he eventually wept facedown on the bed for over an hour, not once did his grief intrude on his dry reason, on the control his brain lorded over his heart. He told himself that this was a good thing. He could not afford to lose himself, not yet, not here.

Hey, Huck Finn, Whatcha Doin'?

I sipped an Austrian pinot blanc (slap of wet lederhosen; stomp of welcomed jackboot) and savored the perfect morning. The air was freakishly temperate. My bowels were enjoying a rare moment of calm. Before me was the familiar stage of my block—the source of so much contentment in my life. And best of all, at my side was dear Adrian Malloy, my new charge, whom I had already dubbed "the green woodpecker." (It was more endearing than "the hayseed" or "the chawbacon.") I had struggled to get the young thing alone since his arrival, but now that I finally had him (after much cajolery), I was so happy that I could barely speak. For a few minutes, we simply sat together in a yummy concord of silence.

At last, I was ready to introduce myself.

"Sasha Buchwitz's father could not have died at a worse time for her," I began wistfully. "Since the death of her mother, Sasha had been broken up with the blues, but when *he* died she fell into absolute ruin. Think Carthage."

Momentarily distracted, I pointed to a scrawny, little *clochard* passing by across the street. He tilted forward as he walked, as though plowing a stiff wind. "That's Vinnie Volpe. Sauced, as usual."

"What does he drink?" Adrian asked.

The question struck me as irrelevant, but only because at the time I was unaware that the lad's father had been a roaring drunk, sporting, at his death, a liver the size of a pumpkin.

"Cheap wine," I answered with haughty disdain. There was no reason that the boy had to know that I, too, was forced by too-tight purse strings to drink less than the very best.

I resumed: "Sasha's father left her this lovely home, but he also left her in a psychological state swiftly diagnosed as paranoid schizophrenia, accompanied by acute clinical depression. Rather than take proper medication, she become addicted to certain pills. 'Mood ameliorators,' they were called back then. They were given to her by a corrupt psychiatrist, a Kurd by the name of Dr. Osman. Some were ups and some were downs, but she found them all equally tasty. Which was, of course, very bad. They made her condition worse. For twenty-three years I lived in her basement, during which time I rode the roller coaster of her extraordinary moods. Finally, from amid the Babel in her head, the devil spoke out loud and clear, commanding her to hack my head from my shoulders. I moved out immediately, to a nearby tenement, where I lived for almost three years. It was a critical period, during which I fell in love for the second time and became the person I am today—one which quite closely resembles a human being."

The boy smiled vaguely. I noticed in his round, intelligent eyes, as before, a dull dreaminess, the manifestation, I sensed, of a veil that hung between his conscious mind and his most secret nature. Part of my job that summer would be to shred that veil. Otherwise, he would remain a stranger to himself—which, as everyone knows, is suicide for a young artist.

Across the street a fat grimalkin emerged from her basement den. Her sequined gown was filthy, but her carriage was royal. She was trailed by a cortege of mangy mutts. She wore flip-flops on her bare, dirty feet.

"Her real name is Magda something," I said, "but we call her Mother. She's lived on the block longer than memory. Sasha's father said her teeth were as soft as soap."

"How would he know that?"

"He was her dentist."

"Oh." He grimaced and pointed to two dozen broken spirits spilling down the steps of an old church across the way. "Who're they?"

"Junkies. Fresh from their morning rehab."

"Really? God, they look so normal."

"Because they are. Just like you and me. Only hooked on heroin. We're hooked on other things."

"I'm not hooked on anything."

"Patience, lad. You've only just arrived."

He looked bewildered.

I patted his naive knee, then brightened at the sight of a raddled bottle-blonde wobbling by on spike heels.

"There's a poem for you," I whispered. "Paula Twitchell. A trollop. She lives in the high-rise on the corner. She has a secret." I cupped a hand around my mouth. *"She's a man."*

Astonished, Adrian repeated the statement back to me in question form.

"That's right," I replied. "And despite her jumbo Adam's apple and platter-like hands, no one seems to notice. Maybe they don't want to."

"Boy, *I* sure couldn't tell."

"It's indicative, really. Rich boys from New Jersey drive in on a Saturday night. When they leave her bed chamber, they're all puffed up like peacocks. They have no idea that their date for the evening was actually *Paul* Twitchell, a boy who grew up playing hopscotch right here on this block."

"Indicative of what?" the boy asked, his brow in furrows.

"The folly of judging a book by its cover," I replied with a smart, little smile.

In a basement room, just down the hall from Michael's dungeon, Mary Pilango lay half-asleep on her futon. Although the day had already begun, she was not ready to be awake. Her eyes fluttered open and shut, and her cares sank under a swell of oblivion. She was adrift in Lethe, her muscular limbs snug and cool under cotton sheets. Later, she would wake up and write a song. Now, she would sleep. There was nothing to be done. There were no consequences. The day was long.

Mary heard a rustling and remembered that she was not alone. She had made love last night for hours with great emotion. Blind fumblings, wet lips, hairy armpits. Deep slumber with a little head resting on her hard pectorals. At one point in the night, she had moved aside her own arm as though it were someone else's. Who was it that had drained it of blood and turned it into a tube of meat? Mary might have opened her eyes and seen for herself, but she could not find the will. Why surrender so soon? The day was long. More sleep. No consequences. Nothing to be done.

Portraits of women began to cartwheel through Mary's drowsy brain. Betty Schwabb, the political activist, whose breasts hung like hound's ears all the way down to her linty navel. Luscious Tanya Hill, quadruple threat: actress-model-manic-depressive. Jodi Landerman: Her love was like a fast ride on an Israeli gunship. Ah, sweet Minerva Townsend, reggae in her hips and ass. Hiroko Hiroyuki, scentless, wordless, brainless. Louise D'Aprix—she liked men, but on sleepless nights she flew down the stairs, brain atwirl, her big body eager to undress. And Toby Twain, her soul mate, her baby. For better or worse, she adored Toby. Soon, Toby would be out of jail.

Meanwhile, in the little room that lay between Mary's and Michael's, the selfsame Toby Twain foraged violently through a desk drawer, smashing aside pens, coins, keys, and a dozen guitar picks, until she found what she was looking for: Mary's little black book. Only it was red. She pulled it out and wildly flipped the pages. Nothing but women's names. She grabbed a pen and a piece of paper and, sitting down on a bench press, began to write. They weren't even alphabetized! Who were they? Toby wondered. Where did they all come from? Had Mary slept with *all* of them while she was away, lonely behind bars? As Toby wrote, rage curled her other hand into a claw. But she released it. Her jealousy had hurt them both before. There had to be more constructive ways of winning Mary's loyalty than by hurling heavy objects at her gorgeous gypsy head.

A half-hour later, Mary remembered with a jolt that it was Toby who had slept over. She was *already* out of jail. The night before, Mary had opened the front door and there was Toby, smiling with hope. The damp, beseeching look in her eye was typical of one newly clean, learning to brave again the perils of human company. They went straight to bed. The first touch of Toby's peasant lips on her stomach brought back all that was right in the old arrangement. The orgasm that followed was nothing short of transcendent. When Toby finally crashed into sleep with her head on Mary's chest, her mouth ajar like an infant's, Mary felt a pang of familiar happiness.

Awake now, Mary reached out a blind hand to her, but it slapped the empty sheet. Odd. Toby never rose early. She heard a rattle in the middle room. She reached for her eyeglasses.

"Toby?" she said. "What're you doing in there?"

A blithesome pop tune burst into the air.

"Cock-a-doodle-doo!" Toby sang cutely, as she appeared in the doorway, naked, laying an arm along the jamb like a seductress. One her way back to the bed, she dropped a folded piece of paper into her backpack.

When Mary and Toby banged open the basement gate, Adrian and I were startled. Mary was dressed, as usual, in basic black. Toby wore cockled East Village motley and a silly *chapeau*. Prison had

41

not been good to the little druggie; she looked painfully thin and veiny. I doubted that behind bars she had fetched, in shower-room trades, even a skein of yarn or a decent bar of chocolate. Mary greeted me with a curt nod and tried to escape, but I stopped her with a Mussolini-like gesture. I will not tolerate even a moment's incivility among my lodgers.

"You haven't met your new housemate," I said. "Adrian Malloy. He's a lyric poet. Adrian, meet Mary Pilango."

"A pleasure," Mary said. Although she was a soprano when she sang, her speaking voice was distinctly baritone. She smiled as politely as she knew how and held out a mannish hand, bearing the kind of nails one would expect on an expert fingerpicker.

"Same here," Adrian said, leaning down and shaking.

"This is Toby Twain," Mary said proudly, as though the lass's mere ability to stand upright were an accomplishment in itself.

"Hi," Adrian said.

"Hi."

"So you're a lyric poet," Mary said.

"Yeah, but— Well, I'm just starting out. I've never written anything very good. I mean, I'm not—"

"Nonsense," I interjected. "He's brilliant. In fact, he brought with him hundreds of odes and sonnets stuffed into a trash bag."

Mary grinned, showing a dazzle of straight teeth. "What a coincidence. When I wrote poetry, that's where I kept *my* stuff."

"That's where yours belonged," I snitted. "Adrian's belong in print."

I was well aware of how badly our young poets needed encouragement. As I have said, they were lonely anachronisms in the boom-boom eighties.

"Anyway," Mary said, "we're starved. See ya." And with that the two Sapphists set off arm-in-arm down the block toward the Parnassus Diner, where the open-minded Cassandra would be happy to serve them a trout omelet, or whatever else they might desire.

"Beautiful girl," I said, shaking my head. "But, my God, she's a slut. Rare among lesbians, you know."

"Actually, I didn't."

"Oh, yes, dykes are usually monogamous unto death. Like tapeworms and geese. But she's a musical genius, so I overlook her wantonness."

"What's her music like?"

"It recalls a young Joni Mitchell. Only when she hits her high notes it doesn't sound like someone left the kettle on."

Adrian just stared. He was unused to my wit. I cleared my throat and, with uncharacteristic machismo, unloaded a ball of phlegm into the street. Just as I was about to suggest that we follow the girls to the Parnassus, Miranda appeared on the sidewalk, holding a white paper bag. She wore tights under a pair of boxer shorts, and a top that revealed, near the straps, the swell of her spunky little bosoms. Adrian's face changed. I would have known that dopey look anywhere. It was the face I made at the early sightings of my darling Christopher. The lad desired her. Or at least he thought he did. Hardly surprising. Her body offered all the economical packaging of a boy's. She would be a comfy bivouac in his inevitable march to the Greek border.

"Breakfast!" Miranda sang.

Adrian rocketed to his feet. Without tossing me so much as a "How do you do? " Miranda skipped up the stairs. Adrian disappeared right behind her, slamming the door.

A minute later, lonesome, I hoisted my guts, slipped inside, tiptoed down the hall, and silently cracked open the swinging door to the dining room. Miranda, opening a take-out food container, laughed at Adrian's frown.

"You said you wanted something healthy."

"Well, yeah, but—"

"The soy has protein and the seaweed's full of zinc."

"I guess where I come from healthy means something else."

"What, steak and eggs?"

"Yeah, pretty much."

When they were halfway through their meal, during which they had engaged in the most inane small talk, the telephone jangled. Although the contraption was just inches from her elbow, Miranda did not answer it. Hardly surprising, as the only calls she ever received were from her mother in Texas, begging her to quit painting, move home, and marry the son of her next-door neighbor.

"B. K. claims you're a genius," she said. "Like William Butler Keats."

(Even today I shudder.)

"Not really," Adrian replied. "Not yet. I just got out of college."

"What did you major in? English?"

Adrian subtly spit a cube of tofu into his hand. "Actually, no. Astronomy."

"Why?"

Good question—I would have asked it myself, had I been invited to join them. But I already knew the answer: A love of science is hardly incompatible with a gift for poetry. Keats, for example, studied medicine, Goethe identified a common constituent of natural rust, and James Joyce was an avid scatologist.

Before the boy could say as much, Louise hollered from upstairs, *"Miranda! Phone!"*

Miranda grabbed the invasive instrument, ready to protest that she was twenty-five, an adult, and had no desire to return to the killing fields of Houston. (At the time, Houston tallied its daily murders the way San Diego, say, logged fender-benders.) And if she ever did move home, it wouldn't be to marry a chubby Mormon podiatrist.

"What do you want now!" Miranda began hotly.

"Miranda Buchner? Jerry Sheridan here! I'm a friend of Jay Darden's."

Jay was an old pal of hers from art school whom she had not seen in three years.

"Oh, I'm sorry." she said. "I thought you were my mother."

"Not the last time I checked. Look, I was visiting Jay's loft in Williamsburg the other day, checking out his stuff, and I noticed a few amazing oils, only they weren't his. They were yours."

Miranda had given Jay a few pieces when she graduated, but nothing she liked.

"Anyway, here's the story," Jerry explained. "My mom owns a gallery uptown on Madison Avenue. I've worked there for years, but, between you and me, it's match-the-couch stuff. I've decided to strike out on my own. I just rented a space in Soho."

"Great," Miranda murmured, hardly daring to hope.

"I thought if you weren't committed elsewhere, maybe you could be my first show."

"Really?"

"Absolutely. Your oils have a tactile element that absolutely defies narrative."

She wasn't sure what that meant, but her heart began to buck. She threw Adrian a joyous look, but like me he had no idea what Jerry had said, so the best he could do was smile and bob his eyebrows.

She tried to sound adult and professional. "Sounds interesting, Jer."

"So what's the best way to do this? Should I drop by your studio?"

Miranda did not have a studio. "I've got a better idea," she said, with a hint of panic. "Why don't I bring you some slides? I've got really good slides."

"Cool, let's do it over dinner."

They picked a time and place.

After she hung up, Miranda gobbled down the rest of her meal (and the rest of Adrian's, as well) while she explained what had just transpired on the telephone. Before Adrian could even congratulate her, she jumped up and pushed through the swinging door, slamming me forcefully into the opposite wall. When she saw me plastered there, the back of my head having cracked an old canvas, she growled with evil intent and plunged down the basement steps.

Adrian, wondering why he had been abandoned, pushed at the swinging door, too. This time, I dove aside and was barely grazed. He dashed past me without so much as a glance. I gave chase, following him into the cellar. I stopped at the bottom step, right behind him. I do not believe that he even knew I was there, but I could be wrong. I breathed his head. In just two short weeks, his virginal, heartland aroma had been supplanted by the cloying bouquet of cheap Central American shampoo.

We watched in silence as Miranda approached a door. Her little knock was like that of a ghost tapping a rainy window pane. A moment later, Michael opened up, wearing only a pair of ragged denim shorts. His legs were muscular and hairy.

"What is it?" he brusqued. Miranda faltered. His bare chest, so close, unnerved her. "Come on, spit it out, but not on my head, okay?"

"Oh, yeah, I'm really sorry about that. I wanted to say something funny and I couldn't think of anything."

"Obviously not. So, what is it? You came to apologize?"

"Yeah, but I have a question, too."

"Okay, what? I'm in the middle of something."

"You are? What?"

"None of your god damn business."

Miranda blurted out her good news. She paused, waiting for him to congratulate her. When he did not, she asked her question: "Do you know a cheap photographer who could take some slides of my work? I told the guy I had slides, but I don't."

"Sorry, no."

"Oh," she breathed.

"And if in the future you have any more exciting questions, use the *outside* stairs, okay? The inside ones are off-limits—you know that."

He shut the door.

She stood for a moment, stabbed through the heart. Adrian, realizing at last that it was Michael with whom Miranda was unrequitedly in love, spun around, embarrassed, and slipped past me.

I stayed compassionately put.

When the pigtailed beauty reached me, I said, "I'm proud of you, my darling. A show of your very own. How wonderful. You're on your way now. I promise to fill the place with my friends." I moved in for a hug, but she stopped me with a stiff-arm.

"Yeah, right," she snarled, pushing past.

She knew that Cassandra was my only friend and, stout though the old bird she was, she could hardly be expected to fill an entire art gallery. I felt foolish standing there alone in the dark, so I plodded up to the sitting room, where I opened Mr. George Meredith's *The Egoist,* with whose ornate prolixity I wrassled away the long afternoon. The only interruption came in the form of panicked flights to the toilet. My condition was growing worse by the day. I feared now that its source was not, as I had assumed, the jitters of new love or even a virus, but rather a hungry cancer of the bowel. It was undeniable: very soon I would have to visit a doctor and be probed.

That evening, the young orphan sat on the carpet of his cave, his back against the bed, surrounded by his father's papers. He had already worked through the incidental notes and a bundle of scientific photos and was now ready to begin more serious study. He took a sip of his ice water and opened a published book that bore his father's name on the front cover. The introduction was a fond satire of his father's college advisors, "the authorities in thick glasses, with leather patches on their elbows and minds," who had tried to dissuade him from dedicating his postgraduate work to the study of hydra. There was no future in it, they told him, because everything there was to know about the little polyp had already been discovered. It had, after all, been studied for centuries. His father had forged ahead anyway, and by the time he was forty, he had published eighty papers on the creature. He had dedicated himself to this work, he wrote, because he believed that the hydra's power to regenerate held locked within it miraculous potential for mankind.

Voices from the floor below. Adrian crawled over, cracked the door, and listened to the sound of Carl Alan Dealey, actor extraordinaire, running past Louise's room.

"Hey, Oblomov left his bed!" Louise cried out. "Will miracles never cease? What's the occasion?"

"Back, madwoman!"

"What's in the paper bag? If it's something illegal, you'd better share."

"It's a handgun. I'm gonna blow my brains out."

"Oh, me too! Me too!"

Miranda joined in: "Louise, don't joke like that. Not with Carl. He might be serious!"

When Carl finally reached the third floor, he froze at the sight of Adrian on all fours. (Who wouldn't?) Pulling from the paper bag a black vinyl case, Carl spoke with unexpected sweetness: "Hey, Huck Finn, whatcha doin'?"

"Reading some marine biology," Adrian replied, crawling back to his papers.

Carl burst in. "You goin' out tonight by any chance? Got a date? I thought maybe you had a date."

"I wish. I just moved here. I don't know anybody."

"I've lived in the city for ten years and neither do I. Mind if I borrow your window for a while? Mine's too conspicuous." He crossed to the window, unsnapped the vinyl case, and removed a pair of binoculars.

Adrian, fascinated, rose to his feet. "What are those for?"

"I don't believe in love" was Carl's non sequitur. "Never have. Like one day I spotted this frat brother of mine in Central Park. I never liked him much, but he's balder than me, so I stopped to gloat. Anyway, he's with this hot, little chick. His girlfriend, he says." Carl adjusted the focus. "Whoa, I can see right in the window of the church!" He shook his head. "Anyway, I didn't like the looks of her from the start. She's a schoolteacher. I said to myself, 'This woman is not to be trusted.' You go around with some hot little schoolteacher, you know what happens?"

"What?"

"You end up marryin' her."

Adrian joined him at the window. "So?"

"So all those married guys runnin' around with pasted-on smiles. 'Hey, look at me! I've got someone to grow old with!' It's pathetic. No thanks, who needs it? Wow, I can see the speedometer on that motorcycle!"

"But aren't you afraid to grow old alone?"

"What's the alternative? Some little heap of wrinkles runnin' in, takin' a piss while I'm tryin' to shave? Think *that* cures loneliness?"

"Maybe. What're the binoculars for?"

"Just doin' some consumer testing. B. K. thinks I'm some kinda misanthrope, doesn't he, just 'cause I hate the human race?"

"He thinks you're a genius. Like some guy named Frenchy something. So what about the binoculars?"

"I'm no romantic. This is an exception to the rule."

"What is?"

"I'm gonna try the love thing out. I've found the right girl and I'm gonna try it out."

"What is she, an ornithologist or something?"

"A *what?*"

"I thought maybe she was into bird walks."

"No, I just need these to see her."

"Huh?"

Carl sat Adrian down and told him all about the naked girl across the way. "She's just like me," he concluded. "A homebody, but we're also different. In good ways. She keeps a clean apartment, for instance. Which I do not, but can appreciate."

"Wow, you're sort of insane, aren't you?"

"Me? What about you? Readin' about clams on a Saturday night."

Witnessing this genial flapdoodle through a peephole in the bathroom wall, I chuckled to myself, charmed by the bond I saw forming between the two young men. Content that Adrian was making his way in The House Beautiful, I returned the Hogarth print to its nail on the wall and stepped out of the bathtub.

Before I had even reached the landing, however, melancholy dropped over my head like a hangman's hood. Why did my lodgers dislike me so? Adrian was proving to be no different. With Carl and Miranda he sparkled and giggled; with me he was calf-eyed and passive. Was there something about my person that offended him? Was my flamboyance a threat to his sexual confusion? Was my high estimate of his talent daunting to his insecurities as an artist? I thought of talking it over with Pip, but he was busy whipping up tomorrow's brunch. Something special. A "big supplise," he had promised. Anyway, the last thing he wanted to do was talk about Adrian.

On my way to my bedroom, I heard the clacking of a typewriter. It had hardly stopped for the past twenty-four hours. Lashed by her cursed blood, Louise was already thigh-deep in her new novel. How I envied her. I had never undertaken anything so ambitious. In the congealed mercury of the hallway mirror, a sadeyed old fairy stared back at me—a ludicrous being, a useless thing. My goodness, why so bereft of hope? Mozart burst lively in the air, the music that Miranda played when she painted. I took to my bed and slept for the next fourteen hours.

How's Dr. Marker?

The thermometer soared and I was forced behind shutters. Deriving only the vaguest of relief from my prewar fan, I wore nothing but a silky kimono, a pair of satin briefs, and large Thai slippers—the spoils of a lecture tour Dr. Wolf Zeller had made of the Pacific Rim. (Often my lodgers complained of my summer attire, claiming that it was worse than indecent, but I told them to blame the Gods, not me: I was *born* a heavy perspirer.) I endured the heat wave, as I endure all things unpleasant, with chilly wines and dusty books.

Having at last finished *The Egoist* and craving something less strenuous, I dipped once again into Sasha's collection of detective fiction, something I had not done since just before her death throes. Frankly, I considered such fare to be well beneath me, but, as a sort of homage to the good woman, I decided to give it another whirl. Sure enough, it *was* well beneath me. The tales were as resonant as peanut shells and no tastier. Just as I was ready to abandon the project, however, I stumbled on a work by Mr. Raymond Chandler. At first I was put off because the story took place in and around Los Angeles, California—a city which I despise and have never visited. Yet, after just a few chapters, I discovered that the man was a miracle worker, able to endow the citizens of that desert outpost with actual *souls*. As improbable and impressive an achievement, I felt, as Mr. Orwell's, when he endowed barnyard animals with revolutionary fervor.

My only break from the long hours of happy confinement, spent commingling with sly Mexicans, feckless shines, and platinum frails, came after the sun cooled. Only then would I brave the streets, huffing it through the crepuscular soup to Pip's place, where he would pamper me with another of his scrumptious stir-fries or feathery crepes. Although I was unable to digest the treats, it in no way diminished my pleasure in gobbling them down. After dinner, we spooned in air-conditioned comfort on his creamy leather sofa and watched black-and-white movies, the artistic nuances of which I would murmur into his uncomprehending ear. It was my first brush with domestic bliss and, I must say, it suited me well. At last I grasped *Homo sapiens'* stubborn urge toward monogamy. Why had it taken me so long to partake of its heavenly fruit?

When the film ended, I would whisper into his sleepy, confused ear, "Movie over," and we would retire to his bedroom, shed our duds, and engage in the most spirited of hanky-panky. He was a veritable geisha, that Pip. If ever a middle-aged man enjoyed, *gratis,* more intense erotic pleasure than I enjoyed that summer, I would like to meet him and shake his trembling hand. I will offer no specifics as to what took place on his king. I am not one to kiss and tell. But I will say this: The young man was a veritable contortionist, twisting himself into all sorts of impossible postures, learned no doubt at the wee feet of those fabled magicians who fashion balloon animals during Tet.

The only cankers on the tender leaf of my happiness were Pip's sporadic flares of temper, which centered on the same two tired issues: his jealousy of Adrian and his desperate desire to move into my home. Somehow he had come to see the two as related, convinced that I was already sexually involved with the green woodpecker and that this was why I refused to let him move in. Absurd, of course, but flattering, as I was obviously too old and ugly for Adrian. But even if the boy *had* been open to making love to me, it was irrelevant. I was spoken for. As for Pip's moving in with me, however, that was still out of the question. My house was growing hotter by the minute and, as I had told him again and again, the proximity of so many prying eyes and twitching ears would inhibit the frequency, not to mention the volume, of our bedsport.

Pip was undeterred. (Never fight a land war in Asia.) His anger always returned, and always at the worst possible moments. Just as love's sad satiety was gently nudging me toward slumber, he would sit upright, slap me, and lash out, "You no love Pip!" And before long it was, "You make love with Adlian!" And by way of finale, "Pip going to kill himself! You be all alone! No one cook for you!" The young man's agony was so acute that it was absolutely impossible for me to take it personally. Clearly, its source predated our meeting by many years. It lay in the blasted tunnels and boiling paddies of his boyhood. Napalm turned inward, I called it, and I was the victim of its indiscriminate blowback. Still, his agony saddened and bored me, and I longed for it to end.

It was the Fourth of July and I had no plans. At midday, *Farewell, My Lovely* eased down onto my booth-top and I gazed misty-eyed through the window of the Parnassus Diner. My mind had drifted back to the day, exactly five years previous, when young Christopher and I had ventured out in search of fireworks. I had spoiled the festivities by flying, Pip-like, into a hissy fit. Later, refusing his offer of dinner, I had slouched home with my tail tucked between my thighs, while he took off on adventure bent. In the end, he celebrated the anniversary of our nation's freedom by betraying me with a piece of teenaged female fluff. The wound was still fresh.

Every Fourth of July since, I had marked the anniversary by feeling profoundly sorry for myself. But this year things would be different, I decided, drying my eyes and throwing back the last of my Rob Roy.

"Hey, old girl," I hollered at Cassandra, "what do you say we go out tonight, turn this crazy town upside down?"

The dear old sorceress ambled over, smiling coyly. "Aw, B. K.," she said, "I'd like nothing more, but I got plans. Emiliano's takin' me out for spaghetti and meatballs."

Emiliano was her new boyfriend, a rude mechanical with a face like a scorched boot and heavily tattooed forearms. I had met him only once. I thought them well suited.

"Oh, well," I sighed pathetically.

Clearing my plates, which held the remnants of my lunch (chicken Marsala and a plate of mashed), she said, "Why don't you call Peep?"

"Pip. I just left him. A few hours ago. And not on the best of terms."

"Oh. Too bad. How 'bout Rusty?" She was referring to Adrian, whom she had yet to meet. "I bet he could use a friend."

I explained that the young bard was elusive, rarely spending more than a few moments in my presence.

"You know," she said, batting her fathomless Greek eyes, "you can change that if you want. All you gotta do is trim your toenails nine Sundays in a row."

In no mood for her magic, I said good-bye and lumbered home. Entering the foyer, I was surprised to see Louise, Miranda, and Adrian skipping down the stairs toward me. When they spotted me, they froze, like children caught with a belching bong. Eyes narrowing with suspicion, I asked them where they were going. They looked at each other with ill-concealed horror. Louise confessed that they were off to an art fair.

"Give me a minute," I said.

Over their objections, I ran upstairs and threw on a pair of madras shorts and a lavender wife-beater. I met them outside, where I offered to "blow" them to a cab. Unfamiliar with this innocent Jazz Age idiom, which means nothing more than to "treat," the trio blanched, but when a taxi screeched to a stop and I opened the door for them, I noticed with satisfaction that they did not hesitate to tumble in.

The fair was located in a downtown square. In honor of the holiday, the town fathers had swept the square clean of aspiring prostitutes and dying vagrants and filled it with artwork of the most execrable kind—the sort of handicraft that adorns the dormitory rooms of the universities on Long Island. But the art was not the point. At least not for me. I craved fellowship.

I laid a hand on Adrian's shoulder and asked, "Have you ever seen so much garbage in all your life?"

He barely managed a smile. He disliked me intensely. Why? What had I done? We passed a display of turquoise jewelry, the vile excretion of a hairy-calved throwback wearing a peasant blouse without a bra (if Sir Isaac Newton had been married to the wench he wouldn't have had to wait for the apple). I coughed and a spurt of molten Marsala bathed my uvula, along with a healthy wash of last night's stir-fry. I batted back tears and swallowed hard. At that moment, much to my surprise, I spotted Mary Pilango sitting ten feet away on a park bench. She was stroking the back not of her ex-con girlfriend Toby Twain, but of another of her vagitarian squeeze-toys, an actress named Tanya Hill, who, with lowered head, was busily employing a woman's best rhetoric—tears.

"I don't understand you!" she managed through the brine. "How can you be so stupid?"

Mary smiled modestly, as though she had been complimented, but I could tell she was deeply uncomfortable.

"You know, stupid is one thing I've never been accused of," Mary said, leaning back and letting the sun toast her gorgeous olive face.

Louise led us on to the next booth, a display of rainbow-colored clocks—the enameled output of precisely the sort of artisan whom I would never allow to darken my threshold. As the trio inspected the wares, I glanced back at the lovers. It was clearly a moment of pained intimacy between them. Knowing better than to intrude, I darted behind a sapling to listen.

"But we have so much fun together," Tanya cried, "and you're just throwing it away! I can't go on like this!"

"Oh, so *you're* just throwing it all away?" Mary smirked.

Tanya punched Mary's sturdy thigh with a bejeweled fist. "Don't turn it around! How can I keep seeing you when you treat me like this! When you sleep with every girl you meet?"

Mary looked away, thinking. Her gaze landed on a ragtag band of Hare Krishnas serving free grain to a crowd of impatient hippies.

Tanya watched Mary closely, her eyes shooting daggers from beneath her raven curls and tilted black beret. "Say something!" she demanded.

Mary shook her head as though enduring an insistent, hysterical child, which, because Tanya was an actress, is precisely what she was.

"Well," Mary began, "I don't sleep with *every* girl I meet. Some don't find me sexy. I have no idea why."

"Because you find all of *them* sexy! You're like a man! You're like a fucking *dog!*"

Mary turned, suddenly angry: "Look, I put my cards on the table, didn't I? The first night!"

"Yes, but you—"

"No, *not* me—*you!*"

"But—"

"Did I in any way misrepresent—"

"No, but I thought you'd change! I thought you'd love me!"

Mary groaned and looked across the park to the band shell, where on one side a stringy-haired rock group was descending the steps, lugging instruments, and on the other an ebony chanteuse was ascending, followed by three ragtag Rastafarians toting conga drums. (Their dreadlocks looked like colons.) Mary's face changed. It was a reminder from the universe that she should be home working on her own music.

"You don't love me," Tanya concluded, sniffling. "If you did, you wouldn't need to sleep with anyone else."

Mary shook her head at Tanya's perverse logic. This was the price she paid for being a slave to her loins. Men paid a similar price every day. No wonder they hated women.

Since Mary was so exasperated, I ran away and caught up with my pals in front of a collage made of varnished comic book covers. Louise lifted the sunglasses off her fierce nose to take a look.

"I met this poet once," she said. "He was a lot like Michael, into the whole woe-is-me, starving-artist trip."

"Michael's not like that!" Miranda protested.

Miranda's defense of her beloved stung Adrian. He glanced at me. I shrugged in a Chandleresque way that said, "Dames. Go figure."

"Anyway," Louise said, "he wrote me a love poem on a napkin and handed it to me with this heavy look, like it was written in his blood. Like I was supposed to read it and jump in bed with him."

"Was it any good?" Miranda asked.

"The poem? No, it was crap. The sex was hot, though."

"You slept with him?" Adrian blurted, shocked.

My God, could he really be as unworldly as he seemed?

Louise smiled naughtily. "Who said anything about sleep?"

Adrian's eyes rounded wider. Miranda laughed.

"Why're you surprised?" Louise moved to a display of feather earrings. "I mean, isn't that why *you* write poetry? So women'll have sex with you?"

"No, not at all!"

I took his arm and whispered, "She's teasing you, boy."

"Oh!" He glanced back and forth between the two women. "I'm sorry."

"It's okay. You're cute," Louise said. "So, tell me about your work."

"Well . . . I . . . I don't really know how to describe it."

"Do you work in classical forms?" I asked, trying to help him along. "Spenserian sonnets, villanelles, terza rima? Or are you an innovator?" Adrian merely nodded, which, given my question, signified precisely nothing. Why was he so evasive about his work? Normally, I would have dispensed with the questions and simply searched his room. But I feared that if he caught me, or even suspected me, he might avoid me even more staunchly than he did, or else simply move out.

Miranda held a parakeet wing up to her little lobe and studied her reflection. "But you majored in astronomy, right?"

Adrian shyly nodded.

Louise flinched. "You did? *Why?*"

"To help me as a poet. You know, with imagery and stuff."

Louise frowned skeptically. The boy looked panicked.

Enough was enough. I leapt into the fray, hoping to win his trust. "Well, I, for one, adore celestial imagery in verse," I said. "*Astrology,* on the other hand, I abhor, for the simple reason that if the horoscope were true, there would be only twelve types of people in the world. Which is patently absurd. Everyone knows there are only seven."

They all stared at me as though what I had said were not terribly clever.

"You hardly leave your room," Louise said to Adrian. "You don't spend all that time writing, do you?"

"No. No, I read a lot."

"What exactly?"

"Well . . . lately . . . about hydra."

Fascinated, I asked, "The constellation? Or the mythological monster? Or the literary journal put together at that Scottish war hospital, edited by Wilfred Owen, and chock full of poems by Siegfried Sassoon?"

"The animal. It's a book my father wrote. He was a marine biologist." Adrian's cheeks reddened. "He spent his whole career trying to figure out how hydra regenerate. He had this graduate student with no hands. He worked with my dad because he wanted to be the first guinea pig—to see if his hands could be grown back on one day."

"What happened?" Louise asked, wide-eyed.

"Well—" Adrian was forced to swallow hard. "My dad lost all his grants. He was an alcoholic. He died last month. At fifty-three."

It was an astonishing coincidence: Christopher's father, too, had been a dipsomaniacal scientist. Even more astonishing, my adoptive father had been both a high school physics teacher and a chronic guzzler of rye. Did this explain why I was so powerfully drawn to these young men? Did I see in their wounds my own?

"Is that why you studied science?" Miranda asked. "Because of him?"

"And is that why you don't drink?" Louise asked.

"How do you know he doesn't drink?" Miranda said.

"Do you?" Louise asked.

"Never," he replied.

Soon the conversation turned to matters of far less interest, and since Adrian demonstrably darkened whenever I chimed in, and since nature was calling (bellowing, in fact), I excused myself and raced to a portable toilet, where I endured a storm of diarrhea best left to the imagination. When I returned a minute later, the trio was gone. I was gobsmacked. I looked everywhere, but they had vanished into thin air. On my way out of the square, I was shocked to see that Mary had yet to extricate herself from Tanya. Mary's patience was prodigious. I returned to my hiding place and caught the histrionic blabberpuss in mid-aria: "—and I haven't had an audition in two months, so I really need you now, but when I call, I just get your machine, and I know you're home, but I'm not even allowed to come by and check."

"You know what?" Mary replied. "Check if you want, but if I'm in bed with someone else, that's only going to make you feel worse. And it's not really fair, is it? I mean, how would you like it if *they* dropped by while *we* were in bed?"

Failing to appreciate Mary's reasoning, Tanya raised red claws to the sky and shrieked like a victim in a B horror movie. That was it. Mary had had enough. She rose, told Tanya to "grow the fuck up," and stormed off.

But after just a few steps, Mary stopped dead. I stood right in front of her, crouched behind the sapling. I smiled and gave her a wave. Her face twisted with contempt. She walked back, hoisted Tanya by the arm, and led her away.

I checked my pocket watch. Three o'clock. So many hours left in the day. I missed Pip. So what if we had had a tiff? He was my boyfriend, for heaven's sake. Determined to salvage the rest of my holiday, I boarded a bus and arrived at his building an hour later. The doorman, a pimply young queer from Yonkers named Marvin something, allowed me to enter unannounced. Knocking on Pip's door, I knew the pop-in would surprise him, as it was my first, but I trusted that he would welcome me gladly. When I heard teensy footsteps approaching the peephole, I formed a spontaneous-looking smile and held it. He barked out a vicious Mekong slang and ordered me away till dinner. I whined that I was lonely and begged him to let me in.

"No, you go! You go now! Come back latel! I cook big supplise!"

Reeling with *Weltschmerz*, I returned home and downed an obscenely large helping of Chianti (optimistic Neapolitan start, ashy Pompeiian finish). I downed another and another. Then I burst into tears. Of course, I was overreacting, but it had been a most difficult day. Well in the bag, I weaved up the stairs and, overshooting my bedroom, did not stop until I reached the stairs to the third floor. Adrian stood at the top of them. So he was back! He owed me an apology.

I tiptoed up, but before I could catch him, he knocked on Carl's door. When he got no answer, he opened the door and entered. I heard a tiny electronic buzzing coming from inside the room. I advanced on cat's paws and leaned in for a look. A messy heap lay by the window. The buzzing came from inside it. Adrian hit the wall switch. When the lights burst on, Carl leapt out naked from under the heap, which was actually just a dark quilt pulled over two folding chairs.

"Turn 'em off! Turn off the lights!" Carl screamed. Adrian jumped back, almost hitting me, but he did not obey. Carl lunged frantically for the shade and yanked it down. "Are you crazy? What are you doing? Who told you you could do that!"

"I'm sorry," Adrian said. "I just—"

"What? You just what!"

Carl's pubic hair was rose gold. His manhood was modest but well-formed, showing the subtle jack-o'-lantern scar of a botched circumcision. Around his neck he wore binoculars, an instant camera, and headphones connected to a radio on his belt. His pale, freckled torso glistened like a glazed ham.

"What were you doing under there?" Adrian walked over to where Carl had set up two chairs near the window.

"Leave my blind alone!"

"Your what?"

"My duck blind!"

"What's it for?"

Carl pointed to the window.

"Oh, oh!" Adrian, navigating trash, crossed over to it. "Is she there right now?"

"Be careful!" Carl growled, pushing him aside.

"You've seen her again?"

"I've already got two rolls."

"You *photograph* her? Why didn't you tell me?"

"'Cause it's personal!"

"Do you see her a lot?"

Carl wiped his chest and neck dry with a grimy pillow case. "If she's on her way to work, I see her change at three. She's butt-naked for twenty minutes. On her days off, she wakes up at noon and putters around topless in panties till dinner. Then she goes out. Before she goes out, she showers. I see her naked again."

Adrian grinned with delight. "You see *everything?*"

"Everything." Carl lifted his binoculars with pride. "They're Japanese."

"But why the duck blind?" Adrian asked, pointing to the quilt and the chairs. "She's far away. It's night. With your lights out, no way she can see you."

"Better safe than sorry." Carl knelt between the chairs, slipped on his headphones, and lifted the quilt over his head. "Now get lost."

Adrian, laughing, walked over, flipped off the lights, then walked back to the window. He knelt, too, and slowly lifted the shade. A moment later, he gasped.

"Ain't she somethin'?" Carl whispered, gargling with testosterone.

The woman walked past, naked, eating a bowl of cereal. From what I could see, she was ectomorphic and malignantly conceited, and would one day cheat on her kind Jewish husband.

"She's perfect," Adrian murmured.

Carl's camera clicked and clicked. I stepped away and shut the door. I did not belong here. Too locker room for me. I returned to my sitting room, where I drank even more wine and huffed a dozen more cigarettes. Soon, I heard the powdery thunder of fireworks. I imagined all the inhabitants of the great city out on the streets and docks and roofs and fire escapes, oohing and aahing, roasting wienies, hugging, laughing. How I wanted to be among them! But what right did I have to celebrate independence, when, since the day I had reached man's estate, I had never held down a steady job and was now completely dependent on government checks for my survival?

Remembering Pip's surprise, I staggered upstairs, and, although it ran counter to my urge to bury myself under the covers and never come out, I forced myself to open my closet. With painstaking care, I duded up. I had not worn my navy-blue blazer since Sasha's funeral. I had managed, even with all my recent digestive troubles, to put on quite a few pounds since then—some as a result of the cake carousel at the Parnassus, the rest at the hands of the epicurean Pip—so the fit was worse than snug. I slipped on red linen trousers and a white V-neck T-shirt. Looking every inch the patriot, I weaved off down the block, well in the grip of the grape, encouraging myself with the thought that if Pip could refrain from his reckless attacks for one night, and if my bowels behaved themselves, I might actually steal a moment of holiday fun.

On my second trip past Marvin, the doorman, he asked me, "How's Dr. Marker?"

I had no idea what he was talking about, so I did not answer, but on the way up it occurred to me that Dr. Marker might be Pip's lover. It was an outlandish notion, but one that, after a hellish day, I could not banish. Is that why Pip had refused to open the door for me that afternoon? Is that why there were so many medical books in the den? Is that why Pip was so distrustful of me, because he was a cheater himself? I made a mental note to look into it. But later, every-which-way drunk, and dizzy with lust, I forgot to investigate.

Michael Shannon's hairy tree trunks were crossed at the ankle. Candy, a beige slattern of remarkably unspoiled beauty, lifted herself on tiptoe and peed into the tiny motel sink.

"You gotta excuse me," she said.

He supposed she was right.

She scraped herself with a cheap paper towel, then fell down next to him with a naughty smile. She reached for his manhood, but he stopped her.

"What's the matter, baby?"

"Nothing. Roll over." He turned her by the elbows. She looked frightened. He chuckled. "It's not what you think." She fell onto her stomach and he lowered himself onto her generous rump. He began to scratch her back, exactly as he had scratched his mother's when she got home from work. Sometimes he had scratched until his nails were hot.

"Hard night, Candy?"

"Yeah. You know, summer brings out all kinds."

"How long you been on the street?"

"I dunno. Two years maybe."

"You like it?"

"It's okay."

"Where you from?"

"Detroit."

"Ever get scared?"

"Of what?"

"Catching something."

She turned her head to the wall. "Naw, not really. They come out and test us. Like every two weeks. And a john don't like rubbers, I tell him to find somebody else, 'cause there ain't no way I'm dyin' for this. I got a daughter. She's back home with my mother. When I make me enough money, I'm gonna go back, buy us a house."

"Every hooker's saving for a house."

"Yeah, but I'm *serious.*"

"My aunt, you know what she did?"

"What?"

"She sold her big house in Pennsylvania to come here. She wanted to meet all the jazzy people in New York, she said. But, see, what she didn't know, what no one told her, was that most of the jazzy people here just want to make enough money to get the fuck out. They all want big houses just like hers, as far away from the city as possible." He laughed and rubbed her shoulders at the spot where he felt his own worst pain at the end of a shift. He had always imagined he would do this for a girlfriend one day, but he had never had one. He leaned down and kissed her between the shoulder blades. She shook a pretty smile into the bedcover.

"This how you spend good money?" she asked.

He laughed and continued kissing, covering her back with kisses as small as quarters, until she twisted her head around to see if he was crazy.

I No Undelstand What You Say, Old Man

Manhattan worked its magic on young Adrian and in no time at all he was desperately lonely. I took advantage of this happy turn of events to draw the foundling ever closer to my nurturing bosom. I say "nurturing" and not "heaving" because, as I believe I have made clear, I harbored no erotic designs whatsoever on the boy. I am not claiming that had he slipped between my sheets one night, I would have found the moral strength to order him back to his cave. I am, after all, despite much evidence to the contrary, merely human. I am simply reminding you (as I had reminded the hair-trigger Pip, ad nauseam) that I was spoken for.

The lyric poet advanced toward me slowly, like a newborn kangaroo making its slow, sticky trek to his mama's pouch. Each time I found myself alone with him (usually because I had cornered him in the kitchen or violated his room on some flimsy premise), he showed signs that he did not hate me as much as I feared, and that he had not irrevocably shut his mind to my serving as his mentor, if not muse.

One morning in mid-July, my patience and persistence were at last rewarded. Sitting on the stoop as the sun fell, he opened his heart to me, spelling the glories of Ames, Iowa, where I learned that there lurked, amid the vast unintelligentsia, a rich cultural underground. He spoke eloquently of his childhood interest in the heavens (inspired by the gift of a telescope from his mother) and of his high school years, during which, serving the muse Urania, he spent more time dallying among the stars than playing with his peers. Not surprisingly, he had made love to only one girl. Her name was Sally something. He showed me a snapshot. Like Adrian, she was a pretty, unfreckled redhead. Like Miranda, she was more boy than woman.

Adrian dated Sally from the time he was sixteen until the fateful morning, five years later, when she telephoned from college to say that she had fallen head over heels in love with one Chip Clancy, the Fighting Gators' third-string quarterback. A believer in full disclosure, Sally tortured Adrian with gory details of her and Chip's first night of fornication, which had concluded just minutes before and which might best be described as "heels over head." Adrian's heartbreak was so complete that it had rendered him, ever since, entirely chaste (resulting, I'm sure, in frequent stabs of testicular pain).

As a lyric poet, Adrian was in desperate need of help. Under fierce interrogation, I discovered that he knew almost nothing of the glories of the English poets. This could not stand. I immediately initiated a cram course; a College of One. His first assignment was to read the odes of Keats. An apt choice because, aside from the other similarities I have mentioned, Keats, too, had been up to his lungs in girl trouble.

The next morning, I found Adrian sitting on a bench in the Vale of Health, barefoot and cross-legged, reading "Ode on Melancholy." As he read, his lips moved and his brow puckered with consternation. In an antic mood, I plucked a handful of dandelions from a flower bed and quickly fashioned a laurel wreath. I snuck up behind him and dropped it on his hair. Startled, he

smacked at it as though it were a halo of bees, but when he realized what it was, he smiled and was willing to leave it on for a few
minutes. I plopped down at his side and invited him to share his
impressions.

"Well," he began, "I guess Keats is saying that it's okay to get
depressed, that it comes with life, and you might as well not
fight it."

"Excellent! What else?"

The boy bit his lip and thought hard. "That's it."

The poem's mystery, magic, and music had utterly eluded him.
I was disappointed. As I parted my lips to offer some heuristic prodding, the boy suddenly spun around and looked up at the sky. His
eyes flared with wonder. I turned and looked, too. Oh, no. I should
have guessed it. Miranda. Bare-shouldered, she gazed down from
her bathroom window. But not at him. She studied Michael, of
course, who sat scribbling in a notebook at the patio table. She was
going to spit on him again. It had been childish, but at least it had
made him notice her. She swept her fine hair away from her face,
gathered saliva, then changed her mind and swallowed.

"Hi," she said.

For a moment the unshaven hulk did not move. Then his brow
tensed and his head cocked, rather like that of a naturalist who
believes he has heard, but knows it is unlikely, the call of a rare,
reclusive thrush. When his eyes met hers, the girl did not immediately grope for words. For a change, she remained silent, letting *him*
think of something to say. It worked. Curiosity took hold of him.

"What're you doin' up there?" he asked almost tenderly.

She would not be lured into nervous chatter. "Nothing," she
said. "Watching you write."

He exchanged his fountain pen for a cigarette and tilted back
his chair. He shielded his eyes for a better view. I glanced over and
saw that Adrian was about to speak, but I stopped him with a poke
to the ribs.

"Button your gabber," I whispered. "There might be a sonnet in this. Think *Romeo and Juliet*."

"Not very exciting," Michael mumbled.

"I wouldn't say that," she countered.

He tapped the end of his filterless fag on the tabletop. "You'd hate my stories. They're not very cheery. Not very uplifting."

"You think I only like happy things?"

"Yeah."

"Well, you're wrong."

"Huh. Wonder where I got *that* idea. Probably your pretty smile."

(This was, in fact, untrue. Her choppers were straight and shapely, yes, but as dull as weathered cedar. Later you will discover why.)

"Read me something," she demanded flatly, settling her chin onto her crossed hands.

"Nope." He released twin genies of smoke from his nostrils. "I don't read them to anyone. I throw them in a box as soon as they're typed."

"You never send them out?"

"Never."

"You need a therapist."

"Or a new hobby."

"What are they, anyway? Philosophy or stories?"

"A little of both. More like ranting. Mixed with some raving."

"Let me read one."

"Nope."

"Fine."

She ducked inside.

Standing naked in the bathtub, she held her breath, listening to her intuition. A moment later, obeying it, she slid around the corner into her bedroom. She lifted the shade and peeked down. Michael was still staring up at the bathroom window, wearing a toothy grin, assuming that at any moment she would return and make light of her disappearance. She watched as his smile slowly dissolved. She fancied she detected a hint of disappointment in the way he dropped his little eyes to his notebook. It gave her hope.

"Do you require smelling salts?" I whispered.

"No, I'm okay," Adrian sighed.

"You love her, don't you, boy?"

"Love's a pretty strong word. I just can't figure out what the heck she sees in him."

"Love's not only blind," I whispered, "but deaf, numb, and devoid of taste buds. It's based solely on smell."

"What, you mean *pheromones?*"

Ah, the bardling had *so* much to learn.

I wrestled his attention back to the great ode. Even gently guiding him, I found, much to my chagrin, that he had nothing further to say. He was like no lyric poet *I* had ever met. And so, for the next hour, I lectured him, peeling back in onion-layers the poem's diverse and subtle beauties. I flatter myself that he was much enlightened.

For weeks, there had not been a single message from a woman other than Toby on Mary Pilango's answering machine, but, oddly, she was pleased. Freed from the time-drain, not to mention *chi*-drain, of compulsive sex, Mary found that she had much more energy than usual and that her days lasted much longer (an astonishing twenty-four hours), which meant that she was able to attend more diligently to her bodybuilding and her music, and, more important, to Toby, who, fresh from kicking heroin, needed all the love and attention available in the vicinity.

And for a while they were happy.

Soon enough, however, they were back where they had started—trapped in the same dispiriting cycle of fabulous love-making, jealous accusations, raging demands, and harrowing silences that had made Toby's incarceration the previous spring such a relief for both of them. Once again, Mary had assumed the role of beleaguered caretaker and Toby that of grateful but froward patient, only Mary found now that it brought her little satisfaction, not even for her outsized ego. Instead, her heart raced and her sleep turned fitful and she longed to die. It occurred to her that she might be growing up, that she was ready for something new and better. Uncertain as to how to tell Toby of the change, she subtly pulled away. Toby, despite all of her jailhouse psychotherapy, stalked Mary's retreat.

Finally, unable to bear her own cowardice a moment longer, Mary interrupted her morning push-ups to tell Toby the whole truth. Although she laid it out as delicately as she could, it was still rather too blunt for a newly clean junkie, taking her sobriety one minute at a time. Mary explained that she understood now what made their lives together so unhappy. It wasn't Toby's jealousy or her own promiscuity; it was something far more basic to their beings. The real enemy lay in the warped lessons of their childhoods, in the early longings their sick, selfish parents had been unwilling or unable to satisfy. In short, their damaged edges fit together like puzzle pieces and it would prove their undoing unless they found a way to relate to each other differently. No more parent and child. No more caretaker and patient. They had to meet as equals, two mature adults willing to look inward and live from their deepest capacities for love.

"*You cunt!*" Toby screamed. "You don't *want* me to get better! You're blaming *me* for *everything!* The only thing wrong with us is *you!* I'm never good enough!"

Rather than inspiring an early curtain to the melodrama, Toby's outburst merely kicked off another dreary act. Two hours later, exhausted, they cried like hungry newborns and made love until Toby hurried away for a bagel with her parole officer. Mary spent the rest of the morning bench-pressing far too much weight and pacing her room in tight circles, sucking wind. What next? To reject Toby entirely would be like cutting out a chunk of her own heart, but to stay with her would kill them both. Finally, she fell on the bed, desperate to disappear.

Behind her closed lids, she saw flashes of women on summer streets: tiny skirts, hairy treasures, long legs that had never known the sting of the razor or the shock of the wax, gauzy halter tops sporting bull's-eye nipples. Mary grew dizzy and her heart skipped beats. The room was abruptly airless. As if by magic, she suddenly found herself standing on a corner renowned for its heavy flow of Sapphist foot traffic. The first girl she spotted was a pink-haired punk, bearing a veritable tackle box on her ears and nose. She was plain, but her eyes were damp with sensuality and her ass was luscious. Mary raced up and asked with remarkable casualness if she might take a look at what she had bought at the record shop. Her prey smiled and opened the bag, revealing, unexpectedly, not some growling bit of Scottish anarchy, but the splendid debut album of a folksinger, black as pitch, whose name was on the lips of humorless women everywhere. When Mary told the girl that she was a singer-songwriter too, the girl said, "Cool. I love music. I live right up there. Wanna come over? You can sing me something."

Already Mary sensed that this woman was a dreary jackass who probably didn't bathe regularly. Had she been the mistress of her senses, she would have cut and run, but she was not, so she followed her, thinking only of how her ass would look naked. Deep down, in some private place, Mary wanted to weep until the end of days.

At the stroke of noon, Adrian was perched on the stoop of The House Beautiful, recalling my most recent exegesis on the measured glories of the Boy-Bard. How I had brought Keats alive for him! How he longed for more! But, as the Fates would have it, I was not at home. Today was Pip's twenty-seventh birthday and I was at Saks picking him up a white silk scarf. (They had both the best selection and the most poorly placed cameras.) When Adrian heard the door open and close behind him, he turned, startled. He was staring into a pair of knees—skinny and white, bearing a generous sprinkling of fish-food freckles on each cap. His eyes moved up, along tiny hips, over a cottony vintage dress, till they reached a pair of eggcup bosoms.

"Are you okay?" he asked.

"No, I'm scared shitless," Miranda confessed. "Will you walk with me for a little while?"

Ignorant of the fact that beautiful young women are rarely stirred by young men who respond to their whims like yo-yos, the innocent jerked to his feet. As they headed down the block together, Miranda explained that she was scared shitless because she was off to meet Jerry Sheridan, the art dealer, at a restaurant downtown. It was, without a doubt, the most important business meeting of her life. Adrian, touched, offered to walk her all the way to the restaurant. Miranda gladly accepted, and then, insatiable, asked if he would go even further and sit at a nearby table during the meeting, eavesdrop, and when it was over, tell her how she had done. Adrian happily agreed. By way of thanks, she took his arm. He smiled to the point of bursting. He had no idea that by being so generous and agreeable he had all but ensured that she would never have sexual intercourse with him.

When they arrived at the macrobiotic eatery (specializing in high-fiber, slug-laden cuisine), Jerry Sheridan was already waiting outside. He was handsome in a rodentine sort of way and his skin was obscenely tanned.

"Hey, you brought your boyfriend!" he sang. "No problem. Come on, I got us a table by the window."

Miranda was mortified that Jerry had mistaken a polyester-clad yokel for her beau, but she was too shy to correct the mistake.

Jerry scanned the restaurant, one hand wrapped around the back of his chair, the other tugging at his stiff collar. "Funky place," he said. "Prime location. I'll bet it does great business, huh?" Miranda stared at him with bald confusion. He hit himself playfully on the forehead. "What am I thinking? *I'm* the businessman, not you." He laid his well-manicured hands on the table. They began to twitch. Miranda watched them curiously. "I tell you, I'm a little crazy today. I'm three days off the powder and it's drivin' me nuts." He made a crying face, straight out of vaudeville, and scratched the table with both hands. "Mommy, help!"

"Are you okay?" Adrian asked, startled.

"Sure. Come on, let me see what you got."

Miranda reached down to her straw bag and brought up a plastic sheet containing two dozen slides. As Jerry held it to the sunlight with a look of delight, Miranda turned away and surveyed the restaurant as though it were a vast gray seascape or a desert and she was waiting for the arrival of something, a ship or a caravan, that she knew would never come.

(Later that evening, Miranda admitted to Louise that she always felt blue like this when faced with the possibility of success. And she knew why: because no one on earth cared whether she succeeded or not. Her grandparents were dead. Her parents had never forgiven her for giving up horse portraiture. Her friends *sort of* cared, but they had their own careers to worry about. And Michael, he didn't care about her any more than he did about himself. In her novel, Louise summed up what Miranda told her this way: *"Whenever she has a chance for success, something inside of her dies. It is an embarrassing but undeniable fact, but she would trade all the fame and fortune in the world for a man who loves her. Howl, feminists, howl!"*)

Jerry lowered the slides.

"Do you like them?" Adrian inquired.

"Hell, no."

Adrian was as crushed as if the work were his own. "Why not?"

"Because I *love* them. You're my first show, Miranda."

Adrian cheered and patted her back.

The best Miranda could muster was a strained smile and a "Wow." She took a piece of pita bread, wiped it across Adrian's plate, and stuffed it in her mouth. Mistaking it for a gesture of intimacy, the boy was speechless.

Jerry was not: "Anyway, I've got a lot to take care of. In a few weeks, we'll be ready to start hanging. It'll be fifty-fifty, okay? Standard arrangement. Any questions?"

Miranda shook her head.

"How long will her paintings be on display?" Adrian asked.

"A month. Maybe two."

When the meal was over, Jerry tossed a credit card on the table. The waitress told him that they did not accept plastic.

"What, are we in a time warp here?" He dug for his wallet. "No salt, no meat, no credit cards. Shit, it's like 1969 all over again—except you're wearing a bra."

"Salt's not good for you, anyway," Miranda muttered.

Jerry grinned as though she were joking.

On the way home, Adrian, noticing Miranda's sadness, sought to impress her with a spontaneous recital of "Ode on Melancholy," but after the "rosary of yew-berries" the words escaped him.

The romantic disappointment of Adrian's afternoon propelled him back to work. Late that rainy night, he was almost finished: He had read both his father's books, all of his published papers, every scrap of professional memorabilia, and eleven of the dozen lab books. The eleventh had been especially hard going. As a graduate student, his father had used it to record the response of hydra to various drugs and vital stains. It was filled with such pearls as: *"Toluidine Blue in concentrations of 1:1000 is non-toxic. It stains nematocysts except for a few stenoteles. There are light purple droplets in the epitheliomuscular cells that stain. They are clear and homogeneous. Some big droplets in the digestive cells. . . ."* Even though Adrian knew the lab books had little to offer him, he had saved them for last, as though, somehow, a barren end to his search for his father might lessen the pain of its futility.

Staring out his rainy window now, he found he could not bring himself to open the final book. Once he had read it, his father would be dead, truly. And what had he learned? That before his fall, his father had been a gifted scientist and writer, able to express with felicity the most obscure and complex material. That was no surprise. He had inferred it long ago from the honors his father had won and from his single visit to Maine, when, despite his father's drunken decrepitude, he had seen flashes of his brilliance, winking like moonlight off the broken glass of a garbage dump.

The wind blew and a cockeyed shutter tapped the brick. Thunder rumbled in Adrian's chest. He heard a commotion in the hallway. The door burst open and Carl was there, naked but for his binoculars, radio, and windbreaker. Sweat trickled down his red chest and his eyes blazed. Adrian welcomed the interruption. He had grown fond of his eccentric floormate. Maybe someday they would even be friends.

"She thought she could outfox me!" Carl boomed.

"Who?"

"My girlfriend! Guess what she did!"

"I give up. Get dressed and tell me."

"Installed a shade!" Carl threw his arms out wide. "A shade, Huck!" He started pacing, waving his arms. "And I gotta tell you, it scared the hell outta me. She had a friend over, see . . . who by the way I think would be great for you . . . she's pretty. And I'm watchin' 'em, camera ready, hopin' for a little pre-party girl action."

"What's that?"

"Aw, you know. Make-up, tradin' clothes, tryin' on shoes, comparin' tits."

Adrian suppressed a smile. "Who would have won?"

"Mine. Yours is flat as a board. Anyway, next thing I know, my girl's up on the sill with nails stickin' out of her teeth! She's got a hammer! But once the shade was up and I'm ready to kill myself, I notice there's a gap at the bottom. I mean, no one pulls shades all the way down in the summer, right? Only vampires. So, anyway, I wait there for about . . . I dunno . . . four hours. It's pissin' rain. Finally, she gets back from her party and strips down. And guess what?"

"What?"

"I could still see her!"

"How?"

"Through the gap! Butt and bush! Walkin' back and forth!"

"That's all you saw?"

"That's plenty."

"Aren't you going to miss her face?"

"Hey, the universe hands you lemons, you make lemonade."

"You really like her, don't you?"

Carl paused. His face went solemn. "I *know* her, Huck. Better than most people know anyone. And I love her."

Adrian studied him for a moment. "Carl, sit down."

"Why?"

"Just for a sec."

Carl obeyed, but only reluctantly. His leg twitched as though he were trying to kick-start a motorcycle. His eyes bounced to the door.

Adrian began slowly. "I'm worried about you. I mean, it's great that you love this girl and everything, but don't you think you should try to meet her, leave a note on her door or something, or else just forget the whole thing? I'm afraid if you don't, it's gonna drive you crazy."

Carl's expression was blank. "What do you mean?"

"I mean, what you're doing is—" He exhaled his frustration. "Well, it's illegal for one thing. But it's also a waste of time. Isn't there something more *productive* you could be doing? Taking an acting class . . . or maybe trying to get a part in a play or some-thing? Or maybe you could do volunteer work. Work with AIDS babies or something."

"I gotta get back."

Carl jumped up and ran away.

Adrian looked at his bed. The final lab book waited for him there. It was time to face the inevitable. He walked over and opened it. Written in his father's hand on the first page was the title "Journal of the Never-Never Man." His eyes flared. He turned the page. It was a personal diary. After reading just a few sentences, he slapped it shut, hardly daring to believe what he held. Tears rose to his eyes. Here was a book that he would never finish. He wanted to sing or shout, tell the universe *thank you!*

Moments later, when he opened the book and began to read, the Tip-Toe Night held back her dark, gray hood and watched in reverent silence as father and son, one living, one dead, kissed and greeted for the first time.

In all the long weeks of our intimacy, nothing matched the frenzy into which Pip whipped himself that dark and stormy night. His timing could not have been worse. Our celebration of his birthday had been flawless, full of childlike giggles and thrilling cuddles, and crowned by another of Pip's culinary masterpieces—a leg of something or other, garnished with cilantro, ginger, and bamboo—but no sooner had we finished our pudding than the devil took hold. I confess it was my fault. Tipsy and not thinking, I had mentioned the cute crink in Adrian's brow as he struggled with his Keats. Within minutes, Pip's weeping grew so intense that his legs turned to rubber and I was forced to drag him to bed.

"I want live with you!" he moaned, clinging to me for dear life. "I be good! I love you! I cook!"

I could scarcely believe that we were having this discussion again. It is one thing to live one's life as though it will be repeated for eternity, but quite another to face the Eternal Return every three days, to see the dreary patterns of one's life replayed with ever-increasing, ever-more-enervating frequency. My compassion for him was so profound, however, that I did not let on that I was disgusted. Instead, I addressed the matter as I always did, as though for the first time.

"I know you would, precious thing," I purred, stroking his matted hair. "But this place is so much grander than mine and it's air-conditioned. Plus, at my house, we'd never have time alone. It's absolute bedlam."

"I no undelstand what you say, old man! Talk English!"

"We get interrupt," I said patiently. "All the time—people, people. Crazy people. No-happy people. Artist."

"I no cale!"

"You no cale *now*. But you would later. Trust me. No make love loud no more."

"I no cale! I make love quiet!"

"That'll be the day," I thought.

Rather than insult you with any more of our discourse (more befitting a road company of *Miss Saigon* than a serious work of fiction), I'll cut to the pith. Exasperated and demoralized beyond words, I invited Pip to move into The House Beautiful.

No sooner had he hurled his little arms around my neck and peppered me with kisses than I was surprised by the most unfamiliar surge of happiness. I had not known until that very moment how frightened I had always been of what Dr. Gaby Geitman, my old shrink, used to call "commitment." It all made sense now: After my first college heartbreak, I had been turned into a hopeless Invalid of Eros, unwilling to trust my heart to anyone. That is, until I met Christopher. But he, too, proved to be nothing more than another distant green light, someone who I knew, even if only unconsciously, would never love me in return. Both were risk-free adorations. Neither imperiled my grand view of myself, the high wall I had erected around my heart during the first betrayals and humiliations of my early childhood. But now, surrendering at last, almost by accident, to a creature made of flesh and blood, who desired me and only me, I was revealing the longing for closeness that had always cowered behind that wall. I had never felt so vulnerable and, thus, so alive. I held Pip close. His tears were of relief, mine of gratitude.

Adrian Is an Inquisitive Beauty

If, as Aristotle claimed, "the plot is the soul of the drama," then the soul of the plot is the order in which information is doled out to the reader. As I create only true stories from my own past, when I sit down to write a novel I am endowed with twenty-twenty hindsight; which is to say, I know everything about my subject. Yet, much of the time I pretend that I do not. Otherwise I, as narrator, knowing so much, would divest my tale of all suspense. This is why in all of my novels (both) I strive, whenever possible, to mirror in the telling of my story my own ignorance at the time the actual events took place.

At this point in the action, however, my ignorance in regard to Adrian was so profound that for me to sustain it here would be to smother the tale in its crib, and so, even though months passed before I got a chance to photocopy Adrian's father's diary (or even knew that it existed), I will reveal its contents to you now. Here it is, entirely unexpurgated, but for the entries which I have deemed to be of little or no interest to you.

The Journal of the Never-Never Man

Everything is desolate outside and inside. The Big Mother leans over the world with her frozen hands stretching from the end to the beginning of the sun.

The most vivid memories I have of boyhood are of night. They begin when I am first tucked to sleep in the attic of the farmhouse and they climax immediately once the hall lights are turned out and I am in the dark. That's when the noise began. Surrounding the farm were dense woods, stretching for miles— the whole life of the farmer in this region is to beat back the woods which continually threaten to invade his livelihood. The Maine woods seem to exist as they did on the day after Creation. All of the raw energy of the life-force which sustains it shows itself wherever your eye or ear travels. In other forests you can see fifteen feet ahead of you through brambles and whips. In Maine you can't see past your lids. All the animal voices of the woods, to a boy, are merged into one. In that voice are bobcats, barred owls, catbirds, trees trying their joints, deer, mink, weasel, the whooping loons and grebes, the whippoorwill, the Canada goose, the wind—a thousand sounds calling out in a single song. If you are six years old and you hear it, you respect it because it flourishes in a place where you would hardly dare whisper. In fact, you downright envy it. Especially when you are shushed off to bed at 8 p.m. and the lights are down and you're ordered not to peep.

I have turned out to be a biologist but all this has done is educate out of me the awe which I once held for life. It's different in my poetry. A biologist is able to tell you why a fly is able to sustain itself in flight. Only a poet can describe why it annoys you.

I could give up my whole life right now and go to New York City to write. But it is impossible now, with the baby coming. What do I want? This is what I keep asking myself.

We talked tonight. I showed her a bit of my monster. She was as wonderful as a wife can be. I marvel that anyone can be so good. She is like a brooding Mother that waits until I am naked, then bundles me in love. I want to do so much for her. I could and would, only it is still there, the monster, that red-eyed creature that lives inside me with its dull, mechanical, cold, unchanging brain.

I wrote a poem today that reminds me of my sick friend, alone and sequestered, and of the billion million others just like him, who will not give their hearts because they fear they will be split in two, and so all their lives they never know the glorious suffering in a particle of love.

I haven't sent a poem to a publisher in months. I am out of step with the dry, geometric talk in today's verse—lyrics about dirty underwear and suspenders that won't fasten, elegies to outhouses, odes to the toenail of a long-dead, beloved cat. There are no sponsors for my poetry, no patrons, not for me, and there never will be.

I am searching for God in everything, but my lab work overtakes me. It's like there's lead in every inch of my frame and I feel so distant from God that I fear I will never find him.
When you have completely given yourself up to poetry everything becomes more difficult in some ways. Your acquaintances dwindle to nothing and friends become almost nonexistent but for that one rare person with whom you can share what's truly meaningful.

I fear death only because I fear that I will die before I say what I could have said, and this is stupid because what I could say is not what I do say and it never, never will be.

No poems! They are stuck somewhere down in my feet and I can't bring them up. My whole world revolves too closely around my shoulders for verse to spark. I forced myself to write a line and it was as barren as an autumn stone.

For the first time in months or almost years I am becoming interested in my research again. I don't know whether this is good or bad. Received a new shipment of animals today which pleased me greatly.

She is growing beautifully like a pear. Thank God we can give love and through this know the truth, as the magnet knows the turning of the star and the courting of the many-sided moon.

Two poems rejected. The letter said that my adjectives were "hounded." What does this mean?

My experiments are flourishing, but only because I am not writing verse. I must get my degree by next year if our baby is to eat anything better than peanut butter.

When a man or woman becomes a poet this is ruin. When a poet becomes a professor this is worse.

Welcome, May! You are especially well dressed this year. Last year you came in crippled sticks and icy boots but now you are dogwood-decorated and studded with daffodils.

She has been terribly tense lately and with my cruel streak it has made for disharmony for several days now. We exchange a word or two every so often.

I planned to work on my poetry this month, but my research cuts into my best hours. Today I washed dishes in the lab.

I rushed her to the hospital Saturday at 5 p.m. Finally at 2 a.m., the nurse told me that our son had been born, 6 pounds, 9 ounces, 21 inches. Adrian Charles.

Adrian is an inquisitive beauty. He is vigorous and has small artist's hands.

My child, be always true to yourself, and you will live and die a harmonious, intelligent, perfectly beautiful eternity. Only the unnatural universe is to be feared.

What Adrian discovered, reading these thousand words, struck him as nothing short of a miracle. His father had been not a scientist only, but a poet as well—an anguished, yearning, sensitive, dear, doomed poet. What made this such a miracle was not that Adrian was a poet, too, but—here, again, I reveal to you more than I knew at the time—that he was merely *impersonating* one.

Perhaps, Shrewd Reader, you already knew that the boy was an impostor, but I did not. While I had certainly been confused by the boy's unfamiliarity with the mighty dead of English verse and his unwillingness to show me any of his work and his curious habit of cracking his knuckles at the strangest times—it turns out that he did this only when he lied—not once had I suspected him of entering my colony under false pretenses. I always believe the best of people.

Because Adrian was, in fact, nothing more than an astronomy student pretending to be a poet, the revelation that his father had been a *genuine* poet rocked him to the heels. Here the boy had thought that, as a fledgling scientist, he was following neatly in his father's footsteps, when, in fact, he was only doing so when he dissembled. The irony was breathtaking. Not to mention the coincidence. He longed for someone to talk to about it, but knowing that only artists were allowed to live in The House Beautiful and afraid that his deceit might land him on the pavement, he kept it to himself, which only compounded his feelings of anxious isolation.

I like to believe that if I had met him in the hallway or in the Vale of Health the morning after he had read the diary, the sight of my kind face would have inspired him to come clean. Unfortunately, we will never know, because I was twenty blocks away, squirming in the silky arms of my new lifemate, christening the imminent merging of our households with a round of pre-breakfast bawdy.

It is of the nature of epiphanies that within hours, if not minutes, of enjoying one, our most primitive fears rise up to queer it. I am happy to report that my epiphany survived all the way until six o'clock the following evening. I was sitting impatiently at Pip's dining room table while he pottered about in the kitchen, preparing the Hanoi cousin of the Mexican enchilada. I rose and pushed at the swinging door, asking if he wanted any help. He flung himself at the door, barking, as he always did when I tried to invade his workspace, "No way! No come in! I no need help! It's supplise!" Suddenly, I was seized by a dreadful premonition that we would never pass a single night together under my roof. I had no reason to think this, but I did, and the awful hunch would not go away.

What was its source? Was it based solely on his refusal to let me serve as his sous-chef? Or did it have something to do with my knowledge of all men? Did I fear that he would cast me aside, now that I had been so entirely won? Or maybe it had something to do with my own misgivings. Was the language barrier a bigger deal than I was willing to admit? Rather than share my fears with Pip, which I knew would only trigger another round of mucus-letting, I held my tongue. After dinner, I made my excuses and hurried home. By the time I reached my stoop, I was doubled over, clutching my vitals, which had been reduced to a bag of burning liquid.

After a sprint to the loo, I hightailed it to the Parnassus, where, chugging a shandygaff, I unburdened myself to the sapient Cassandra. A great believer in premonitions, omens, and auguries of all kinds, she flung a hand to her bulging hip and pondered the Delphic matter. A moment later, she delivered her verdict: If Pip was a heartless rogue, soon to reject me, there "wasn't squat" I could do about it, but, if *my* feelings were the problem, I needed to take an honest self-inventory before he moved in lock, stock, and barrel. She also suggested some arcane precaution, which involved boiling a pinecone and shouting into a rain barrel.

We're Eating Each Other Alive

At Astor Place, Mary Pilango was a dark thread in the colorful ribbon of pedestrians flowing to and from St. Mark's Place. Everything from kitchen appliances to great fiction lay displayed on dirty blankets and strips of old cardboard, but her attention was not on the goods—it was, as usual, on herself. She knew what a good shrink would tell her: that she was twenty-nine and a stranger to intimacy, that she used sex not to express love but to shirk the incumbencies of her talent and to elevate her mood, and that although for years she had told herself that she was on the verge of a breakthrough, she had, in fact, made no progress at all: she had yet to perform her best music publicly and had yet to be sexually loyal to a woman for more than a few days. Now here she was, sleeping with no one else but Toby, but rather than a climb toward the light it was a descent into the worst darkness she had ever known. Never before had she felt so hopeless. She could not bear another moment of discord with Toby, but at the same time she was frightened of being alone. Meanwhile, she hadn't picked up her guitar in three weeks.

Mary took off her sunglasses and wiped them clean with the corner of her baking T-shirt. Sweat tickled her ribs. The next vendor stood behind a pile of old record albums. "Come on, right here. Anything you see, two dollars!" Mary knelt to inspect the records, but then she saw who was selling them: a smooth-skinned Puerto Rican in tight jeans and a lime-colored halter. She was too young, too desirable. Mary defiantly moved on.

"Hey, girl, check it out!" The next vendor waved a pair of Bermuda shorts decorated with seashells. "Three dollars! Can't beat the real thing!" Mary smiled and shook her head. The young Carib flashed a blinding smile. "Girl, you need these! Ain't no way you're ever gonna get no legitimate dick without a nice pair of Bermudas!"

Mary chuckled at the misunderstanding, then stopped short, startled by the sight of the next vendor.

It was Lily Puff, an ex-lover, standing behind a heap of wrinkled, dirty clothes.

"Yo!" Lily yelled when she saw her. Her limbs were wasted, and her bleached hair looked as though it had been cut against her will by a hospital orderly. Lily stepped over her wares and gave Mary a trembling hug.

"How you doin', girl?"

"Okay," Mary said, hiding her shock. "You?"

"Good, real good."

"Still in the program?"

"Naw, it was a drag. Buncha assholes. What about you, man? How's the music goin'? Good?"

"No complaints," Mary lied.

"Any gigs? Got any gigs yet? 'Cause when you do, you know I'm there."

"Yeah, I know."

She snapped her filthy fingers and pointed. "I'm there!"

Mary's eyes moistened again. It had been two years since she had performed publicly. "When I get something together, I'll send you a flyer. Take care of yourself, okay?" When Mary was ten feet away, she looked back just in case she never saw Lily again.

Lily caught her eye and called out, "Hey, who was that chick who called me?"

Mary froze. "What do you mean?"

"I dunno."

Mary walked back. "What chick?"

"She was askin' me, like, did I see you, are you my girlfriend or what? Shit like that."

"Are you serious? When *was* this?"

"I dunno. While back. A month maybe."

"She didn't give her name?"

"Nope."

"What did you tell her?"

She shrugged her bony shoulders. "I said you and me weren't tight no more, you know. I thought maybe she was a cop. But she said she was your lady."

"My *what?*"

"I knew *that* was bogus!" She laughed and lost balance and grabbed Mary's big biceps for support. "Mary? One girl? No fuckin' way!"

Mary turned and ran for the subway. At home, she found her little red book. She flipped and flipped, hoping that the culprit's name would leap off the page, but she soon realized that except for the women who were now happily involved with someone else, it could have been any one of them. She had hurt all of them. She looked up and, through the bars of her window, saw Toby outside, about to knock on the glass. Their eyes met and in a flash Mary knew.

Stone-faced, she unlocked the door. Toby followed her inside and asked what was wrong. Mary, back turned, heaved an enormous breath. She was about to utter inevitable words, delayed for far too long. She knew that if she let herself connect even for a second to the pain she was about to inflict, she would stop right there, draw Toby into her strong arms, and they would make love as though they had never been unhappy, as though they never could be.

"We're eating each other alive," Mary said at last. "It's over."

Exhibiting a morbidity of temperament every bit as profound as that of the poet Keats, Adrian passed the sticky morning just as he had passed every waking hour since reading his father's diary: lost in a fog of glum reflection. For all of his twenty-two years, using his father's example as a guide, referring to it the way ancient sailors referred to the stars, he had sought to emulate his father's strengths without ever falling prey to his weaknesses, and so he had devoted himself to science and had avoided alcohol—not to mention every other vice. Not only had he never drunk a drop of liquor or sucked a taste of tobacco, but, averse to disappointing a woman the way his father had his mother, he had made sure every romantic step he took was honest and high-minded. And what had been the result? He was practically a virgin. He was not only ignorant of the adult world but scared to death of it. He was a pitiful excuse for a human being. But now he knew the truth: His father had been a drunk and a scientist, yes, but he was also a poet who worshiped nature and believed in the sanctity of the self. Had he known this sooner, Adrian was certain that he would have lived differently. He would not have been so afraid of the unknown, or of his own nature. But what *was* his nature? he wondered. Who the heck *was* he?

The basement gate banged open, and Mary and Toby appeared. Toby was crying hard, her face scarlet and her hair attached to her wet lips by silken strands of snot. Mary, holding Toby by the elbows, guided her as though she were blind. Alarmed, Adrian looked around. The passing pedestrians were uninterested. Suddenly, Toby exploded into a fury. She yanked her hands away and slapped Mary repeatedly across the face, calling her vicious names. Mary's glasses flew off. Adrian had never seen so much emotion in all his life and he was sure that in Mary's place, he would have either run as fast as he could or fought back, but Mary did neither. She simply took it. Each slap left a red mark, but she did not move. Finally, Toby dropped her head and began to sob. Mary stepped in close. Toby rolled her forehead on Mary's firm chest, moaning about all the things she would miss. A few seconds later, Toby turned away. Adrian exhaled slowly and watched as she staggered down the block, shoulders shaking.

"Are you all right?" Adrian asked finally.

Mary, retrieving her glasses, looked up, startled. Her face was scratched and her lip quivered.

"Sorry," Adrian explained, "I was trapped."

"So was I," Mary whispered.

Adrian was full of energy suddenly, wanting to ask a thousand questions. He sat on his hands and tried not to seem too excited.

"What happened?" he asked. "It was just a fight, right? You didn't break up, did you?"

"Afraid so."

"You did? Why? What happened?"

Mary thought for a moment. "Everything got worse, then it ended. Isn't that what always happens?"

Before he could ask her what she meant, Mary eased the gate shut and returned to her room. A moment later, Adrian heard an unearthly wail of grief from inside. Although he felt sorry for her, he also envied her. When Sally had broken the news to him about her quarterback, he had been just as wrecked as Toby, but all he had done was wish her good luck and tell her to call collect if she needed to talk. As a result, he had never moved on. He was glad that he had witnessed Mary's raw and terrible breakup. It gave him something to aspire to.

• • •

The day of the big move began, as all days do, with the rising sun, but unlike every other day, I was actually awake to confirm it. I had wanted to spend the previous night at Pip's place, so that I could be there when the removalists arrived, but Pip nixed the plan, claiming that my presence would distract him from "pack-pack." After a sleepless night, I rang him up. He answered on the first ring and talked a mile a minute, bubbling with happiness—the most intense he had felt, I suspected, since peace had descended on his homeland, in the form of bomb-addled hordes from the north.

"Happy evel aftel!" he crowed.

I was unable to share in his optimism. Even though the merging of our households was upon us and my earlier premonition that he would never move in seemed entirely groundless, when one has been a lone wolf on the steppe of love for one's entire life, the prospect of sharing one's bed with another human being until the end of time is daunting—particularly when one suspects that one is suffering from a ravenous cancer of the bowel. Plus, there was the matter of my lodgers, who, although riddled with psychosexual problems of their own, were still products of their culture and its countless prejudices. How would they take to Pip? Would they judge harshly his minstrel butchery of the English language? His cut-off T-shirts and short-shorts? His tendency to break into dance at almost any musical opportunity?

"Who is it?" Pip barked into the phone, at the sound of his own ringing doorbell.

"That must be the removalists," I said. "I'll let you go. I'm on my way over."

As I headed off, a bit cross-eyed from a liquid breakfast, I felt my spirits slowly rise. Human beings have a tendency to agonize over their defeats for months, even years, while enjoying their successes for no more than a few minutes. It was time to congratulate myself. I had grown tremendously. Prior to meeting Pip, I had hoarded my heart's treasure; now, at long last, I was *investing* it. Of course, difficulties lay ahead, but at least I was finally in the game, and for that I had every reason to be proud. Soon, I was trotting on air. For the first time in weeks, my guts were pacific.

I decided to blow myself to a taxi.

During the slow crawl along the running sores of the city streets, I regaled the driver (a Nigerian, ceremonially scarred) with every detail of my relationship with Pip. He could not have seemed less fascinated, but I did not let that deter me, for it swelled me with satisfaction. As we neared Pip's building, I was met by a sight that even today makes me want to cry: A police cordon was stretched like a jaundiced membrane across the doorway. Standing before it were a throng of onlookers, a patrol car, and three gigantic cops.

I screamed for the hack to brake. I hastily paid and dashed across Park Avenue. I passed a removalist's van on whose hood sat two Dominican hulks looking bored and angry. I dove into the crowd of gawking proles. I feared the obvious: Pip had killed himself. I wanted to shriek, "Let me pass! Let me pass!" but I knew it would be bootless.

I stopped at the cordon, holding my breath, waiting for a gurney to burst through the front doors bearing the limp, blue body of my lover.

When the doors burst open, there was no gurney. Only Pip, standing as tall as he was able, very much alive. I wanted to cry out my joy, gather him in my arms, but then I noticed that his wrists and ankles were shackled and he was being led by a chubby constable, who, although clearly of Celtic descent, looked every inch like a Toby mug in blue. For a split second, Pip turned his head and our gazes met. He shook his head and jangled his bracelets, as if to say, "Pretend you no know me." He dropped his narrow eyes and the cop forced his head into the back of the car. I was frozen in place, caught between fight and flight. To my left stood a sawed-off creature of uncertain gender.

"What's going on?" I asked.

"Beats me," it replied.

I scrimmaged free of the crowd and hurried to a huge policewoman.

"Officer," I began, "I'm a lifelong tenant in this building. Would you be so kind as to inform me what's happened?"

She stared coldly, studying my face.

Just my luck, a man-hater.

"Some chink killed the guy in 19E. Made chop suey outta him."

Someone in the mob overheard this and began to scream, "Gary Marker! He killed Dr. Marker! That guy killed Dr. Marker!"

My knees buckled, my breath failed, my guts roiled. As I tumbled down the block, I turned like a man hounded and saw Marvin, the pimply doorman, sashaying toward the cops carrying a bag of doughnuts. He would tell them all about me. I would be thought an accomplice! I ran home the entire way. The tongueless caverns of stone and glass cried misery. The heavens cried misery. My heart whispered death. When I reached the stoop, Adrian, rereading his father's diary for the hundredth time, leapt up and asked me what was the matter.

"Nothing!" I said as I bolted past.

I tripped and entered the building on all fours.

The staircase to the second floor cracked as I hit it.

The landing thundered as I fell.

My door slammed and I dove under my bedding and did not move.

For the next eleven days, I subsisted entirely on wine and toast. I could not imagine ingesting anything else, for the simple reason that I was convinced that in the past six weeks *I had eaten at least half of Dr. Gary Marker.*

Before you scoff, consider the facts, all of which were unearthed by the top-notch crime reporters of the *New York Post.*

Pip, whose real name was Yung Su Kim, had moved to our shores at the age of eighteen from Seoul, South Korea.

(I had merely *assumed* that he was Vietnamese based on his aroma and bone structure.) The Kims settled in San Pedro, California, where they opened a dry cleaner's, specializing in Oriental carpets. Yung Su attended the University of California, Santa Cruz, majoring in business administration and minoring in theater. Three years later, bored with the dry cleaning business, he moved to New York City, to a seven-story walk-up on Essex Street.

Almost at once, the enterprising scamp embarked on a career as a boy of the night. One year later, he met me in the shadows of the Fifty-ninth Street Bridge. Mere minutes after we had parted with a juicy kiss, he picked up *another* trick—retired plastic surgeon Dr. Gary Marker. The cocky "Hot enough for you, Marvin?" that Dr. Marker offered the swishy doorman as he and Yung Su strolled hand-in-hand through the lobby that night were the last words anyone remembers passing the doctor's lips. His brother Dr. Ralph W. Marker, an orthodontist living in Shaker Heights, Ohio, was the only human being to notice his weeks-long silence. It was Ralph who called the cops.

When the police raided the apartment that awful morning, they found, using various forensic potions and magnifiers, that the immaculate-looking, lemon-scented kitchen had, in fact, recently been used as a "human slaughterhouse." The traces of blood and hair distributed throughout matched those of the missing tenant. As for the whereabouts of his mortal coil, one theory was that Yung Su had disassembled it and carried it out of the apartment piecemeal, but this was directly at odds with the testimony of Marvin and the other doormen, who claimed that since the night Yung Su had arrived with Dr. Marker, they had seen no sign of Yung Su entering or leaving the building. Aside from an occasional delivery boy, the only person they remembered admitting to 19E was a middle-aged man whom they described as "fat and home-less." (Thanks.) But the man never left carrying satchels or vessels of any kind. In the end, the cops decided that the resourceful Yung Su had simply disappeared Dr. Marker down the garbage disposal.

My conclusion that Yung Su had, in fact, been *feeding* Dr. Marker to me one exotic dish at a time was well within the pale of credulity. How else to explain his compulsive cooking? His unwillingness to let me ever step foot in the kitchen? His modest, inscrutable smile whenever I asked just what exactly I was eating? But most damning of all was the fact that the intestinal turmoil which had made my life unbearable for weeks had promptly and permanently vanished within a day of Yung Su's arrest.

That I had finally given myself, body and soul, to a man who said he loved me and that he had turned out to be a liar, a murderer, and perhaps even a cannibal, was more than my fragile brain chem-istry could withstand. My psyche tottered and toppled and I lapsed into an unprecedented paralysis. I will not bore you with the details. Clinical depression is no laughing matter. (We are all nothing but entrées ordered by the worms, but slow in appearing.) I will leave it at this: I succumbed to a grief almost Tennysonian in self-indulgence and pathos. I stared at the wall for inordinate lengths of time, slept most of every day, vomited frequently (gluten, grape, and bile), and several times contemplated suicide. Throughout, I was certain that at any moment a huge net would whelm my bed and I would be carted off to the cackle factory.

My only comfort during my languishment was young Adrian, who proved the embodiment of Midwestern compassion. His devotion was generous and unflinching. He cooked my toast, uncorked my bottles, and changed my linens. The other lodgers dropped by, of course (as did Cassandra, between shifts), but clearly it was Adrian who cared most deeply whether I lived or died, and so it was to him and him alone that I confided my worst fears. His suggestion that I had simply read too much Raymond Chandler and that Yung Su might have used drain cleaner to dispose of the body went a long way toward settling my nerves. As for all the strange meals that Yung Su had cooked for me and the way that they had gnawed at my innards, Adrian guessed that he had merely thawed his way through Dr. Marker's fridge and that I had been sickened by old meats and by bizarre spices and condiments combined in Korean ways.

A few days later, inspired by the orphan's common sense, I rose from my Slough of Despond, ready once again to join the ranks of the living. I found the courage to bathe. It had been far too long, and the bubbles turned quickly gray. After brushing and flossing my teeth and blow-drying my few, last, sad gray hairs, I wobbled into the kitchen. My legs had lost their muscle tone. Determined to stay awake at least until nightfall, I chose from my wine rack a Kenyan Chablis renowned for its slow start and marathon finish.

The doorbell jangled as I poured. I knew exactly who it was: Benjamin, the dusky South Carolinian who delivered my daily mail. While most New Yorkers are content to have their letters jammed through a slot, I prefer to have mine handed over in the flesh. It reminds me of gentler times, back in my birthplace of Fargo, North Dakota—the Athens of the Prairie.

"Good day, Benjamin," I muttered, as I opened up. He was the first person other than my lodgers to see me in my grief and he was startled by my reduced belly, Modigliani face, and shaky legs.

"Hey, Mr. Troop, long time no see." He handed over my mail, then took a moment to mop his chocolate brow.

I flipped through the letters like playing cards. As usual, nothing but junk: letters for my lodgers, and bills, bills, bills for me. I stopped suddenly on an envelope bearing an official seal.

"Bad news?" Benjamin asked, seeing my look of horror.

"No, no!" I shrieked. "A surprise, that's all. Oh, well, must get out of the sun now. Wrinkles, you know!"

He chuckled at my vanity as I slammed the door in his face. I staggered back to the front room, trailing mail. When I landed on the leather, I clutched to my heart the fateful letter. It was from the feds. After a deep breath, I tore it open and gobbled the text. Tears sprang from my eyes. Exactly as I had feared! I looked up and saw, suspended in front of me, my future. Anarchy galloped toward me on a white horse splashed with blood. It was my lift to the Apocalypse!

I returned to my bed for another three days, during which I endured a torpor such that, had I been under water, I would scarcely have found the will to kick myself to the top. Ah, but how necessary is a world of pains and sorrows to school an intelligence and make it a soul! For, at the tail end of this second confinement, facing the very real possibility that the government might destroy my way of life and, along with it, The House Beautiful, I experienced a remarkable awakening. I realized that I had been deluding myself. I was not, and had never been, cut out for romantic love. I had burst into life lonely, crying, and bloody, and would die that way. My sole purpose on earth was to serve as mentor, if not muse, to the young artists who surrounded me, and to defend with my last breath the roof under which they labored. The works of genius they produced under my care would be the crowning, perhaps the only, achievement of my earthly tenure, and none of these works would be born if my colony was dismantled.

Ah, the Plight of the Poemless!

Erect with revised purpose and having vowed to remain, each day, teetotal until dusk, I bypassed the wine rack and brewed a pot of black tea, ideal for a rainy morning. When I emerged into the front room, carrying my silver-plated service (Rogers Brothers, Ambassador pattern), I was just as surprised to see Adrian lounging on my leather as he was to see me perched aloft my own two feet.

"You're up!" he cried.

"That I am," I replied stoically. "As so are you. Which is good. I was just about to wake you." I noticed that he was holding one of my framed snapshots. I walked closer to see which one it was. "What are you doing with this?"

"Just looking" was his casual response. "Who're these people?"

"I and some college chums."

"You all look so intelligent."

"We were. *La crème de la crème.*"

"Who are these two, holding hands?"

"Do you mind getting out of my chair?"

He jumped up and took the sofa; I set down the tea tray and retook my throne. His sharp buttocks had bent it out of shape. A big wiggle set it right.

"These snowbanks are amazing," he said, still eyeing the photo. "It's Maine, right? And this is the guy from the other picture. He and his girlfriend look so in love. Maybe I should write a poem about *them*. Who are they?"

I did not like this line of inquiry. I was in no mood to discuss the couple and their dishonest relationship, so I dodged it: "Oh, you don't want your poem bogged down by facts, do you? Poets deal in truth, not facts."

"Well, yeah, but—"

"Anyway, we have more important things to discuss." I poured the tea. It was pale. I should have let the water boil.

"Not Hung Su again?"

"Yung! *Yung* Su! No, I've moved on. What concerns me now is the future of our colony. Let me explain. Sasha and I had many things in common, not the least of which is that we were both the lucky recipients of monthly checks from the federal government. She for a genuine psychiatric disability and I for a fraudulent one. You see, I was a patient of Dr. Osman's as well. And in return for an occasional swipe of lard across his Kurdish palm, he was willing to vouch for my insanity. He wrote letters on my behalf, stating that I was a manic-depressive with a narcissistic character disorder of Schopenhauerian proportions."

"Schopen*what?*"

"Doesn't matter." I handed him a rattling cup and saucer, which he eagerly took. I tossed him a scone and a paper towel. "What matters is that Dr. Osman is dead. He passed last April. Of tuberculosis. It ate a hole in his lung the size of a squash ball. And so, this year, no letter. And now the feds are after me. They want to talk to me at the end of next month. Unless I convince them that I'm mentally ill, they'll take away my benefits. It's all part of what the Republicans are doing to this country, forcing the mentally ill back into the mainstream. It's positively barbaric."

Ignorant of the ethical compromises that New Yorkers are compelled to make in the pursuit of a decent life, Adrian exhibited a rare lack of empathy. "But you *aren't* mentally ill, right? You could work."

"How dare you!" I cried. "That money subsidizes your art. If I lose my benefits, your rent will double! You'll be forced to move out! So will the others! Is that what you want?"

"Oh. Wow. Okay. I'm sorry." He bit into his scone. Pebbles crumbled into his lap. It had been in my freezer since a distant Easter.

"Here's my idea," I said. "Let's enact a mock interview. I'll play myself. You will play the crafty government inquisitor whose goal it is to determine whether or not I am psychologically fit for gainful employment."

"What do I do exactly?"

"You ask questions. Whatever you think is appropriate. You've been to a government office, haven't you?"

"I have a Social Security card."

"Excellent."

"It was a long time ago."

"Behave bureaucratically."

"Should I start now?"

"Please."

"Mr. Troop," he said, setting down his scone. "I wanna ask you some questions. You say you're too sick to work. Is this true?"

"Yes."

"You seem fine to me."

"Oh, for heaven's sake, Adrian. These are professional people."

"Well, what would they say?" he mewled. "I don't know. I'm a poet, not an actor."

I reached for a cigarette. "Don't whine. I'll start you off." I assumed the cruel posture of a government flack.

"In all likelihood it will begin something like this: 'Mr. Troop? Have you brought a letter from your physician which corroborates the diagnosis of manic-depression?'"

Adrian nodded wholeheartedly, getting the drift.

"And to this I will reply, 'No, sir, for you see, Dr. Osman died last April.' And then I'll look away like this, as though the thought of his death has brought me to the brink of tears."

"That's great!" Adrian crowed.

"I know," I replied, bobbing my eyebrows.

"Especially if it's a guy. Guys hate to see other guys cry. What next?" He carefully slurped his tea. From the face he made, he, too, found it understeeped.

I sat back with confidence and fingered my fag as though it were a fat cigar. "He'll say, 'Why didn't you bring a letter from *another* doctor? To second Dr. Osman's diagnosis?'"

"Good one."

"I'll cry in earnest now. I'm very good at this." I dabbed at my schnozzle with an invisible hanky and began to blubber. "Dr. Osman's the only doctor I've ever trusted and he attended to me for free because he knew how sick I was! How frightened!"

I made a cruel face. "Frightened, Mr. Troop? Of what?"

I leapt back as though from the jaws of a snapping poodle. "The streets! The subways! The people! Everywhere, everywhere, people! Why do they hate me so?"

Adrian broke into peals of boyish laughter. "That's great!" he giggled. "You're a one-man show! *You* should have been an actor! Like Frenchy Tone!"

"*Franchot,* you dimwit!" I screamed. "Stop laughing at me!"

He froze, eyes bugging. "I'm not laughing at you."

"Oh, really? What would you call it!"

"I'm excited for you, that's all."

"It's *ridicule!*"

"It's not! I . . . I swear! I'd never—"

I jumped up, pointed a finger at him, and blew my jets. "Now you can run off and tell the other tenants that you made a fool of me! Well, I wouldn't have been forced to enact *both* sides of this exercise, if you had any trace of imagination. A poet! Ha! I wonder if you have a single creative bone in your body! I reserve my rooms for young artists who *produce!*"

"I . . . I produce."

"Oh, really? Show me then! Bring me a poem!"

I picked up the tray and stomped off. I regret, even today, that the dear thing was forced to bear the brunt of my frayed nerves. Wholly ignorant of his deception and his struggle for selfhood, I had no idea how my attack affected him. Certain that his fraud was about to be exposed and that he would be kicked to the curb, he raced to his Cave of Quietude and tried to write a poem. But Euterpe will not be forced, tight-kneed bitch. He toiled and toiled the rainy morning away, failing dismally. Eventually, he cried a little and fell into a shallow sleep and dreamt that all his teeth were falling out.

Mary Pilango, crouched behind a rack of barbells, set the needle on a vinyl record. Pure heaven, Louise thought. Candles. Mint tea. Rain. And now music. It was the first tranquility she had known all summer. Her heart was beating at a human rate for a change, and her big shoulders were snuggled into a mound of Moroccan pillows. She had no desire to write ever again. How long would this last? How long before the madness took hold and her blood reignited? Sometimes these reprieves lasted for weeks, sometimes mere days, but she was grateful for however much time the Fates bestowed. So far, it had been thirty-six hours. Outside, the vulgar city roared, but she was safe here, wrapped in the wings of the hospitable present.

"Gregorian chants," her hostess said, flashing a pretty smile.

Louise watched as Mary's superb body dropped cross-legged at her side. She remembered the way her naked breasts looked and she felt a twinge of envy.

"You look happy for a change," Mary said, sipping her tea.

Louise formed her thought and spoke it softly. "You're hard to write about, do you know that?"

Mary frowned at the non sequitur. "I am? How come?"

"Half-woman, half-pig."

"Weird. Tanya says I'm half-man, half-dog."

"The point is, you sing like a goddess and screw like a beast. It's hard to make that believable. Gay women are usually so damned—"

"*Nesty,* I know."

"The other day I almost cut you out of my novel entirely."

"Oh, don't do that. I want to be immortalized."

"Well, unless I can come up with some way to explain the paradox . . ."

"I know." Mary set down her cup and crawled to Louise on her forearms. "The reader loves you, right? *Your* character?"

"Enormously," Louise replied with a big smile.

"So why not have my character and your character sitting together. Just like this." Mary laid her head next to Louise's. She slipped one arm around her neck and laid the other on her generous, soft tummy. "The room is dim. Just like this. My character lays her face next to yours, just like this, and then says something that blows her mind. The reader's, too."

Louise smirked suspiciously. "I can't wait."

"That she's through being a slut."

"Right!" she laughed.

"Seriously. She's giving up random pussy, cold turkey."

"And you think that makes her *more* believable?"

"Naturally, your character's skeptical, but she reserves judgment." She touched her lips to Louise's neck, depositing a fleck of mint leaf. "To show her support, she says congratulations and gives my character a hug."

A pause.

Mary jostled her. "Go on, do it!"

Louise chuckled and hugged Mary.

Mary savored it, closing her eyes. "The reader is moved. They're thinking the Pulitzer Prize for Louise D'Aprix. But my character adds something totally unexpected. She says that even though everything she just said is true, can't she start being a good girl tomorrow? Please? One last day as a beast? That's all she asks for. *Please?*" Mary licked Louise's neck and gently pinched one of her nipples.

Louise laughed and shoved her away.

Mary landed back with a thud—shocked, wounded, baffled.

Had I witnessed this scene (instead of discovering it months later in Louise's manuscript), I would have been delighted. I had long hoped that Mary would learn to keep it in her pants, as it were, and apply herself more ardently to her music. Mr. Ambrose Bierce hit the nail on the head when he defined an opiate as "an unlocked door in the prison of Identity. It leads into the jail yard." For Mary, compulsive sex was clearly the prison yard, but now she had resolved to return her cell and get down to some serious work. Good for her. Unfortunately, because her resolve was still in its infancy, she had faltered at the cell door and lunged for one of Louise's nipples. Thank heaven Louise was shrewd enough to reject the advance. It was exactly what the slag needed. Now all Mary had to do was pull shut the door, plump her mattress, and pick up her guitar.

The door from the first floor—which was never to be used by anyone other than me—opened slowly, sending a widening plane of light down the steep, dirty basement steps. As Miranda descended into a swinging cobweb, she heard church music and Louise's throaty laughter coming from Mary's room. She walked to Michael's door. Without knocking, she opened it and slipped inside, leaving it ajar.

A moment later, the first-floor door opened again, revealing yours truly in silent pursuit. When I had seen Miranda slip down the forbidden staircase, my first thought was that during my breakdown she had begun a clandestine affair with Michael, which angered me. I like to know everything going on under my roof. But when I followed her down and peeked into Michael's room and saw that she was only snooping, I relaxed and forgave all. No one has to tell B. K. Troop about the lengths one will go when bridled by Eros.

Michael did everything possible to convince the world that he was a slob, but he was not. His parquet shone. His sink gleamed. His single was made. Existentialist novels lined the walls. I braved a step closer as Miranda made for the closet. A dozen shirts hung there, most of them white. A shoe tree held loafers, boots, and sneakers. She fell on all fours and reached behind them, but found only more books, pushed to the wall in regular piles.

I stepped away as she crawled out and made for the desk. An electric typewriter. Office supplies, neatly organized. In the lower drawer, a baseball mitt, and beneath it a jigsaw puzzle of Brueghel's *Fall of Icarus* that I had given him for his last birthday. She shook the unopened box, then fell to her knees again, reached under his bed, and pulled out a folder. Inside, there were typed pages stapled into bunches. She held the manuscripts up to the drizzly light at the window and read the titles. She chose one and returned the others.

Afraid to mount the squeaky stairs ahead of her, I tiptoed into to a dark corner and hid. As she passed by me, she whispered almost tenderly, "I hate you." I did not know whether these words were meant for Michael or for me. Once the coast was clear, I raced up to the kitchen, and, although it was not yet dusk, I poured myself a bracer. Day one, and I had already broken my pledge, but my nerves were shot and the day was drizzly and overcast.

When I awoke hours later, the sky had cleared and a fresh Atlantic breeze blew through the open window of my bedroom. My first thought was of food. Clearly, I was myself again. I trotted off to the Parnassus Diner, where I was greeted by Cassandra like a loved one thought long dead. Over a bowl of fettuccine carbonara and a gin gimlet, I told her all about my troubles with the feds and the desperate peril into which I would be plunged were my monthly checks to be withheld. She laughed and said that it would all work out. I did not believe her, and I told her so in the most self-pitying and aggressive way. Happily, she was not offended. Like her mythical namesake, Cassandra was used to having her prophecies dismissed.

Sound asleep, Carl looked as though a poison dart had felled him in his tracks. His naked limbs were sprawled and his head snored on the wet windowsill. The phone was resoundingly silent. At his side lay a pool of black-and-white glossies, each showing his beloved or just her groin in various stages of distant undress. Adrian stood over Carl's bed, not speaking, just staring and waiting, as though he hoped his presence alone would be enough to jostle the mad, secret masturbator awake. Sure enough, it did. Carl suddenly sat up, slammed the window, and groped to the floor for a cigarette.

"You're not a happy man, Huck. How come?"

"B. K.'s all freaked out about some meeting with the government, and, even though it's not for a few weeks, he asked me to help him prepare for it, so I did, but not very well, and the next thing I know he's screaming at me, saying he wants to see one of my poems. But I *can't* give him one because . . . because I lied, Carl. I'm not a poet."

(Had I been stationed at my peephole, I would no doubt have bicycled on the porcelain and fallen flat.)

"I know," Carl said.

"Really?"

"You don't drink. You don't laugh. You dress funny. You read about clams on a Saturday night. You're like no writer *I* ever met."

A claw of red crept across Adrian's neck and cheeks. "How can I write a poem? I don't know anything *about* poetry. I'm not even sure I like it all that much."

"Ah, the plight of the poemless! Yeah, I do a play every year for the same reason. To prove to B. K. I'm really an actor. Last year I played a Potawatomi Indian chief in some shit-hole downtown. Smoked a peace pipe and everything."

"Maybe you could help me find something in a book that—"

"Forget it. There isn't a limerick on the bathroom wall at Penn Station he hasn't already memorized. How do you think he got so fat? He *eats* poems. He ought to be teaching at Harvard. No, Huck, just go ahead and write one. It doesn't even have to be that good."

"Just good enough to convince him I'm the reincarnation of Keats."

"Hardly. You should have seen me in that play. Trust me, I was no Jay Silverheels."

(Despite his modesty, Carl really was enormously gifted. Louise put it best in the chapter where she first introduces his character: *"His problem was simple. He was an actor, as Oswald was an assassin, as august is sultry, but he was born in the wrong body. Inside: sound and fury. Outside: the blandness of a Bible salesman or a golf instructor."*)

Adrian looked up fearfully: "Carl, if I don't give B. K. a poem, I think he might kick me out, and if he kicks me out, I'll never find another room this cheap. I'm living off student loans as it is. I'd have to go back to Iowa and start graduate school, and I really don't want to. And . . . and if I move out, who knows who might move in? It could be someone really loud, someone even more annoying than I am. Or someone who calls the police when he sees you spying on your girlfriend."

Carl's face tensed as he imagined it. "What kinda poem you lookin' for exactly?"

"I don't know. B. K.'s just been through a pretty bad breakup. A love poem might cheer him up."

"I can only write what I know."

"What do you know?"

"Myself, I guess.

"That's it?"

"I could make it sound universal."

"I'd really appreciate that."

"But, listen, Huck, in the meantime? Start *acting* like a poet. It could go a long way with B. K."

Adrian sat back, trying to imagine how poets acted.

After dinner, my noggin well oiled, my nerves a bit duller, I climbed the steps to the third floor. I wanted to apologize to Adrian for my inexcusable conduct and suggest that we wait a full week before we conduct our next mock interview. This would give him time to reflect on his miserable performance and come up with ways to make sure that it was not repeated. When I reached his door, however, I heard footsteps from overhead. Odd. The roof, too, was off-limits. Why was everyone suddenly flouting the rules? My Lord, one short nervous breakdown and the place had turned into Beirut. Then I had a sudden, terrible thought. I flew upstairs, fully expecting to find the green woodpecker standing on a ledge, teetering, about to test his wings. I know it sounds absurd, my immediate assumption that he was going to attempt suicide, but my impossibly high standards have been known to inspire desperate solutions in the young and susceptible.

What I found instead was Adrian, Louise, and Miranda laughing together on a woolen blanket. The evening's breeze had blown away the storm and left behind a clear, black sky. In front of them lay blocks of low rooftops stretching toward the smokestacks of Queens. Behind them towered the gleaming glass of skyscrapers of Midtown. Above them was a brighter than usual scattering of stars.

The trio looked at me with concern.

"Relax, kiddies," I said. "It's just little old me."

I plopped down on the wet tar just a few feet away.

No one invited me to share the blanket.

In fact, no one spoke at all.

My presence had exerted a chilling effect.

"There it is," Adrian said, finally. "Five thousand years ago that wasn't there. There was some other star. Someday, it will be gone and the star Vega will be there and we'll call *that* the North Star.

"It'll be *gone?*" Miranda asked.

"It won't be in that position. It has to do with the earth's axis. It's called precession. Our axis moves. It all moves. All of it's changing."

"Except the Big Dipper," said the still-serene Louise, dropping a chocolate mint in her mouth. "If you tell me it's gonna disappear someday, I'm gonna write my congressman, whoever that may be."

"It's definitely gonna change." Adrian pointed again. "You see, it's seven stars that happen to fall into a form because of where we are in relation to them. Now see the middle five? They're a group. You can only see three of them right now, actually, but they're about seventy-five light-years away and they're gonna stick together. But the star there at the top of the handle? That's much farther away and it's moving in a completely different direction. And that star at the bottom of the bowl? That's about two hundred and fifty light-years away and it's also moving away. Which means it's all breaking apart. Soon it won't look the same."

"Soon?" Miranda asked.

"About fifty thousand years."

"Oh, I thought you meant *soon* soon."

"The bowl will sort of flatten out like it's been hit by a hammer."

"The Big Spatula," I intoned.

Adrian chuckled. (Was he merely currying favor so that I would not evict him?)

Louise offered her bag to Adrian. "Mint?"

"No, thanks."

"Miranda?"

Miranda quickly shook her head.

I shook my head, too, although Louise had not offered.

"Tell us more," Miranda said to Adrian.

"About what?"

"Anything."

His face softened as he sat up higher on his slender forearms. His hair blew back and his dreamy eyes grew bright. "You see the second-to-last star in the handle? It's really two stars."

Miranda squinted. "I only see one."

"They're actually far apart. It's called an optical double. They line up because of where they are in relation to earth."

"So they look like the same star but they're not even friends?"

"Right. But there's more. Because each one of those is actually *two* stars. They're binary stars. Two stars so close that gravity keeps them inseparable."

"My parents are like that," Louise muttered.

"Not mine," I said. "My adoptive parents despised each other. They slept in separate bunks."

Howling silence.

I felt invisible.

I lighted a fag.

Miranda threw a furtive glance at Louise. The bag of candy lay swaddled in darkness. She made for it with a creeping claw.

"God," Louise said, "I don't remember anything about astronomy except there was a cute jock named Trey who sat next to me. Once during a lecture, he turned to me and said, *'I'm* gonna be a star one day.'"

"I took geology," Miranda said, quietly digging into the bag and pulling out five mints.

"And here's something else," Adrian continued. "The better our instruments get, the farther we're gonna be able to see and the more we're gonna be able to learn. But not about the future. We're gonna learn about the past. We'll be able to see things that happened at the beginning of time, but whose light hasn't reached us yet. We'll see the first light of creation."

"It's all so enormous, isn't it?" Louise murmured. "So *humbling.*"

Miranda spoke soberly, chewing mightily: "Maybe if I studied astronomy, I'd stop thinking about Michael all the time."

"No," I sighed, "studying the Big Bang would just make you want him even more."

"Shut up!" she screamed. *"Who invited you?!"*

Miranda had never spoken to me so harshly and I could not for the life of me understand what I had done to deserve such hatred. So I had snooped on her while she was snooping on Michael—on what planet was this a capital offense? Watching her jam nine more mints into her mouth and knowing only too well the agony of unrequited love, I decided to cut her some slack. I would not shout back. I would let her outburst go unpunished. I flipped onto my side, planted an elbow, and propped my big head on my palm.

I studied Adrian. His breathing was slow. Despite the fiasco of our mock interview, he looked happier than I had ever seen him. It had been years, I guessed, since he had seen the sky through the eyes of a beginner. Stars had become mere facts to him, mere data to be memorized, but now, narrating the heavens, sharing a few simple lessons with his friends, he was a boy again—back to the days when constellations were as exciting to him as the monsters and heroes who lent them their names.

I watched as Adrian smiled, closed his eyes, and imagined that the night breeze was blowing away like dead leaves every habit of mind he had ever acquired, every dreary pattern that rendered him dull and predictable. If he lay perfectly still, he thought, soon the wind would whisk away the past entirely, leaving behind only what was essential. He could begin again, become anyone he chose. He opened his eyes. Miranda was crumpling the empty candy bag. Louise looked like she might be sleeping. And there was I, a modern-day odalisque, staring at him with X-ray eyes, reading him to the very marrow.

"B. K.?" he whispered.

"Yes, lad?"

"Can I have a cigarette?"

Miranda flinched.

I extended the white, soft pack of my generics and she grabbed my wrist.

"You don't smoke!" she said to Adrian. "What are you doing? They're horrible!"

"Maybe he *craves* something horrible," I explained.

Miranda yowled as I yanked my hand away and tossed him the pack. Adrian caught it with both hands like a bridal bouquet.

"Relax, it's just one," he said to her.

"That's what everybody says!"

"Don't worry, I won't get hooked. I have willpower. Maybe *too* much."

I thought of my darling Christopher. He, too, had had plenty of willpower, yet within days of my teaching him to inhale, a veritable nicotine-gibbon had appeared on his back. I leaned across Miranda with Sasha's gold lighter. Adrian shielded it from the wind and I flamed the weed.

"You're a piece of shit!" Miranda growled at me. "I've lost all respect for you!"

"Dear me," I countered insouciantly. "Whatever shall I do?"

"Louise, say something!"

"If he wants to kill himself," she shrugged, "let him."

Adrian hacked a ball of smoke.

"Easy does it," I purred. "Let me show you."

"Lessons?" Miranda cried. "You're giving him *lessons!*"

I crawled over her to get to Adrian.

"Get off of me, you whale!" she cried. "You're crushing me!"

"Inhale more slowly. Let the poison linger among your pearly whites . . . tickle your uvula . . . caress your epiglottis. Good. Now suck it gently into your sacs, taking oxygen with it."

"Get off! I can't breathe!" Miranda screamed.

I rolled off and shouted. "Look, it could be worse! He could be addicted to some *smelly philosopher!*"

Her mouth dropped open. She had pushed me too far and had paid the price. Oh, how the truth hurt.

"Addicted?" Adrian said, coughing again. "I'm just messing around."

"For the time being, yes," I said, "but soon you will be hopelessly enslaved. And let me warn you, boy, addiction is a dance with death. I've been battling these enchanted sticks since the loss of my milk teeth. Not to mention a tussle I had with nasal spray in the late seventies that left me baying like a wolfhound on the Brooklyn Bridge."

"God, you act like it's heroin or something."

"It might as well be."

"Then why did you give it to me?"

"Because you asked," I replied profoundly.

"So if I asked you to give me some heroin, you'd give me *that*, too?"

"Sorry, plumb out."

"Boy, you're some great mentor," Miranda muttered.

"I want him to grow up," I said.

"And addiction'll help me do that?" the boy asked skeptically.

"Yes. You've opened the door a crack. In a few months, when you realize you can't shut it, you're going to go dead inside. Your self-loathing will be immense. Your joy of life will drain away. You'll have to claw your way back to mental and physical health. Choose life all over again. You'll understand the truth of human existence.

"Which is what?"

When serving as mentor, it is always best to let the charge make his own way though the labyrinth—that way the victory will be his and his alone. I did not answer. Instead, I changed the subject, to something that I hoped would interest everyone: my government interview. My hopes were ill-placed. It interested no one. Fifteen minutes later, we were all in bed, snug as bugs in rugs, when I felt an urgent need to void my bladder. I popped down the hall and was surprised to see a light shining from below the bathroom door. I banged a fist.

"I'll be out in a second!" Miranda shouted.

"Well, I hope so."

I walked in place with diminishing volume, slid aside an oddly placed umbrella stand, fell to my knees, and applied my face to the hole. I was level with Miranda's boyish hips and sparse vanilla pubis. She turned her bare bottom to my face and leaned into the tub. The view reminded me of one of her paintings. The hot water blasted from the bath spigot. She waited until the steam rose, then turned and gathered a wad of toilet tissue as big as her fist and dropped it quickly into the toilet bowl. She cocked an ear to the door and listened.

I held my breath and watched as she puked quietly chocolate mints onto the toilet paper.

At last I understood why she had been so nasty on the subject of addiction and why her chompers were the color of mice. She vomited again, and another splash of chocolate came up. She wanted another go, but she knew that I hated waiting for the toilet, so she reached to the medicine chest and pulled out a bottle of antacid. She gargled, spit, stashed the bottle, rinsed out the basin, and turned up the cold water in the bath at the same time as she turned off the hot. She knelt and soaked her hair so that she would look freshly shampooed. She grabbed another wad of tissue, wiped the rim of the toilet bowl, and flushed.

I was about to lurch away from my peephole when she froze

and turned to the full-length mirror. She turned sideways, laying a hand on her tummy. Flat. Better than flat. Collarbone sharp, too. Legs and arms tight. Perfect. She pressed two fingers beneath her ribs and felt that the muscles were sore.

"I'm killing myself," she whispered flatly.

I moved the umbrella stand back to its odd spot and stomped in place with ever-increasing volume.

"Miranda, dear?"

Wrapped in a towel now, she flung open the door. "All yours," she said wearing a phony smile, but the smile turned instantly upside down when she saw that I was naked.

Smoking a cigarette on the front stoop, Adrian was faintly nauseated and his sinuses stung, but he liked the way he felt: like a movie hero, one more manly than himself, and taller, and with way more than one woman on his sexual résumé. He exhaled a puff and pretended to brood. Pedestrians passed, returning from their revels or on their way to more. Cars passed by, too, most of them taxis. The city went on like this, day in and day out, like a perpetual motion machine, regardless of anyone. A person had only one choice, Adrian thought: join in or be rendered irrelevant. He flinched when the gate opened and Michael, slump-shouldered, skipped up the stone steps.

"Past your bedtime, isn't it?" Michael asked.

"Yeah, I guess. Just smoking one last cigarette. What about you? You're going out now? Where are you going? Isn't it kinda late?" Adrian felt his heart race and his hands tremble. Was it the nicotine or his sense that Michael was headed out for a night of dangerous fun?

"For me, it's dinnertime," Michael said.

"Oh, right. You're nocturnal. But what's there to do? Where're you going?"

Michael studied him with a penetrating eye. The lad twitched with self-consciousness. Michael looked across the street to the steps of the crumbling church.

"Whoring," he said.

Adrian's surprise bordered on horror.

Michael smiled at him. "Wanna come?"

(In terms of Adrian's needs as a man and an artist, the offer was not without its merits. Keats, too, had frequented brothels—many critics feel that these visits gave much-needed landing gear to his flights of fancy. In fact, remembering all that a momentary descent into sin had done years before for the foundering Christopher, I had even flirted with the idea of finding Adrian a whore myself.)

"Isn't it dangerous?" Adrian asked.

"Sure, but what isn't?"

"Lots of things."

"I mean, that's *enjoyable.* Coming with me?"

"I wouldn't like it."

"You'd get laid. What's not to like?"

"Taking advantage of someone like that."

"They have the advantage. You pay them."

Adrian wondered why he felt a sudden urge to giggle. "No way. I couldn't. It's disgusting."

"How do you know? You've never tried it."

"I've never murdered anyone either."

"Really? Why not?"

Adrian gestured him away with an effeminate wave. "You're making fun of me. Great. Anyway, look, just go. I'm not coming. It's just . . . wrong."

"What are you, a poet or a preacher?"

"You don't have to go to whores to be a poet."

"No, but you should understand them."

The words resonated.

"I think you should try to *help* them," Adrian managed feebly.

"If anyone needs help, it's you, kid. Your head's so far up your ass, it's a wonder you can breathe." He walked a few steps and looked back. "You're sure now?"

Adrian wanted to spring up, just for the sake of experience, but he looked at his boots instead and told himself that no matter what he mustn't budge. He wanted to live more fully, yes, but not if it meant hurting another person.

Michael walked away, chuckling into the humid air.

As Adrian retreated to his cave, glancing at the flicker beneath Miranda's bedroom door, he had no idea that the girl he adored was curled naked under paint-splattered sheets, reading by candle-light the slice of her beloved's corpus that she had pulled from beneath his solitary bed.

Paint the Town Black

By Michael Shannon

After penetration, she speaks only twice. First, "You can go faster, baby."
Then, "I'm beat."
Then she covers her mouth, coughs, and gets up to clean.
I lie motionless after the gate slams shut. The air is sick with morning
light. The tick of a cheap clock fights my heartbeat in the pillow.
Outside one is always inside, crawling between walls. Anyone who sees
beauty in this place is blind or lies. No one who values life and has the money
to choose would ever live here, without green, without breezes that sweep down
from above the clouds, without hints from the seasons, without a single vista
that has not been fouled. The city is a concrete platform on which goods are
sold—a massive, multilevel, shiny, decaying mall. What is a man to do when
he lives in a mall but has no money to buy and nothing to sell?
My eyes are dark and small. When I am alone, they are void of life.
Beneath my brow which is black and above my cheeks which are pitted
with scars, my eyes are striking. The irises hang heavy and the whites are
visible beneath them. But when animated they are tiny flames. I catch
them sometimes in the bar mirror and I step back alarmed at their urgency.
I scare women with them, which is why they do not trust me. Sometimes

I picture myself decapitated, my head lying on a pedestal with the eyes burning like eternal flames on a grave, unbended by the fickle wind.

What is a man to do when he lives in a mall but has no money and nothing to sell? Answer: He can tell what he sees.

In the afternoon the telephone wakes me. "Come on," she says. "A party. Saturday night. We'll paint the town red."

I happen to be free.

The party is at the home of a rich playwright's daughter. She meets us at the door with the beaten look of a mediocre child born into a famous family. She slouches as though her father squatted on her back. Her smile is overfriendly. She points out the punch bowl.

Within minutes, my friend finds an unemployed actor to talk to who is as desperate for fame as she is.

I recognize some of the guests. I have not seen their movies or plays, but I know their faces. They glance at me with skittish eyes, ready for me to recognize and approach. I sit alone on the sofa with my punch.

A teenager sits next to me and tells me why she did what she did with her character in her last movie. When I open my mouth to reply, she runs away.

A model takes a liking to me. Lifeless skin, perfect teeth, dreadlocks, strangled voice, eyes covered with cobwebs. Finally, she asks delicately if by any chance I have some cocaine. I tell her no and she vanishes.

A stage manager with two nickels for earrings tells me that I smell good and asks why I won't flirt with her. I tell her this is how I flirt.

A bleary-eyed actor poses by the window smoking a joint. His last movie was a hit, so he feels entitled to be antisocial. None of the others intrude on his legend. They want to be accorded the same privilege when they have their hits.

"I know you!" I want to scream, standing on a crowded table. "You are lost, desperate, stumbling through the desert. There's sand in your mouth, your knees are bloody, your lips and lids are scorched, yet you lurch on, grinning wide at the silence. You suck at a spiny cactus, then lick your lips, and back you go, and every time you plunge into a mirage and choke

on the hot sand, you laugh at the sun and say, did you like that joke? But soon night will fall and a cold wind will blow. You'll look in every direction for cover and know at last what you've been told a thousand times and always denied: You are dying. Yes, even you."

I tell my friend I'm leaving. She insists on coming with me. "Fine," I say. "Let's paint the town black."

A clean, dark room. A huge pair of handcuffs on six-foot chains hangs off the wall and an ominous leather curtain conceals the Orgy Room. The clientele are the usual—a few transvestites, some drunken girls, a pack of homely men over forty. The star of the evening is the only young woman who has brought along a slave. He wears a leather suit that exposes his jellied stomach and chest. After a few minutes of parading him, she jerks the leash and hauls him behind the curtain. In slow motion, a dozen men rise from stools. "Follow me," I command. My friend reluctantly obeys.

The room is twenty feet wide with stalls in back. The men are already there, clustered around a stall in a semicircle. Inside, the mistress is calling her slave names while he laps hungrily at her shaved crotch. A man at my left, silver-haired, sighs.

"She's calling him names," he whispers, spittle forming at the corners of his chapped mouth.

"I hate this place!" my friend hisses.

"Really?" I say. "Not me. I feel completely at peace."

"Well, we're different then! Very different!"

I walk alone under the gray dome of the sky. I am so happy to be free of her admiration I could scream. And for a stupid moment, I feel immortal.

Death does not exist for the mind because the mind lies. When confronted with the universe, which never lies, the mind is a paltry thing. When you sit at your mother's hospital bed or cradle her as she dies or stand at the lip of her freshly dug grave, the mind is like a sad, runny-nosed friend who tags along, stumbling to catch up.

I need to be reminded.

A punk club. The usual chinless crew, daubed with paint, decked in black, moving to agonizing music. Their hair is dyed and ravaged, their skin pierced and cartooned. Their parents must have beaten them, either with their fists or in more violent ways. They dance without partners. These kids know better than most that life ends, but they are too afraid to live, so they play roles instead, in a vain attempt to abstract their despair into something mythic and eternal. Because their roles are ghoulish, they are shunned. Because the middle class's are not, it is not.

Leaning on the bar, I think: Maybe if that little rich girl in the papers last month had been pounded in her childhood like these kids were, not by fists necessarily, but more constructively, with wisdom perhaps, had been told that living is a hell of suffering and that the universe owes her nothing, she might have lain down in that hotel corridor and let that crazy rapist do his business. Or else she might have fought back in a way that he could have understood. Instead, when life introduced itself to her in the form of a man, off-white, saying, "fuckyoutakeoffyourclothesyoustupidblondebitch," she squeaked her protests like a bunny pinned under a tire. It was like having her hairs pulled out one-by-one for her to admit into the shrine of her imagination that a stranger, au lait or otherwise, was actually going to enter her body and squirt out a load of his gooey madness. Better the knife! was her mind's genteel response as it shut itself down. And the universe obliged.

I stand alone in a dismal square, my grief in pieces inside me, like a swarm of free radicals. I breathe deep and try to open my heart to the end of existence, because without death there is no reason to say anything, build anything, love anyone. It is the only purveyor of value. It is God.

At the party, I told a girl full of beauty and hope that she and I and everyone else were all the same person.

"Why, who do you think I am?" she challenged.

"Unconditional love," I said. "And animal fear."

So Write a Poem

Through the kitchen window, I spotted Michael sitting alone in the sweltering garden, swigging a can of beer. Not yet recovered from his previous night's corruption (another drunken shiatsu performed on another dusky voluptuary), he looked sleepy. Pen touched paper, but no ink flowed. Suddenly, his chin snapped, as he nearly nodded off. Excellent, his defenses were down. Still, I must tread lightly. My personal dramas bored him witless. I loaded my anxieties into a Trojan horse of good cheer.

"It's a beautiful world, Stout Fellow!" I proclaimed.

"Oh, shit. What is it now?"

He had seen right through me. Evidently I was a bit *too* cheery.

"Nothing," I said, creaking into wicker. "Mmmm, look at you all stinky and manly." I dabbed at his dripping ribs with my hanky. He swatted it away.

"Stop buttering me up. What do you want?"

I squirmed myself comfortable in the chair. "Just this: Last week I received a letter whose importance can best be described as 'life or death.'"

"I'm skeptical."

"It seems that Uncle Sam has decided to question my insanity."
The lout smirked.

"It's not funny!" I shrilled.

As I laid out the details of my case, my fears scrambling out of
every equine-orifice like suffocating soldiers, he grew increasingly
restless. It was only my conclusion that roused him: "These disability checks are crucial to my budgeting. If I lose them, I'll be
forced to charge you all twice as much rent."

Nothing focuses a philosopher's attention like a threat to his
purse. He snatched the letter from me. As he read, his brow grew
grumpy.

He threw down the letter. "So what do you want from *me?*"

I picked at my blouse, which already blossomed with flop
sweat. "A mock interview. You ask me pertinent questions and I
answer them. Then at the end you tell me whether I seemed mentally ill or not."

He leaned back, holding his fountain pen between two finger-
tips like a canny interrogator. He was already in character. How
marvelous.

"Mr. Troop, tell me a little about yourself. I see in our records
that your doctor—"

"Serxwebun Osman. A Kurd."

"Yes. He's diagnosed you as a manic-depressive."

"That's right. An untreatable one. Lithium-intolerant. I also
happen to have a colossal ego and suffer from bouts of depression
of Delmore Schwartzian proportions."

"We didn't receive a letter from him this year."

"Yes, I know. Dr. Osman died. Last April. Of consumption."

Michael tightened his mouth, as though this were *very* bad news.
He jotted a note on an invisible clipboard. "Physician dead . . .
applicant . . . claims."

"Claims!" I was genuinely insulted. "I saw him buried! And if

he *were* alive, he'd have vouched for me, I can assure you of that. He considered me quite ill."

"In the past, yes. As for the present, that's impossible to confirm, isn't it, his being dead and all?"

Good point. My mind groped for a counter. In a flash I had it. "Sir, I know what you're thinking, but I'm fairly certain that Dr. Osman's death was in no way an intentional act of hostility toward me."

"Excuse me?"

"To destroy my eligibility. I mean, after all, he was sixty-three years old and, like most Kurds, infected with tertiary syphilis, which leaves one open to all sorts of other bugs. So for me to take his death *personally* would be . . . well . . . it would be—"

"Are you crazy or not, Mr. Troop?"

"Yes, of course! But I'm not *stupid.*"

I had performed brilliantly. A smile crept across Michael's lips. He regrouped.

"Why haven't you found another doctor, then?" he asked. "Someone *else* to vouch for you?"

An excellent question. My mind went blank. The best I could manage was: "I . . . I don't like doctors. I don't trust them. They remind me of my daddy."

"Daddy?"

"My adoptive daddy. He held a doctorate in physics and molested me until I was nine."

"I see." He leaned back, exhaling. He was demoralized. Victory was nearly mine.

"Do you live alone, Mr. Troop?"

I knew where this was heading. My God, he was wily.

"Yes, I do."

"House or an apartment?"

"House."

"That must be expensive."

"It is."

"But you don't have a job?"

"That would be against the law."

"But if it weren't, you'd have one?"

"Of course not. Impossible. I'm a psychological and biochemical fiasco. Absolutely unemployable."

"So you support yourself solely on the funds that *we* provide you? You expect me to believe that?"

Lacking a leg to stand on, I compensated with volume. "It's the truth! I'm extremely frugal! I scrimp! I collect Green Stamps! I save tinfoil!"

"Is that so?"

"My budget is so close to the bone, there are days when I subsist on nothing but crackers and marmalade!"

Michael eyed my fat midriff and burst out laughing.

My vanity stung, I rose, face livid, and stamped my plimsoll. "Michael! Stop it at once!"

Still laughing, he threw down his pencil. "Why'd you break character? You almost had me convinced."

"You think I'm as rich as Croesus, don't you? Well, there are expenses you can't imagine! I could charge you all so much more, but I don't! I sacrifice for you! So that you might pursue your work free of care! But no one appreciates it!" Near tears, I sprinted to the door at cricketer's speed. "Thank you so much for destroying my confidence!"

"Okay, okay!" he screamed after me, laughing even harder. "You're off your rocker! I believe you!"

A metal fan rattled on the windowsill, rippling the thick August air. Louise dabbed the canal between her plump, dripping breasts with a hand towel, then resumed her frantic typing. Miranda, lying on her back on the floor, wearing only panties and a T-shirt, talked to the ceiling: "And, see, this girlfriend of mine is a writer, and I think she's really good, only she has no confidence. Anyway, she gave me this story to read and I think it's . . . it's interesting . . . different . . . so before I returned it to her, I made a copy for myself."

(So had I, weeks before. In fact, I had secretly run a copy of every single story Michael had ever written, all ten. [My favorite was "Sad Lazarus," which depicts the crushing moment when Lazarus realizes that he is no longer dead. He berates Christ in the most ungrateful way, calling him a "Jew meddler."] I kept the stories stowed in Sasha's dresser, along with the manuscript of Christopher's aborted opus, all the pages that I had secretly photocopied of Louise's new novel, and the outpourings of a few other gifted lodgers, now departed.)

Louise nodded and typed what Miranda had just said.

"I know it was wrong," Miranda continued, "but you remember my uncle George? The editor? Well, I was thinking maybe he could help my friend. But is it wrong? You know, to send the story to my uncle without telling her?"

Louise hit the carriage return. "Yup."

"But if I tell her, she won't let me send it. She never sends anything anywhere."

"So go ahead and send it."

"But you said it was wrong."

"It is. But without some help, Michael's gonna die in that basement."

"Michael?" Miranda exclaimed, popping herself up onto her elbows. "I'm not talking about Michael!" Louise threw her a glance that pushed her back to the floor. Miranda pointed a toe at the ceiling and admired her pretty foot. "I can't believe how smart you are."

"What's the story like?"

"Smart but kinda creepy."

"What a surprise."

While Miranda ran to call her uncle, Louise imagined how their conversation would go. She set it down forever, as fast as her fingers could manage it.

• • •

Michael laughed when he saw Adrian standing outside the security gate, lighting a cigarette by extending his neck toward the flame.

"You look like a baby giraffe. The match goes to the cigarette," Michael said, unlocking the gate. "Not the other way around."

"I'm not interrupting anything, am I?"

"As a matter of fact, you are. I was writing."

Adrian apologized as he was led down the dim hallway into the middle room. Crates of record albums rose to the ceiling around a cluster of barbells and weightlifting contraptions.

"Are all these records yours?" Adrian asked.

"Mary's."

"What about the weights?"

"Mary's." Michael opened a small refrigerator. "Beer?"

"No, thanks. God, it's hot in here."

"Yeah, I know." He handed Adrian a wet bottle.

"I said no. I don't drink. My father died of cirrhosis."

Michael crossed into his bedroom. "So? My dad weighs three hundred and eighty pounds. I still eat."

"Well, yeah, but genetically—"

"Look, if you're gonna interrupt my work, the least you can do is drink lunch with me. And, incidentally, no candy cigarettes allowed." He plucked the burning generic from Adrian's hand and tossed it into the sink, where it landed with a hiss.

"What's wrong with them? B. K. smokes them."

"He's a homo." Michael grabbed a pack off his desk and shook it at Adrian. "Here, try one of these on."

Adrian took the filterless cigarette warily, as though drawing a potentially fatal lot. He inspected it. "Aren't these too strong for me?"

"Better to get cancer from one of these than a hernia sucking on those stupid filters."

"You know, I'm not really a smoker. I'm just sorta joking around."

"So be *real* funny." He scraped his lighter and offered a flame. Adrian inhaled just as I had taught him. "Well?" Adrian gagged. "Yeah, it's like inhaling skulls." Michael forced the beer bottle into Adrian's hand, then plopped down on his unmade bed. "Here's how." After a few gulps, Michael wiped his mouth with the back of his hand. "So, what's on your mind?"

Adrian, having taken a tiny sip, wiped his mouth just as Michael had. "B. K. wants to see some of my poetry."

"And you don't have any, because you're not a poet."

"How did you know that?"

"Lucky guess."

"I think B. K.'s starting to suspect it, too. If I don't give him a poem soon, I think he's gonna kick me out."

"So write a poem."

"I tried. I . . . I . . . just can't. Carl wrote one *for* me. Only I don't think it's very good. I'm not sure." He pulled a piece of paper from the back pocket of his wrinkly corduroys. "What do *you* think?"

Michael took the page, unfolded it, then read aloud:

I Like Extremes

I like extremes extremely much,
Like nothing else I've found.
I flourish in extremity,
I fail on middle ground.

I'd rather fall in Zanzibar,
Be flayed in Timbuktu,
Than heart attack in Lauderdale,
Or stroke in Kalamazoo.

Michael laughed.

Adrian threw up his hands. "I knew it. It stinks. What am I

supposed to do now? If I give it to B. K., he'll evict me. He thinks I'm a genius."

"Relax, I'll write you something better."

"You will?"

"Isn't that why you're here?"

"Well, yeah. I guess so. God, thanks. That's great. It's so nice of you."

"But first you've gotta do something for me."

"Oh. Okay. What?"

Adrian knew the answer before it came—although he did not know that he knew.

"Come whoring," Michael said.

Adrian tilted his bottle, and beer spilled on the floor.

At this point, the young charlatan really ought to have run upstairs to my bedroom and confessed. (If he had, he would have been met with a most merciful bosom.) He later claimed that this was an option he had considered when he walked home from the public library that day, after struggling for two full hours to write an ode to morals. The Fates intervened, however, moving Mary Pilango into his path outside a busy pizza parlor. Adrian was fairly certain that she was the first lesbian whom he had ever met, and he found her a very tasty piece of Paganism, indeed, so even if she had no sound advice to offer, at least it was an excuse to speak to her.

As he explained his predicament, Mary took a slice of pepperoni thin-crust from the Sicilian Bigfoot behind the counter and folded it lengthwise in its wax paper. On the street, as they walked together, she gave him counsel.

"There's no reason to confess," she said, "or go to a whore. Just write a poem."

"I told you. I've tried. I can't. I'm not even sure I *understand* poetry."

"Maybe you're reading the wrong poems."

"B. K. gives me really great ones to read, but nothing I say satisfies him. I feel like an idiot. What do you think about prostitutes?"

Mary held the slice over her head and let the oil drip into her mouth. "I've dated a few."

"Is it *wrong* to go to one?"

"If a grown woman wants to rent out her body, that's her business. Anyway, even though you seem pretty freaked out by the idea, it might not be the worst thing for you, poetically speaking. Flowers grow out of manure, you know."

Mary stopped in front of a busy outdoor restaurant. Ten feet away, a waitress was clearing a table. As Adrian gabbled on, unburdening his various worries, Mary stopped listening. The waitress had impaled her. Sturdy and curvy, she wore a peasant dress and sandals adorned with iridescent sparkles. Mary felt her heart skip as the waitress bent down, straight-backed, and slid a stack of filthy plates into a bus cart. Suddenly, a commotion. In the corner, a rude Yuppie fatso had pulled a glass off another waitress's tray and sent its contents tumbling. His upwardly mobile posse, all male, leapt back with a roar, as dishes, glasses, cutlery, and ice cubes splattered their laps and shirtfronts. Without a pause, Mary's waitress strode over and took control. In a matter of seconds, she had brushed the avalanche into a rubber tray, cleared and wiped down the table, and calmed the angry men. All the while, her face was as still as a statue's.

Adrian's voice returned: "—and even though part of me's really pissed that Michael's making me do it, another part of me thinks, 'Well, it *would* be something different.' And, you know, like you said, about manure and flowers and—"

"Look, I'm not gonna tell you what to do," Mary said, her patience snapping. "Advice is a waste of time. People just do what they were gonna do, anyway."

"Not always."

"Always."

"Well, I don't see how I have much choice. I mean, I can't write a poem. What about you? Do you write poetry? Song lyrics are sorta like poems, right?"

Mary's mouth slowly fell open, as she realized for the first time that he was not at all the guileless juvenile he pretended to be.

"You're a manipulative little shit, aren't you?" she asked, with a hint of respect.

Adrian smiled and his face colored.

"No way I'm bailing you out," Mary declared. The light changed and, before he could protest, Mary tossed her wax paper and ran.

She didn't stop running for the next six blocks. Mary always looked to her body for clues as to what she was feeling. Why was she in such a panic? she wondered. Why was she running so hard? Was she running toward or away from something? Since her breakup with Toby, she had kicked cunnilingus with strangers cold turkey, and she had never felt so peaceful in all her adult life, and now, suddenly, she was a wreck again. Why? Mary saw the waitress again in her mind's eye and knew at once what had captivated her—not the woman's prodigious beauty but her *poise*. Her aura of imperturbability. Unlike Toby, she did not need help. She did not need to be saved. She was whole, complete just as she was. It occurred to Mary in a flash that, were she to be involved with a woman like this, it might be *she* who broke weak. It might be *her* wound that was opened daily. She felt a stab of empathy for Toby. Suddenly, Mary was running faster, weaving wildly through the dawdling pedestrians, to nowhere in particular.

Poor Louise. She had been awake for three straight days and had only just shut her eyes when I had trooped her downstairs and jammed a mug of cold coffee in her hand. Still terribly upset from the morning's role-play with Michael, I gave her a quick rundown of what had happened and demanded that she do better.

"It's crucial," I said, "for my insanity."

In a flash, we were off and running. She leaned forward, eyes red and bleary, her voice thick with fatigue, and said, "Mr. Troop, may I speak frankly?"

I crossed my legs and sipped from a cup of Lachryma Christi (a cedar ladle of vinegar tannins punctuated by three hard thumps of iron).

"Be my guest," I said. "Speak any way you'd like."

"I'm not a person who pays much attention to files. I believe in *eyes.*"

I did not like the sound of that one bit. Thinking fast, I tried to make my baby-blues appear dewy and ingenuous.

She frowned, as though she saw something quite different in them.

"Keeping in mind your present mental state," she said, her voice brassy and official, "if you were *compelled* to seek employment, what sort of position would you pursue?"

Suddenly my bottom seemed too big for the chair. I writhed a bit. "Well, I don't know, I'm so far from decisions of that sort. I'm an untreatable manic-depressive and quite full of myself, so the possibility of gainful employment has always seemed so remote—"

"Just answer the question."

I picked up a Japanese paper fan and madly flapped it, mind churning. Finally, it came to me.

"Well, I suppose if I were *forced* to work, I'd pursue a position as a dentist."

She blinked.

Ha! Advantage Troop.

"My dear friend Sasha Buchwitz? Her father was a dentist. She told me all about the things he used to do. The procedures and little tools and so forth. I'd only want a *modest* practice at first—"

Louise waved her arms. "Cut! Cut! Cut!"

"What's wrong?" I whined.

"Are you out of your mind?"

"No, but I want you to think so."

"Obviously!" She threw aside her red mane and moved forward in her chair. "They'll see through it. Give them a real answer. Tell them you'd make a great secretary."

"I happen to be an excellent typist."

"So?"

"So they might make me *become* one!"

"Never! They'll think you're nuts for admitting you're employable. Only a lunatic would tell them the truth."

"You're not taking this seriously—"

"I am! If you're too *obviously* crazy then—"

"You're not!" My voice rose sharply. "You're talking in riddles. It's positively *Kafkan!*" I popped to my feet. "Thank you for reminding me that I'm not as creative as you are. That I'm just a *secretary!* That I'm nothing!"

I burst into tears and fled the room.

Before I even reached my bedroom, I knew that it might be a good idea if I took a break from mock interviews. Clearly, my nerves weren't up to it. And was it any wonder? I had been through quite a lot that summer. A better strategy would be to prepare for my Inquisition by *not* preparing, by taking my mind off it, thereby lowering my blood pressure so that I might remain lucid when face to face with my Inquisitor.

So, for three full days, I did absolutely nothing. I pottered about The House Beautiful, polished my pillboxes, finished my last Chandler (dreadful), even stared at the boob tube. I discovered, however, that in my current state I was just as unfit for leisure as I was for action.

Truth be told, I was lovelorn.

Although it had been weeks since the arrest of Yung Su and although I knew it was better to have loved and lost, et cetera, deep down, I was still in pieces. At one point, I even considered visiting him in the slammer, bringing him a smoked ham or a Korean comic book, but why? It would never be the same between us. Not only was he a murderer, but he had lied to me about almost everything.

Historically, lost in such a funk, I would have slipped on a blazer and cap and cabbed it down to my favorite nightspot, which lay in the Stygian shadows of the Fifty-ninth Street Bridge. There I would have plucked a boy to elevate my mood, but I had learned during my hard year with Christopher that no amount of booze, disco dancing, and Asiatic love can mend the broken heart. If it could, Bangkok would be Lourdes.

Alas, my malaise was also aggravated by the fact that what had allowed me to rise from the ashes of my breakup was that I had fully embraced, to the exclusion of all else, my role as mentor, if not muse, to my young lodgers. In that regard, I had spent virtually every waking moment since my confinement fretting about their future and girding myself for the battle to keep a roof over their heads, yet my lodgers, creatively speaking, had never wanted less to do with me.

Louise's novel was gushing out of her with such force that, fearing it might clog her spigot, she refused even to discuss its evolving story. (One morning, sunning on the tar, I read through all that I had so far stolen and photocopied, and I could only marvel at her originality. You obviously agree, or you would not be reading these words, for a great deal of what you have read up to this point was inspired by or culled from Louise's wise and witty tale.) Miranda was painting around the clock, preparing for her big show, and as she had often expressed grave doubts as to my good taste in the visual arts, she naturally refused to involve me in her process. Michael, on the other hand, was usually quite willing, when pushed, to chat about his twisted philosophical tales, but lately his self-loathing had reached such a critical mass that I no longer enjoyed his company. Mary was another story altogether, as she had been entirely closed off to me since the day she moved in. (As I said, it is always this way with lesbians. I don't know why. Is it their natures or do they envy my basket?) But even if she had liked me, it would not have made a difference, because ever since she had returned home from spotting her waitress, she had not put down her guitar, writing song after song in praise of huntresses, unshorn shanks, rainbows, first menses, and juniper trees.

At times like these, feeling shut out, I had always been able to rely on Carl as my last resort, but his weeks-long obsession with the doll across the way, coupled with the resounding silence of his telephone, had taken a terrible toll on his spirit. More and more, he looked like a dying man. During my last visit, he merely smoked and grunted, and often his eyes, right in the middle of my most vital utterances, darted to his baby oil. These days, he rose from his soiled linen only to fill and void his tubes.

This left only the green woodpecker.

Terrified that at any moment my patience would snap for the final time and I would order him to put out (poetically) or hit the streets, he had been evading me at every turn, literally running away or playing possum whenever I approached. So one morning, frustrated, yearning for some distraction from my cares, I waited in the foyer for him to go out for his daily blueberry muffin and tea. When he appeared, I leapt out and announced that we were going to resume our tutorials. They would take place every day at three o'clock in the Vale of Health (which the cruel August sun had turned into a Vale of Hades). I gave him no choice; he was my hostage.

Our work resumed, both of us squeezed under a beach umbrella—I tippled iced grape and puffed generics; he gulped cold cola and sucked Michael's filterless atrocities. Desperate to please, the young fraud applied himself to whatever I put in front of him, and soon he was romping through fields of iambs like a colt turned into a spring meadow. He was actually quite impressive on "Ode to a Nightingale," successfully identifying its core themes, spotting the source of the Fitzgerald title, and humbly accepting my corrections in pronunciation ("Lethe" does not rhyme with "sheath"), but most promising was that the third stanza actually moved him to tears. He said that phrase "Where youth grows pale, and spectre-thin, and dies" reminded him of his dear, dead daddy. This pleased me enormously, I told him, because if poetry does not touch one emotionally, then it is without value, which is why I detested nearly every poem published since the demise of Mr. Dylan Thomas's liver.

"Really?" he said, rolling his cola can against his brow. "How come?"

"Because free verse is like playing tennis without a net. And *balls.* It's not that poetry without meter and rhyme is bad poetry. It's that it is *not* poetry. It is what scholars once referred to as *prose*—no matter how you chop it up on the page. Some of it is excellent prose, by the way, but it is prose, nonetheless, speaking where it should sing. And verse that does not sing cannot touch the heart for very long. It might for a year or two, or even a decade, but not for centuries."

As our lessons continued into their second week, the bond between us deepened, but there was still an invisible barrier between us that I could not penetrate. What was the cub withholding from me? What was he not saying? It occurred to me here, for the first time, that he might be a phony, not a poet at all, but I pushed the suspicion aside. (As I have said, I like to believe the best of people.) My second thought was that he might be growing sexually attracted to me and was afraid to act on it. So one afternoon I tested the waters. I asked him whether he had ever had slept with a man. He replied, "God, no." I suggested that he might understand "Endymion" better if he had kissed a grown man at least once. Rather than let the idea percolate, he grimaced as though I had suggested that he swallow a squashed, putrefying frog.

One afternoon, frustrated by his lack of openness with me and by the fact that he had never, ever, not once, asked me how my preparations for my government interview were going or offered to conduct a second mock interview, I demanded, once again, that he show me one of his poems. This might very well have been just the thing to nerve his spirit and jump-start his unlearned quill; instead it merely flung him in the direction of Michael, which, as you shall soon learn, was not wholly a bad thing.

141

You're Not Gonna Kill Me, Are You?

To keep up with his scruffy Virgil, Adrian was forced to walk quickly, moving past lurid bodegas, prowling autos, and loose-hipped men who eyed the night as though they had something evil to sell it. Unseasonably chill winds dove and swirled, yet he did not fasten his jacket. It was as though he were not a participant in the night's adventure but merely a character in someone else's novel. Everything felt unreal and otherly, even his goose bumps. If he did what Michael asked of him, he would never be the same, he knew that. He would be someone else. *Who,* he was not quite sure.

"Hold on," Michael said, disappearing into a brewhouse.

Adrian cupped his eyes to the window. Inside, a clutch of carbuncled oafs floated in relief against a backdrop of neon beer signs and a wavy wall of smoke.

"Wanna date, sweetie?" a voice lisped.

Adrian whipped around. A smirking ogre, a half-century old, gave him the glad eye. Her dimpled thighs bulged in fishnet stockings. Her airborne breasts were clearly factitious. One of her hands was laid protectively across her spongy midriff. Adrian shook his head three times.

"What, your momma won't let you?"

He wanted to speak, but could not.

"You a faggot?"

Michael emerged, handed Adrian a machine-bought condom, and told the slut to beat it.

"Let me ask you something," Adrian said, catching up with Michael as he crossed the avenue. "Am I supposed to *kiss them?*"

"Not on the mouth."

"Good. I had no idea they were so ugly.*"*

"Some are and some aren't. You know, like *people.*" A smile crept across his lips. "For instance."

Twenty feet away stood a buxom blonde, smiling hungrily at Adrian. She was red-hot and ready to moan.

"You take her," Adrian whispered. "I'll go see a movie."

"You don't like her?"

"She's too tall."

Michael chuckled, and turned a corner. Adrian, following him, spotted three men dressed in pink and yellow finery, laughing together in a parking lot across the street. One rested his foot on a bumper and waved a joint as he spoke.

"Pimps," Michael explained.

"I think I'm getting the flu. I might go home."

"Go ahead."

Adrian dropped his head and brooded. The only thing that seemed more impossible than making love to one of these horrible women was writing a poem. He pictured himself back in Iowa, sitting in classrooms, staring at endless calculations scratched across chalkboards. He would have nothing to look forward to but four more years of school and another five or six of dissertation work—and what for? So he could become a professor one day and bore the crap out of the next generation. No, he couldn't do it. If he went home now, it would be as though he had never left, as though his summer in New York City hadn't changed him at all. But it had, and it was time to prove it—in a way that he could never take back.

Suddenly, a zitty Puerto Rican appeared out of nowhere and laid a hand on Adrian's zipper. He jumped away.

"Whoa, chill out," Michael said to the thing. "My friend's new to this. Give him some breathing room."

A few other girls, uninspired by Adrian's innocence, drifted away toward a slowing station wagon. The first stayed put, posing confidently, examining Adrian from head to toe as though *she* were the buyer.

Michael threw his charge an inquiring look. "Well?"

"I thought it would be different," Adrian whimpered. "Safer feeling."

A young blonde sauntered by, brushing Adrian with her shoulder and a whiff of her perfume. She was unlike the others. She looked like a cheerleader on her way to a practice: white stretch pants, a lavender sweatshirt, white sneakers, and a plastic hair clip holding back long, silky blond hair. She skipped across the roaring avenue, her hands against her chest, as though hugging a stack of schoolbooks.

"Is she one?" Adrian asked.

"On that corner, she'd better be."

The impulsive lad gave chase, inspired by the sudden idea that if he had to do something like this, he might as well settle an old score at the same time. She was exactly the sort of girl who had never given him the time of day in high school. Now was his chance to avenge himself. He reached her just as a slinky black-amoor slid out from beneath a hotel awning.

"And how are you this fine evening?" the man asked.

Leaned down to a crawling car, she didn't answer. Another entreprenoir appeared, this one wearing the urban nephew of the traditional Highland tam-o'-shanter.

"Good evening, my dear. My name is Patrick W. Brammer III. Is this sorry motherfucker botherin' you?"

The first man spun at him, his voice rising into a comical falsetto: "I'm talkin' to the young lady! Didn't nobody ever teach you no manners?"

A third man, a Latino with a radio growing out of his ear, slowed down as he approached, as wide-eyed as if the girl had been stark naked.

Adrian touched her arm. "Excuse me?"

She turned at the gentle sound of his voice. Her eyes surprised him. They were like shattered green marbles.

Suddenly, Michael was there, taking the lass firmly by the arm and addressing the men.

"Stoned," he explained.

"No shit!" the first man cried.

The man with the tam shook his head. "Bitch is *fucked up!* You can get a better woman than her right over there at that hotel. They got 'bout twelve ho's over there. Not too expensive neither."

"Yeah, except she's my sister," Michael said.

The boy's hands flew up as though Michael had pulled a gun. "Your *what!*" he squealed.

The other men laughed and fell over clapping.

As Michael escorted the little beauty across the street, Adrian scuttled at her side, studying her face: apple cheeks, pretty, down-turned mouth, flawless, pale skin. He could hardly believe his luck.

"Hi!" she said, when she noticed him gawking.

"What are you doing around here?" Adrian asked. "This is a bad neighborhood."

"I know. I live in Jersey."

Michael stopped on the corner, caught Adrian's eye, smiled almost tenderly, then drifted away, leaving him to fly or fall on his own.

"So what are you doing around here?" Adrian asked.

"I thought I could make some money."

"What do you mean?"

"That's my car," she said, pointing like a proud teenager at a rusty coupe.

"So?"

"I said I wanted to make some money, right?"

Adrian detected a hint of a Southern accent. His brow furrowed and he remembered something he had seen on TV.

"Are you a cop?" he asked.

"No way!" she trilled. "Are *you?*"

Adrian saw Michael smoking under a streetlight, looking a bit impatient. The moment was now. Adrian stepped closer. Blood surged through his thighs. "You want to make money. I assume you mean through sex, right? That's what you mean?"

A giggle lift her onto tiptoe. "I can't believe it! This is so *weird!* I have never, ever, ever, done anything like this. But I need money so bad. I'm moving to Boston with my friend, Susie, so tonight I went to work with her." She pointed to a peephouse across the street. "You know, just to sorta check it out. Anyway, I was in this booth for, like, two hours and you know how much I made?"

"How much?"

"A *lot!* Anyway, Susie went home, but I thought maybe I could make even more money. But I have never, ever, done anything like this."

"Neither have I. I'm not gonna be very good. Where do you want to go? We can't go to my house."

"You're not gonna kill me, are you?"

"What? No. My name's Adrian."

"I'm Divina."

"That's a pretty name."

"Thank you."

Moments later, as he was about to step into her jalopy, he saw Michael gesturing him over.

"Just a second," Adrian said.

"Everything okay?" Michael asked.

"Can you believe how pretty she is? We're going to a motel. Do you know a good one?"

"Calm down. That way. Toward the river. You'll see it on the right. It's fairly clean."

Adrian was halfway back to the car, when Michael stopped him. "Hey, Adrian!"

"Yeah?"

"Breathe!"

Adrian smiled back, then sucked some wind and ran.

Divina drove like a deranged, eyeless woman, jerking the steering wheel this way and that. Her worldly possessions (aqua hairbrush, purple barrette, strawberry bubble gum) flew back and forth across the floor mats. Adrian watched her carefully, ready to intervene. He tried to settle her with small talk.

"How old are you?"

"Twenty."

"Where're you from?"

"Atlanta. But see, my father married this bitch from Jersey. I live with them. She hates my guts." She laughed. "Are you *sure* you're not gonna kill me?"

"Watch out!"

She yanked the wheel, missed an oncoming car, and screeched into a motel parking lot. Inside the office, a tired-looking wretch of little force and negligent finish sat reading a racing form behind a plastic window. Without looking up, he slid a note card and a ballpoint pen through the slot. Adrian scrawled my address. When he saw the blank for his name, he paused, then printed the first name that came to him—his father's.

The tiny room, yellowish and dim, reeked of disinfectant.

"So, how much is this gonna cost?" Adrian asked as he neatly folded his jacket over a chair.

Divina kicked off her high-top sneakers. "Whatever."

Surprised, he laid his condom on the bedside table. "My friend said I'm supposed to pay you *before.*"

"Whatever," she repeated, as she slipped off her pants.

Her naked body glowed like white marble in the half-light. She stood at the foot of the bed, her back arched slightly, her flat tummy bowed out, her knees knocking. The smile she showed was both shy and eager. Lying on his back, Adrian stripped off his pants in clumsy haste, and, before he even had time to be frightened, she was in his arms, wiggling, kissing him deeply on the mouth. His hands moved greedily over her small curves. Suddenly, she was sliding down his body, her breasts tickling his thighs, her lips grazing the coppery down of his stomach.

(I am dying, Egypt.)

Adrian stretched to the bedside table for his condom, but was stopped by a spasm of pleasure. His head fell back and cracked against the headboard. Her mouth sank onto him and he was pinned by blissful heat. He wanted to cry out as her mouth rose and fell and rose. Frantically, his mind spun back to Sally. She had never done this. She had said she never would do this. "Icky," she called it. Then the pleasure stopped and Divina crawled onto her knees. She threw a leg over him, as though mounting a pony.

He grabbed her elbows. "What are you doing?" he whispered. "We need protection!"

She smiled and said that she wasn't sick. Was he? He emphatically shook his head. She eased his hands away and pushed down, scraping him into a blinding ecstasy.

The chenille wrap I wore had been a gift from me to Sasha on her penultimate birthday. Unfortunately, I had chosen the precisely wrong Swiss pinot blanc for a chilly summer night (kiss of wet mountain goat; echo of yuletide yodel), and so, despite the lushness of my wrap, when the wind blew, my crunchers clenched in my slippers and my buttocks flexed.

Michael sat at my side, his forearms resting on his knees, his head down. He had just told me everything. (Well, almost everything. He had told me about Adrian and the whore, but not about the deal that inspired it.) Now he was annoyed that Adrian was late getting back; he wanted to go out and find a whore for himself before it was too late. (Preferably one with tight, aching deltoids.)

"You're not going anywhere tonight," I said sternly. "Adrian's going to require intensive aftercare."

"What do you mean?"

"He'll need you."

"You talk to him."

"Sorry, bub. Whether you like it or not, living in an artists' colony comes with certain responsibilities. Miranda needs you, too, by the way. Even more."

"That settles it," he muttered gloomily, leaking smoke. "I'm moving out."

"Honestly," I tutted with disdain. "Why must you act like such a brute? If you actually *were* one, that would be one thing. It might even be attractive. But there's nothing brutish about you. You're simply a scaredy-cat. A giant quakebottom."

He threw me an awed look, amazed at my insight.

"She likes me too much," he said finally.

"Oh, isn't that droll?"

"Talk softer. People are trying to sleep."

"Just you, you insufferable godwit. And it's time for you to wake up. The way you ignore her is positively obscene. Have you looked in the mirror lately? Forget stopping a clock, your face could stop time itself. Liking you ought to be the *first* thing you look for in a girl. It's a rare quality."

"Tits are important, too," he smutted.

"Unlike jugs, devotion *lasts,* my boy. And don't insult me with vulgar talk. You're nothing but a future-fatso who, if he had even half a brain, would hold on to Miranda and never let go!"

My counsel was harsh, yes, but as one who at last knew himself to be exempt from romantic love, I had never valued it more highly.

He squinted at me. "Who put the bee in *your* bonnet?"

"You did! And let me tell you something else. You'd better watch out or you're gonna end up just like me. A sad, middle-aged flabpot trying to make it to the grave with a shred of dignity and a few healthy hairs. Chew on *that* for a while!" I stood triumphantly. "Now you've put a bad taste in my mouth. I'm going upstairs to rinse and spit." I looked up and down the block. "My God, what have you done to him? Where *is* he?"

"Probably floating in the Hudson."

"I'm sure that's clean compared to where he is." Then I looked down and threw the poor dog a bone. "Listen, I'm all for a bit of fluff from time to time. It's probably exactly what the lad needed. I just wish you had let *me* supervise the experiment. I am, after all, his mentor.

"If not muse."

"I would have found him a nice geisha—servile, hair-free, scentless. Good night. I want every detail at cock's crow. If he never returns, I won't tell the police that it was all your fault, but in return I will expect you to conduct two more mock interviews with me."

I turned and vanished.

For the next half-hour, Michael mulled over what I had said. Every word was brilliant and apt, of course, expressed with the greatest economy, but rather than spur him to action, it merely made him more determined than ever to abandon Adrian and find what little further satisfaction he could before the sun rose. He flamed another cigarette, wondering if there would ever be an end to the dark turn his life had taken. He knew he was capable of something better, but a deep orneriness made him unwilling to budge. It was a defiance he had nursed since childhood—a twisted belief that to give someone what they asked for was a defeat. It was the same wisdom that had told him, as a boy, never to cry when his father beat him senseless, that told him even today that change was impossible until there wasn't a single person left on the planet who cared whether he changed or not. Michael was smart enough to know that it was a devilish, faulty voice, but it was the oldest one he knew.

A taxi came to a stop and Adrian jumped out.

"It was incredible!" he shouted.

"Shhh."

Adrian talked more softly, but just as excitedly, as Michael led him down the steps, through the iron gate, and into the basement: "Her name's Divina. She'd never done it before. So it was almost like a date or something. Remember you told me not to kiss her? Well, I did. Because she kissed me. A lot! And it felt totally natural. And—Well, this is kinda weird, but you know how I pictured the girl hating it and me just taking advantage? Well, it wasn't like that at all. She *loved* it!"

"How do you know?"

"Well, I'm not sure how to put this."

"What, she *came?*"

The boy nodded enthusiastically.

Michael, face hardening, told him to sit.

Adrian obeyed but kept talking: "She went crazy. And then afterwards we smoked together and she said I was the best lover she'd ever been with, and, since she wasn't some prostitute trying to make me feel good, she had no reason to lie. She's just a girl from Atlanta living in Trenton with her dad and his second wife and she needs to make extra money to get an apartment in Boston. During the day, she works in a bank, and she said she's never gonna have sex for money again unless it's with me. I mean, if I want to, and even then she's not sure she'd charge me."

"Shut up!" Michael shouted.

Adrian, startled, fell silent and at last ventured a breath.

"How much did you give her?" Michael asked.

"Well, kind of a lot. More than she expected."

"What do you mean?"

"Well, she didn't really name a price. She said whatever I thought was fair. So we drove to a bank machine and I gave her two hundred and forty bucks.

"Two hundred and forty."

" And twenty-eight for the room. Boston's expensive."

Michael spoke slowly, fighting a smile. "Look, I . . . I hate to break this to you . . . but there's no such thing as a first-time hooker."

"Come on, that's ridiculous. There has to be. I mean, logic says—"

"Just listen. It's a classic con. She walks out on Forty-second Street, looking like Miss Teen Ohio, and waits for the sharks to attack. You don't think her name's really Divina, do you?"

"Hey, all that occurred to me, but—"

"You think a girl that's never hooked before would walk out on that scary corner the way she did?"

"She was disoriented."

"She was high as a kite."

"A little drunk, maybe.

"Bullshit. She's a middle-class junkie who's got some sick trip going on about sex, so she tells every john she's with that it's her first time. It protects her suburban psyche and, best of all, it gets her customers. Generous ones, like you."

"But she liked it."

"Oh, right, the shuddering orgasm, I almost forgot." Michael shook his head. "Jesus Christ, you're a rube."

Adrian was angry now. "She gave me her phone number! Why would she do that?" He dug into his pocket and came up with a slip of blue paper. "I could call and tell her parents. I could call the cops!"

Michael took the number, crossed to the phone, and punched out at the number.

"What are you doing?" Adrian cried. "You'll wake up her dad! He works at the post office. Call tomorrow!"

Michael listened for a few seconds, then handed the phone to Adrian. Adrian heard a breathy woman's voice. At first, the recorded words were hard to make out, but soon they were not: *"Doctor, what are you doing? I'm afraid! Are you going to stick that inside me? You can't. I'm so tight! It'll hurt! Oh! It hurts! Go slower. Oh, yeah! Doctor, it feels so good!"*

Adrian, humiliated, tossed the phone onto the bed.

"As for Divina—" Michael handed him the slip of paper turned over. It was a receipt for a gasoline credit card.

Adrian read the name *Marla Dietz*.

"All I can say is, thank God you wore a condom."

A look of horror blossomed on Adrian's young face. He jumped up, ran to the sink, yanked down his pants, blasted the hot water, and, using his hand like a duck's bill, began to splash himself. Michael lay back on the bed and, despite the late hour and the gravity of the matter, laughed harder than he had in years.

The next morning, I cracked Adrian's door and was relieved to see that he had returned in one piece. He did look unhappy, though, twisted up in a tornado of linen, clutching a damp washcloth to his chest like a treasure map. His torso was musclier than I had imagined. Sadly, his pin-striped pajama bottoms showed only the faintest sign of morning arousal, so I learned nothing of importance. If only my presence had awakened him, he might well have told me all about his descent into sin, and I could have consoled him with the fact that the young Keats had also hired many a whore, and that, after one particularly foolhardy transaction, he had been left with a stubborn case of gonorrhea. Urethra afire, the Boy-Bard had rushed to the remedy of the day, pouring liquid mercury down his pee-hole. The consolation for Adrian would have been, of course, that things could be worse and that carnal disgrace goes hand-in-hand with poetic genius. But, alas, it was not meant to be; the boy dozed like a drunken sailor. I trotted downstairs and roused Michael for the details, but he told me to go away and never come back. It was only months later that Adrian finally confessed all, but by then I had already read all about it in Louise's manuscript.

Some Chick Flick

I posed dramatically before Sasha's full-length mirror. My outfit was tasteful and conservative: navy three-piece, white button-down, black mules, and an emerald silk scarf. I threw a variety of poses like an expert runway model, expecting at any moment to be lavished with praise. When none came, I glanced at Louise's face and saw that she was scowling.

"All wrong."

"How dare you?!" I huffed.

"You look too handsome."

I wheeled back to the mirror with alarm, as though I expected to find a stranger staring back at me. Louise flipped through the hangers in my closet. She pulled out a turquoise wool suit, a favorite of mine from the Ford administration.

"Wool?" I cried. "In August? Are you nuts?"

"No, *you* are, remember?"

I dug her reasoning. She handed me a bright blouse, which I had purchased during a spending spree on The Castro. It was made of tangerine polyester, with lapels the size of condor wings.

"You'll clash and sweat," Louise said, smiling. "And be sure to misbutton it."

I threw on the getup and flew downstairs, looking every inch like a color-blind Punchinello. Waiting for me in the front room was the surly Mary Pilango, who had consented, with a minor financial incentive (thirty bucks off her rent), to conduct my final mock interview.

"How's life?" I asked, as though I were not already privy to every last detail of her valiant combat with sex addiction.

Mary answered as politely as she knew how. "None of your business. What are you wearing? You look retarded."

I snapped fire to fag. "Watch your tongue, sister. You need all the friends you can get."

"What's that supposed to mean?"

"It means that promiscuous lesbians, even recovering ones, are aberrations with whom the civilized rarely choose to associate."

"Let's get this over with."

"Let's." I carefully unfolded an origamied sheet of typing paper. "I've prepared some questions. Ask them exactly as they are written out. I'll respond to them just as I will during my interview. At the end you will tell me whether I seem fit for gainful employment. Got it?"

Mary nodded. I handed her the sheet. She sat back and crossed her sturdy legs.

"Now, Mr. Troop," she began, effortlessly assuming the dull gaze of a government cleric, but reading with little natural talent. "I have reviewed your file carefully and, frankly, I'm not at all convinced you're entitled to these benefits."

"Oh, really?" I tarted smugly.

"Please relate to me the symptoms of your mental illness. Tell me about the misery you endure."

Yes, she was an abysmal actress.

"In the grips of mania, I hear voices," I stated flatly.

"Fascinating, Mr. Troop," she said, a smile wriggling at the corners of her licentious mouth.

I snapped my fingers at the sheet.

Mary looked down and read her next line: "Voices? You hear actual voices? This sounds to me like schizophrenia."

"I'm afraid so. A recent development. Often they are the voices of my adoptive parents arguing in the cellar, but they've been dead for ages, so I know that I must be imagining it. But I check anyway. I find the cellar empty, except for the odd spider or sewer rat."

She simply stared; I had dazzled her.

She snapped her head down and read her next line. "What else do you endure?"

"Panic. I am undone by the most trivial of events."

"For example?"

"Well, let's say a neighbor's kitty cat wanders into my garden. I become concerned that he might strangle himself on my fence. What would I do? What if its owner blamed *me?* What if the fuzz were called in? What if, during their investigation, one of them pinched a pillbox from my collection? Would anyone believe me? My word against a cop's? My mind goes on and on like this, a runaway carousel, until I'm ready to end it all, just to be free of the worry. And I think, good heavens, my peace of mind certainly is a precarious thing, isn't it? If it can be undone by a harmless kitty?"

Mary covered her mouth with one hand, stifling a belch or a laugh or perhaps even the upcrawl of Toby's final, stubborn hairball. The secret to the verisimilitude of my monologue was that most of it was culled, word for word, from Sasha's ramblings during her darkest days. Smiling serenely, I laid my big hands on my lap, one over the other. "I must run along now, if you don't mind."

"Thank you, Mr. Troop. I've heard quite enough."

I floated out of the room.

A moment later, I popped back in. "How did I do?"

"Great. Can I go now?"

"Would you let me keep my disability checks?"

"Oh, yeah. You seemed nuttier than a fruitcake."

"In what way?"

"*Every*. It was real. Can I go now?"

My jaw clenched. Anger sized in my chest. "It wasn't real! I was acting!"

"I know that."

"But you said it was real."

"I just meant that—"

"*You said it!*"

She jerked back in her chair, more indignant, I think, than frightened. "All right, fine, I said it! But it's not what I meant! Jesus Christ, get a grip, you freak!"

I pointed a finger and advanced. "If you run back and tell the other lodgers that I'm worrying myself sick over kittens—"

"Why would I do that? I know it was just a game!"

I reared back like Rodin's Balzac. "A game! It's my *life! Your* life! All of our lives! How dare you patronize me!"

"Oh, go fuck yourself."

My hands became claws and they whirled savagely as I lunged. "Get out! Out of this house!"

She laughed in my face. "Right, like you'd ever be able to find anybody else willing to live in that pit."

"Could, too!" I screamed childishly, losing all sight of land.

"Then how come the room was empty for nine months before I moved in? Huh? Hate to tell you, but the word is out—you're nothing but a crazy, smelly, impossible old drunk!"

While Miranda and Adrian waited, they engaged in the most banal of chitchat. Miranda lamented the rising cost of taxi fares; Adrian sang of his struggle to master the Italian sonnet. (She still thought he was a poet and he preferred to keep it that way.)

When Jerry Sheridan finally walked up, he shouted, "Hey, cutie!"

Miranda showed no sign of being flattered or amused.

Adrian shouted back, "You're pretty cute yourself!"

(Even though the joke fell flat, it was one of the very few he cracked all summer, so I could hardly leave it out.)

"Wait'll you see what I've done with it," Jerry said as he led them down the garbagy Soho street lined with spotless galleries. "It was a sty. A bar for seventy-five years. Tin ceilings, tiled floors covered with about ten coats of maritime paint, old gas jets. I yanked it all out. It's like new." He stopped and pulled out a big ring of keys. "Christ, I feel like a prison guard. Let's see. . . ." A moment later, he pulled aside a gate and gestured for them to enter.

"Not too shabby, huh?" he said, following.

The room was long and narrow. In the back, a flight of glass steps led to a loft trimmed with a faux-iron railing. To the right stretched a thirty-foot stainless-steel bar.

"What's that for?" Adrian asked.

"See, that's the concept. It's more than a gallery, it's a social establishment." He moved to the bar with both hands raised. "Now imagine. People everywhere, drinking, smoking, flirting, partying their asses off, and, when they turn around, what do they see?" He turned around and made an exaggerated face of surprise. "Your work!"

Miranda opened her teary eyes wide and forced a smile. "Neat."

Jerry stormed away. "And . . . and . . . and up here, we've got hairstyling. One of the best stylists in town, Yvette Metz, is bringing her whole crew down from Madison Avenue."

"*Haircutting?*" Adrian repeated.

"That's the genius of it! Because once the customer's all powdered up and ready to go, what's he gonna do?"

"Go?" Adrian guessed.

"Nope, he walks right down here—" Jerry slammed a fist on the bar. "And orders a Manhattan. You know why? Because Manhattans are free! A free Manhattan with every cut. And what do they do while they're drinking? Huh? You know. I just told you."

"They turn around and look at my paintings," Miranda murmured.

"You got it! That's synergy, baby! I can't believe nothing like this has ever been done before. Actually I do believe it. You know why? Guess why."

"Because it's illegal?" Adrian said.

"Yup, hair and booze don't mix, at least according to the health department. So that's why we put in the loft. The hair's up there and the liquor's down here. Plus, I had to bribe a few people." He rubbed his hands together and walked behind the bar. "Who wants a shot of vodka? I've got a bottle here somewhere."

He knelt, disappearing from view.

Miranda looked up at the dark silhouette of an old-fashioned barber's chair. She hugged herself, then turned and uttered words she had heard only on the late show: "Make mine a double."

Poor Carl was getting worse with each passing day. He lay in bed, hour upon hour, too demoralized lately even to reach for his baby oil. When he was hungry, he ordered in. When it was time to relieve himself, he could barely muster the energy to lift the toilet seat. One afternoon, the phone actually rang, shredding the smoky air. He sprang for it, but was disappointed to discover that it was a wrong number. Welcoming the sound of a woman's voice, however, he wasted three full minutes discussing the caller's broken dishwasher, before confessing that he was not, in fact, Sam of Sam's Home Repair.

After returning from the art gallery, Miranda rushed to her room to weep, and Adrian dropped in on his floormate. When he saw Carl lying on the floor naked, idly scratching his emerging beard, he asked politely if he was having a nervous breakdown. The poor player replied that this was a distinct possibility, and he added hoarsely, "The shade's never been down this long in the afternoon."

"Maybe she's got the flu," Adrian suggested, fumbling for a cigarette. He did not really want another one, but at least it would cut the stench of Carl's armpits.

Carl lifted his legs and flexed his gigantic calves. "Hey, Huck, look."

"Yeah, I wondered about those. How'd you get 'em? You run cross-country?"

"I flex 'em when I beat off. It makes me come harder."

Adrian puffed smoke. "You need a psychiatrist."

"Tell me about it." Carl moaned and rolled onto his stomach. "I also gotta quit show business. I'm thirty-three! What a joke. My friends from high school are loaded, even my kid brothers are loaded. What have I got?"

"Talent."

"That and twenty bucks'll buy me a cyanide capsule. Know what I oughta do? Join the family business. Work for my dad, like my brothers do." He exhaled longingly. "My rich kid brothers."

"What kind of business?"

"Women's lingerie."

"You think you'd be happy?"

"Happy schmappy. I could hold my head up."

Urgent shouts rang out in the back yard.

Carl, afraid that something had happened to his girlfriend, hurled himself at the window. Across the way, two floors below her apartment, an inebriated galoot stood on the fire escape holding a plastic garbage bag of stolen goods. A policeman in the garden and another on the roof pointed revolvers at him. The burglar seemed disoriented, as though he had just woken up. His dungarees hung so low that the crack of his derriere was exposed. He looked down at the first cop, then up at the second, like a curious ape studying new faces outside his cage.

"Give it up!" screamed the cop on the ground. "You got nowhere to go!" And he was right. The old-fashioned fire escape was made up of iron balconies, disconnected from one another.

"Don't move! You've got two guns on you!" the other cop screamed. His walkie-talkie crackled.

The creature paid no attention. The windows next to him were gated, so he looked up to the next balcony, his gaze bleary and unjudging. He tucked the garbage bag under his T-shirt, then pulled his shirt over the bag and tucked it into his jeans. Now he looked like a *pregnant* ape. He grabbed the iron support above his head and began to climb. His high-top sneakers caught the brick facade.

"Stop!" shrieked the cop on the roof, falling onto his stomach and bringing his gun down. His partner in the yard holstered his gun and leapt onto the supports of the first balcony. His hard shoes slapped and scraped the brick. Finally, he pulled himself up using only his arms, but his grip snapped and he fell to the ground in a tumble of soft limbs and violent instruments.

Faces stuck out of windows everywhere.

"Shoot him!" a bare-chested Slav shouted from his sill.

A biddy squealed, "He's goin' inside!"

Adrian, peeking out at Carl's side, looked down and saw the top of my head poking from the bathroom window. (In preparation for my interview, I had been teasing my hair into a late Gig Young.) Louise and Miranda watched, too, slack-jawed, from the kitchen window. Michael appeared below us in the yard, wearing nothing but briefs. (Superb tush.)

"Why don't they shoot him?" Adrian asked Carl. "Shoot him in the leg or something!"

"It's illegal to shoot a fleeing felon in New York," Carl snapped. "You have to wait till he surrenders before you blow his brains out."

The thief finally reached the next balcony. He pulled out his bag of loot, then, with both hands, crashed it through the nearest window. At the sound of the breaking glass, Carl's beloved appeared at her window, one story above.

"Shit!" Carl ducked below the sill and forced Adrian down with him. "Do you think she saw us?" They both inched up.

"He's going inside!" Carl's girl cried to the cop on the ground.

"Sexy voice," Carl whispered.

"He's going inside!" she screamed. "Why don't you do something!"

"I approve," Adrian murmured irrelevantly.

"You stay away from her," Carl snapped.

Suddenly, the criminal backed out the window, his arms over his head. A third policeman, positioned inside the apartment, had gotten the draw on him. The perp backed up right over the edge of the fire escape and spilled, limbs flailing, to a crisp thud on the cement. People screamed. Some cheered and clapped. But then, miraculously, the hulk stirred and started to climb to his feet. The cop on the ground ran, leapt, and kicked him hard in the face. The man landed in a flower bed and by the time he had rolled over, ready to stand again, the cop had a gun jammed into his smashed, bleeding schnozzle.

Carl's beloved was unable to get a clean look at him through the iron scroll. "Did they catch him?" she screamed.

"Yes!" Carl yelled impulsively. "He's down!"

She turned with a swish of hair. She saw Carl and for a moment their gazes connected like a laundry line. She smiled gorgeously.

"Oh, goodie," she said.

Carl smiled back, then slowly retracted his head and shut the shade. When he looked at Adrian, there were tears in his eyes.

A moment later, overexcited, he was hopping in a circle trying to jam a foot into the sleeve of a wrinkled Oxford shirt. "Time to go a-courtin'!"

"What do you mean?"

"I'm gonna woo 'er!"

He tossed aside the shirt and raced to his bureau, where he dug for clean pants. Adrian felt a burst of happiness for his floor-mate. At last, action! This was what made the city great. No matter how bad things got, good fortune was always lurking just around the corner.

Carl ran his fingernails through his matted hair. "I'll run into her by accident. 'What a small world,' I'll say, 'I just saw you on your fire escape.' And she'll say, 'Small? Tell me about it. It's practically claustrophobic!' And, oh, we'll have a good laugh!"

"You're *really* gonna do it?"

"Yup! You coming with me?"

"Can I? I'd love to! Can I?"

They heard another chorus of shouts from outside.

"Keep low!" Carl sang, as they slid together to the window.

The backyard had erupted in applause and cheers as the cops led the felon away. I stood in the yard at Michael's side, clapping my hands.

"Hang the rascal!" I cheered.

Carl looked over and saw that his beloved was naked again, crossing to and fro, talking excitedly on the phone. God, how he loved her.

Within minutes, Adrian and Carl were sitting on a foreign stoop a block away, sucking smoke together, their attention fixed on the woman's front door. Deranged with ardor, Carl had refused to shower, which meant that he still stank, but Adrian, fearing that it would hurt Carl's confidence, chose not to tell him.

Soon, their prey emerged, wearing tight black slacks and a little white T-shirt. Even from this distance, Adrian could make out the sprouts of her nipples.

She set off down the block and the lads followed.

Carl grabbed the back of Adrian's shirt. "Heel!"

"We might lose her!"

"Not a chance."

They followed her onto a city bus.

Forty minutes later, she got off and so did they.

They followed her down a crowded avenue. Adrian nearly collided with an old man, but dodged him by jumping off the curb into a pile of dog-dirt.

She turned a corner.

"Wait," Carl said. Adrian scraped the sole of his sneaker on the pavement. "One, two, three, and go."

They rounded casually.

She was standing outside a movie theater, looking up and down the block and checking her watch.

They ducked into a doorway. "You don't think she has a boyfriend, do you?" Adrian whispered.

"Impossible. Only one guy's ever been over and he was a homo."

"How could you tell?"

"She walked around naked in front of him and all he did was tell her what clothes to wear."

Adrian nodded. Every day another lesson.

"Anyway," Carl explained, "if she did have a boyfriend, she wouldn't hang out with her gal-pals so much. The first thing a woman does when she falls in love is drop her female friends."

And yet another lesson.

They watched as the woman fidgeted, annoyed that her friend was late. Finally, she gave up, bought a ticket, and disappeared inside.

"Are we going in?" Adrian asked.

"Yeah. You pay."

When they entered the lobby, she was right in front of them, back turned, eyeing the sugary treats at the counter. She purchased a gigantic candy bar.

"That's pure fat," Adrian noted. (His friendship with Miranda had raised his awareness of such things, long before it was fashionable.)

When she moved away, Adrian jolted after her.

Carl grabbed his shirt and jolted him back. "Easy!"

They proceeded together slowly. The dim auditorium was only a third full. She stood in the right aisle near the front. In the middle of a row sat a young man with dark hair, munching popcorn.

"Shit, maybe she *does* have a boyfriend," Carl whispered.

But when the young man turned profile, they both saw, despite glasses and obscuring hair, that he was, in fact, a young *woman*.

"Ever seen her in the window before?" Adrian asked.

"I can't tell."

"She looks cute. Maybe we could double-date."

"Okay, after the movie, we'll bump into them and introduce ourselves."

Adrian nodded and they strode silently down the aisle. When they were about a half-dozen rows away, Carl slid Adrian into the seats directly behind them.

"Unless some old lady with a hat sits in front of us, we're golden," Carl said. "Now scrunch."

"What's the movie?" Adrian whispered.

"Some chick flick."

The lights faded.

As the trailers began, the dark woman whispered something that made the shoulders of Carl's beloved shake with laughter.

"What do you think she said?" Adrian asked.

"Something funny."

Adrian nodded.

The dark woman whispered again, but this time she inspired no laughter. Instead, Carl's girl poked her in the ribs. The dark woman smiled and tucked her own hair behind her ear, and with a shock Carl saw that it was Mary Pilango. He made a sputtering sound and covered his eyes.

"What?" Adrian whispered, not having seen.

Carl lowered his fingers from his face just in time to see his beloved lean over and apply her mouth to Mary's. He savagely kicked the seat in front of him, making a strangled sound.

"Poke out my eyes!" he cried. "Poke out my eyes!"

"*Stop!*" Adrian begged. "She'll hear—"

But it was too late. The center of Carl's existence for the past two months turned around, and looked straight at Carl. From her facial expression, it was clear that at that moment she disliked him with intensity.

After the movie, Mary Pilango did not make love to the object of Carl's worship (they had met just the night before at a feminist hootenanny, at which Mary had played one of her tunes, to meaty applause and husky cheers), for the simple reason that when they had kissed for the first time, in the theater, Mary had felt no tenderness at all, only lust, and this was no longer enough. To make love to this girl (her name was Felice and she was a Martha Graham dancer) would be to betray not only her new resolve, but her feelings for the unflappable waitress. That she could have felt even the vaguest sense of loyalty to a perfect stranger who might not even be into girls, was, of course, patently absurd, but, try as she might, she had not been able to forget the waitress or to banish the notion that they were meant for each other.

The moment she returned from the movie, having declined Felice's offer of "herbal tea" (dyke code for heavy petting), Mary stopped fighting the inevitable and telephoned the owner of the outdoor restaurant where the woman worked. Pam was a mustachioed ex-snail-darter activist whom Mary had bedded a few dozen times a few years back. Pam was blunt to an obnoxious degree and would tell her flat-out if her fixation on the waitress was based on visceral wisdom or cardiac folly.

"Sure, she's gay, you horny bitch!" Pam barked above the crowd. "Why do you think I hired her? Her name's Caroline!

She's only been in town a few months! What? What?! Station three! Tell Trish station three!"

"Look, you're busy," Mary said. "Just tell me when she works."

"What! Hold on. Hey! Phone!" Then she lowered her voice to a conspiratorial hush. "Good luck."

There was a muffled sound, then a woman's voice sounded, close to the receiver, quiet and cautious.

"This is Caroline."

"Oh. Oh! Hi . . . my name's Mary . . . you don't know me."

"I'm aware of that."

Another burst of clatter. Mary waited for it to pass. Her throat constricted. "I'm a friend of Pam's. And I was— Well, I passed by the restaurant a while back and I saw you and I was. . . ." She couldn't find the right words.

"Hold on," Caroline said. When she spoke again, all the noise was gone. "I'm in the supply closet," she said. "I hope the cord doesn't break."

"Well, I was just saying that I passed by last week and I saw you and. . . ."

"Yeah?"

"I was stunned." Mary waited for some response. When none came, she went on: "I . . . I'd like to meet you. There's something about you." Another silence. Mary wondered if she had heard what she said.

"What sort of something?" Caroline asked.

Mary turned to her bedroom as though the answer were hidden there in the humid shadows. "Something I like. A lot. And need, I think. Something strong." In the silence that followed, she realized that she was squeezing the phone with tremendous force. She drew a deep breath and relaxed her hand. Color returned to her knuckles.

"All right," Caroline said, finally.

"All right what?"

"Let's meet."

She said it so casually that Mary's energy lurched to fill the space. "Really, you will? Great. When? Where?"

"Friday."

"Friday?"

"We'll go to the beach."

"The beach?"

"I have a car."

"A car?"

"Knock it off, parrot. I'll drive. You bring the crackers. See you at noon. Here."

She hung up.

For ten long seconds, Mary did not move.

The future, it seemed, had arrived with a bang.

Chuckling to himself, Michael slipped a folded sheet of paper under Adrian's door. On his way downstairs, he was surprised to see Miranda, standing alone in the hall. She held a paintbrush, heavy with violet. Her tattered long-johns, beneath which she was clearly naked, were splattered red and amber.

"Come here," she said.

When he didn't move, she walked over, took his hand with surprising firmness, and hauled him toward her door. He had never been inside Miranda's room. What she was doing could mean only one thing. She was about to confess her love for him. What would he do? Sleeping with her would be fun, certainly, but then what? How could he possibly avoid disappointing her, since he never avoided disappointing himself?

What he saw inside amazed him. Everywhere, from floor to ceiling, on blazing white walls, hung Miranda's paintings, two dozen in all. What struck him first was their passion. The bright colors were applied so thickly that in places the paint rose inches off the canvas and seemed still to be wet. In the center of each lay a hungry black oval.

"My show's soon," Miranda explained, her voice unsteady. "I'm scared."

Michael moved closer to the canvases. He moved around the room. Each was a world of its own. Some reminded him of flowers, others of autumn trees, others of fires. But the oval at the center of each brought him back to Mother, Woman, Birth, Death, Copulation.

"You have nothing to be afraid of," he uttered finally.

She blinked her owl eyes. "Really?"

He lanced her with a look. "They're beautiful. Sexual, too. They're like a mating song. They could attract bees."

"I just paint what I feel," she said, smiling demurely, cheeks reddening.

He stared, wondering if she could really be so unaware of the raw power of her work. He felt himself grow tender around the heart. He was about to say something that he knew he would regret, but there was no stopping it.

"If you need help hanging the show," he said, walking toward the door, "I'm available."

The silence vibrated.

He turned back. Her expression made him wince—it was all joyous circles. He wished he could take it back, but it was too late.

"Oh, Michael," she said, tears pooling.

She had taken the offer all wrong. He hurried away, certain that if he lingered an instant longer he would punch her in the face or they would make love.

Miranda did not move after the door closed, but then her nose twitched and an intense curiosity took hold of her. She walked toward a wall. I dared not move. I hoped she had merely noticed an imperfection in one of the paintings, but, before I knew it, we were iris to iris. Embarrassed, I took a giant backward step, but I slipped on the porcelain and fell. I hit the spout, ripping my hip. Lying there in tremendous pain, I heard angry shouts. I knew that within minutes the peephole would be plugged.

After the movie, Adrian and Carl enjoyed a speechless dinner, punctuated by long soul-sick sighs from Carl. On the way home, Carl finally spoke, giving voice, yet again, to his desire to quit show business. Adrian did not know what to say. Maybe Carl *should* quit. He had never seen him act, but he suspected that if he were truly as brilliant as I had claimed, he would get a job occasionally. (He had no idea that talent is the second greatest obstacle to a professional acting career. The first is a small or normal-sized head.)

"Well, you've gotta do what you've gotta do," Adrian replied with a shrug.

They parted in silence.

Back in his cave, Adrian found the folded sheet of paper under his door. He opened it and saw that it was the poem he had been promised. Without reading the words, he counted the lines and eyed the rhymes and was pleased to discover that it was a sonnet. If it was any good at all, his place in The House Beautiful would be secure and he could actually apply himself to the business of building a life in the city. He fell cross-legged on his bed and began to read:

What Then?

What, then, my sentimental female friend,
If all you daily beg of me I gave?
Would you at last know peace, or might you tend
Instead to curse me for my kindness, rave
That I had robbed you of your longing, left
You cold without a cause to stoke your heart?
A woman satisfied's a soul bereft.
Without a battle, she's without a part.

Without a part, she merely sweats and squirms.
A joyless soldier in a trench, she waits.
But then a man declares his selfish terms
And off she runs to mingle with his hate.
A woman only seeks what starves her needs.
She's only really happy when she bleeds.

Adrian whimpered and threw down the poem. For this ugliness he had contracted, perhaps, a terminal virus? He wanted to wring Michael's neck. Instead, he fell facedown on the bed, and for the first time that summer wished that he had never come to the city. If he hadn't, he would have gone on with his life. It was a teeny life, yes, ignorant, cowardly, and predictable, but he would never have known that. He would have completed his degree and become an astronomy professor, eventually married, had two children, reared them in an ignorant, cowardly, and predictable way, and, if he was lucky, died without ever suspecting that he had missed anything. Now it was too late. He had entered The House Beautiful, and even if he were evicted tomorrow, he would carry it inside him forever. He would never be able to forget that somewhere there was a place where people woke up each morning without any idea of what the day held, where the only limitations to one's dreams were self-imposed, and where each hour held the glorious possibility of creation.

No Words Came

I awoke the morning of my interview as queasy as a man on death row. I forced down a soft banana, a poached egg, a twelve-milligram sedative, and a mug of Provençal Bandol (tickle of *haricots verts;* squeeze of cigar). Washing the dishes, I felt an intense urge to stick my head in the oven. My distress was quickly dispelled, however, when I staggered to my desk to confirm the exact hour of my interview and discovered that it was still ten days away. I had misread the letter.

I awoke Adrian. He babbled the reasons that he did not have a poem ready for me, and I told him that while it was deeply discouraging, it was quite all right, as long as he met me at once in the garden for a tutorial. Having finished with Keats (for the time being), I decided to move on to that great pansy iconoclast, Mr. Percy Bysshe Shelley. By way of inspired segue, we began with "Adonais," Shelley's elegy to Keats. The lad liked the poem, as it introduced him to the radical idea that there was an upside to being dead (a favorite theme of Michael's). I then gave him a treasure plucked from Sasha's extensive library—a well-worn edition of *Prometheus Unbound*. I tore off the New York Public Library pouch and he accepted the gift with gratitude. I sat back, crossed my legs, closed my eyes, and asked that he recite the entire work to me.

As the boy staggered through the lengthy work, I stopped him whenever I felt like it, to disrobe an obscurity, caress a pronunciation, finger a nuance. In point of fact, his recitation was not dreadful. It conveyed an emerging understanding of prosody. From time to time, his voice even quavered with feeling. He seemed particularly touched by the idea of a man's liver being devoured daily by an eagle. (It reminded him, no doubt, of his father's, devoured daily by domestic lager.) Once or twice, I slid into a snooze, but I had warned him in advance that this was no excuse to stop reading. His gentle voice, combined with Shelley's measured feet, soothed my anxious brain. It even occurred to me that Cassandra might be right—maybe *I would* get to keep my government checks, maybe The House Beautiful was safe.

An unfortunate new subtext to our lessons that week was Adrian's acute worry over his floormate's eroding mental health. Since the day Carl's love plan had gone awry, his door had been shut. Whenever Adrian knocked or pleaded, he heard only silence. When he tried to force the door, he found that a chair had been jammed under the knob. As far as Adrian could tell, the young man had not left his room for seven full days now. (In fact, Carl sneaked out every night to eat and to empty his chamber pot—a Nazi helmet that a former tenant had left hanging in the closet.)

One afternoon, Adrian reached his breaking point.

"I'm really worried about Carl!" he cried, tossing aside the book. "We've got to do something! Last night there was a weird smell outside his door."

I saw the look of stark fear on his face and knew that this was no laughing matter.

"Was it a *mortal* stench?"

"I'm not sure!"

Together we dashed up the stairs. I lunged at the door with all my might and, much to my surprise, it burst open freely. I spilled to the carpet. I opened my eyes and saw Carl looking down at me, wearing a double-breasted business suit. For the first time in memory, he was wearing his toupee, which made him look five years younger. His eyes shone and no fag dangled from his lip.

"Are you all right?" I asked.

"Sure," he chuckled. "What about you?"

He helped me to my feet. I found my footing and took a look around. Adrian, entering timidly behind me, was just as surprised as I was. Carl's sty was the picture of order and tidiness. A pile of folded laundry sat on his dresser and a vacuum cleaner stood in the corner, still plugged in.

"Holy shit!" Adrian exclaimed. "What's going on?"

"The phone rang" was Carl's happy reply. "I got an audition."

The boy and I looked at each other. Was such a thing possible?

He crossed away and completed an expert hospital corner. "I'm gonna go out today and get me an acting job."

"You can just *do* that?" Adrian asked.

"Of course, he can," I snorted. "He's a genius. He's just been waiting for the right role."

"And this is it. It's for a new TV show, starting in the fall. Ought to set me up pretty good out there."

"Out where?" Adrian asked.

"L.A., baby."

"Los Angeles?" I cried. "The City of Bottoms? I forbid it!"

"That's where it shoots."

"But the place is atrocious! It's like one long drive to an airport that never comes. Or so I've heard. I refuse to visit. You'll despise it."

Carl fluffed his pillow and tossed it on the bed. "It doesn't matter what I like anymore. I'm gonna let the universe decide."

"Good God!" I exclaimed. "Don't tell me you're going to let one little heartbreak drive you to spirituality. Why, if I had done that, I'd have spent my whole life since college wearing a diaper and living in Nepal."

"How did you know about my heartbreak?" He threw a cold glance at Adrian. "You've got a big mouth, you know that?"

"I didn't tell him!" the boy protested.

"Oh, leave the green woodpecker alone," I huffed at Carl. "I know everything that goes on here. Everything! You think this place runs by itself?"

Carl strapped on his watch. "I gotta run. And let me tell you, the director wants it louder, I'll do it louder. Softer, I'll do it softer. On all fours, I'll do it on all fours."

"What if you don't get the part?" Adrian asked, already worried.

Carl looked him squarely in the eye. "Those are questions I don't ask anymore, Huck. I'm what's known as a *positive* person."

He grabbed his briefcase and hurried to the door.

Adrian spun around. "Good luck, buddy!"

"Don't need it."

After the door closed, Adrian look worried. I smiled and laid a captain's hand on his shoulder.

"He's going straight to the top, kid. I'd stake my reputation on it."

The sun was visible only as a pale disc shimmering dimly through the gray. It would shower soon, but Mary didn't care. They had been driving for a full half-hour now and, as impossible as it seemed, Caroline had yet to speak a word. Mary savored it. So few women were easy with silence.

In the end, it was Mary who spoke first. "I love the sun as much as anyone," she murmured, studying the heavy clouds, "but I think overvaluing it is a sign of spiritual poverty."

Caroline smiled.

"I'm serious," Mary insisted.

"I know," she replied, "that's why I'm smiling."

Mary elaborated: "Seasons are part of life, right? At least for anyone who grew up with them. For most people. And cold is part of the deal. So's rain. So is . . . I dunno . . . humidity. We make do. We even learn to love it. I mean, who doesn't feel a little trembly during a storm? Who doesn't get nostalgic when it snows for the first time? Remember when Nixon set the clocks back to save energy and we had to walk to school in the dark? Every time I wake up early and it's dark and cold out, I think of those mornings. But some people, all they want is sun. All the time. I don't get it. They move to California or Florida or Hawaii and when you ask them how they like it out there, all they talk about is the weather. It's nuts. I mean, Buddha said to exist is to suffer, not to be perpetually tan."

Caroline smiled gently.

Mary liked the way she listened, so calm and receptive. Finally, Caroline said: "I've been thinking of moving to Hawaii. I hear the weather's sublime."

Mary was rendered speechless. It was only when the corners of Caroline's mouth twitched that she realized she had been joking.

They pulled into a parking lot. It was raining now and there were a dozen cars there, filled with people waiting for it to stop. It was not a slanting rain, driven by wind, but sloppy summer drops falling straight down.

"We'll have it all to ourselves," Caroline said matter-of-factly, as she kicked off her sneakers and grabbed a towel from the backseat.

"We're going *out* in this?"

Caroline nodded and jumped out.

Mary faltered. She was unused to letting her date be in charge. But she supposed she didn't really have a choice, so she pried off her heavy, black shoes. When she stepped out of the car, Caroline greeted her with a playful curtsey. Drops splashed Mary's Mediterranean face. She would be drenched by the time they reached the beach. Her anxious consideration was interrupted by a rapturous scream from Caroline as she took off running across the parking lot, limping on the sharp gravel. Mary ran, too, and the sharpness of the stones shocked her. Years had passed since she had been barefoot in summer. As a kid, her feet had been as tough as hooves. Caroline, laughing at the grimaces Mary made, slowed down, caught her hand, and, with a jolt, towed her toward the sand. It was oddly exhilarating, someone else taking the lead like this. They hit the beach, and Caroline pulled her down on the sand. They rolled onto their backs and gasped for breath. Caroline cried out to the churning, crying sky: "Look how beautiful! And it's all ours!"

The tables were topped with Italian tile, the windows, running with rain, were made of stained glass. Adrian sat back in the hard chair, sipping a glass of wine (the first of his life), wondering what had brought him here. Maybe it was the example of Carl's new positivity. Maybe it was some latent talent of which he was only dimly becoming aware. Maybe it was mere self-disgust. Regardless, no more excuses, no more wheedling. He was about to take control of his life. This was more than just a first creative act, it would be his entry ticket to a long, happy life in The House Beautiful.

He uncapped his pen.

He studied the photograph of my college chums (which he had pinched from my mantel), studying all the faces, but most intensely those of the young couple on the snowbank. Were they in love? How did that feel? To be in love in the late 1950s?

He waited.

An hour later, he was home, dripping wet, running up the stairs. He hated to bother Louise while she was working, but she was always working. He burst into her room and, within no time at all, he was getting exactly what he deserved: Louise had backed him into a corner, her eyes scrambled and homicidal.

"You're a god damn liar!" she screamed, "Do us all a favor, go back to Cedar Falls and stare at the stars!"

"Ames! No! I hate it there!"

"Then stay!"

"I need a poem."

"That's not my problem! Go write one!"

"Do you know of a class?"

"Haven't you learned anything? Teach yourself! Trial and error, that's all it is!"

"That's all?"

"No! It's everything else, too!"

"Like what?"

She stepped off and began to walk in tiny circles, waving her arms. "Why are you asking *me?!* Can't you see I'm insane?" And she was; she had averaged just two hours of sleep a night for the past week. "Just write a poem, for fuck's sake! But make sure it *costs* you something!"

Ten minutes later, Adrian was back in the café, at the same table, staring down at the blank sheet. The moment was now. No more fear, no more self-judgment. He would tell the truth, his own truth, no one else's, and it would cost him something.

He stared for two hours.

No words came.

Mary and Caroline gazed out at the sea, holding their towels over their heads like cowls. "Who is this stranger?" Mary wondered, stealing a peek. Caroline stared at the sea with a look of melancholy, as though some precious part of her were being blown about by the fitful winds. But if she was, indeed, sad, she seemed so *comfortable* with it, as though she knew it was something to be left alone, not fixed or cured. (See "Ode on Melancholy.")

As Mary studied Caroline's profile, she thought of the sort of women with whom she was usually involved. They talked constantly about themselves, always explaining who they were, instead of letting her discover it for herself. It was a ploy to gain her trust so they could jump into her heart, feet first. She realized that, unconsciously, she had long ago accepted that she would never find an equal with whom to share her life. That's why she had slept with them all. Why not, since nothing would come from any of it? And now there was this peaceful, quiet stranger. Mary didn't even know her last name.

She wondered if the reason she had never made love last was that she had never known what that would look like. How could she find what she could not imagine? How would she recognize it? And so she closed her eyes and tried. She was lying in bed, side-by-side with a woman in a dark room. There was no talk. The warmth of each other's bodies was enough. The cadence of their breathing blended with the beat of their hearts. Outside, the world was crude; inside, everything was pure and true. No matter what dramas came and went, what tears were shed for whatever reasons, she and this woman would never be adversaries.

As if the universe were telling her that Caroline was the woman with whom she might create just such a union, there was movement in the clouds and a fiery sun appeared, trailing an entourage of blue.

"Where did *that* come from?" Caroline whispered, awed.

"I don't know. Make something up," Mary murmured with a smile.

"Well—" Caroline smiled as she collected her thoughts. "God got weary of so much gray, so she went to her palette and added a stroke of blue and gold."

"What, are you a painter or something?"

"Something. A sculptor."

As the sun sank, Mary lay next to Caroline on the sand,

caressing her features with both hands, as though recording every detail, in case they never met again.

"Have you ever been faithful to anyone?" Caroline whispered at last, eyes closed.

Mary told her, honestly, no.

"Do you want to try?" Caroline asked. "Because it's the only way I can do this."

A surge of feeling rose in Mary's throat. She rolled away and hid her face. It was only with quick frantic gasps that she stopped herself from weeping.

You Have No Idea How Much It Hurts

As Helios climbed the sky, sweat trickled down the contours of my big belly. Soon my blouse would be soaked. Excellent—it would only add to the dismal effect. I ran a final check: woolen turquoise suit, misbuttoned tangerine blouse, pinkish ascot, lilac socks. Louise was right: The *federales* could not possibly accuse me of sanity. I grabbed a macramé purse (knotted by Sasha, painstakingly, during one of her forced stays in the boobyhatch), then slid into a pair of authentic Dutch shoes. (I had purchased them one drunken afternoon with my San Francisco pals, in a facetious attempt to start a bohemian book club called the *clognoscenti*.)

I clomped into the hallway and found that I could not bear to greet my destiny without a parting word of encouragement. But whom to pester? It was noon. Louise was, by divine grace, asleep. Miranda and Michael had departed early. Carl, a changed man, no longer allowed tobacco in his chamber. Mary was in bed with her new girlfriend, Caroline, sleeping or spooning, or writhing in the saltclasp of a desperate 66.

On my way up to Adrian's cave, I noticed that the paint above the staircase was in poor condition. A jagged plate of canary, the shape and size of Madagascar, was in imminent danger of falling. (When I had spruced the place up, I had neglected to scrape off the old color before applying the new.) I made a sudden bargain with the Gods: If I prevailed today, I would repaint The House Beautiful top to bottom. In fact, I would restore it in every way to its original condition at the turn of the century. I felt such excitement at this resolution that I decided to go even further in my pledge. I would also crash diet and plaster all my peepholes.

I did not know it at the time, but Adrian had finally made some progress. For the past seven days, he had spent his nights reading Romantic poetry, fumigating his lobes with nicotine, and sketching stabs at verse in the blank pages of one of his father's lab books. Each morning, he tore them out and threw them away, but what mattered was that he was making a genuine effort. Although he had only been asleep for a few hours now, the sound of my clogs stirred him. Assuming that I was coming to demand his long-overdue poem, he was already on his feet, shaking like a leaf, when I banged in.

Seeing his skinny, compact little torso, I lifted an eyebrow and thrummed, "Hail to thee, Lithe Spirit."

I was disappointed that he did not laugh.

"I got up early to write," he lied, wiping a hand across his damp copper hair.

I noticed that his boxer shorts housed a bladder-bone. I looked away. Today was too important to jeopardize with lust.

"In fact, I . . . I'm going to have something for you to read any day now," the mountebank stammered. "I've been working on it, buffing it up."

In a generous frame of mind, I hoisted him gently off the hook. "Splendid! By all means, take your time. Impatience is the bane of the young artist, you know."

He was confused by my sudden *laissez-faire* attitude. Had he been driving himself insane for nothing? I stepped over a mine-field of crumpled poems, oily food containers, and volumes of verse (lifted from my library). I spun around, arms floating at my side, and threw him a coy glance, waiting for his reaction. When none came, I twirled like a runway model, striking his shoulder with my knotty bag. Adrian, still astounded by my indifference to the delivery date of his poem, was speechless.

I was forced to be direct. "I'm leaving for my interview now. Do you like my outfit? Do you, boy?"

"Yeah, you look great."

I froze mid-twirl. "Pardon me?"

He detected a hard edge in my voice, but he wrongly assumed that I was annoyed that he had not offered me *more* praise.

"Really great." He touched my suit jacket, beneath which I fairly dripped with sweat. "Very colorful, very cool."

I stamped like an angry Clydesdale. "I don't want to look *either,* you little dunce! I want to look *mentally ill!"* I threw my hands up in distress. "Your opinion is worthless! You flatter and pander and—"

"But you're so sensitive!" he wailed from the heart. "I never know what you want to hear!"

"The *truth,* for God's sake!"

"All right!" he cried. "You look crazy! Like a total clown! Your suit's hideous!"

"Hideous?" I whispered. "It cost over two hundred dollars! It's genuine wool!"

"I . . . I meant hideous with an orange shirt!"

"That's not what you said!" Red-faced, gnashing my teeth, I turned and clip-clopped to the door.

"Good luck," he muttered feebly.

"I expect your poem in my hand by Monday!" I barked. "And it had better *sing,* that's all I can say. Or you can kiss the curb!"

My parting shot was heartless, yes, but I had not climbed an entire flight of stairs to be insulted.

The telephone jangled on the other side of the world. Dozing flat on her stomach, Louise decided to let someone else answer it, someone awake on the other side of the world. But the ringing persisted like an unheeded alarm. Finally, she staggered to the door, and the next thing she knew, she was sitting on my queen, listening to a man's velvety voice. His name was George Buchner and he wanted to speak to his niece. Louise told him that Miranda was not at home.

"Would you please tell her I've got to leave town again, but I'll get down there as soon as I can to see her show?"

"Will do." Louise's mind cleared. "So, George, what's the word on Michael's story? Did you like it?"

"I guess you're a friend of Miranda's."

"Friend, housemate, romantic advisor."

"A fan of Michael's?"

"Fan, housemate, colleague."

"You're a writer, too?"

"Indeed."

"What sort of writer?"

"The sort who actually writes. Now, listen, about Michael's story—"

"I don't really think it would be fair for me to discuss it with you."

"Of course not, but as intellectuals we both understand how quickly fairness kills a good conversation. Come on, George, what'd you think? I won't tell, I promise."

He laughed. "You're a real character, aren't you?"

"How did you know?"

"What's your name?"

"Louise D'Aprix. I'd like to drop by and show you my novel."

"Ambitious, too," George chuckled.

"It's almost finished."

"What's it about?"

She was awake now and her blood was beginning to snap, crackle, and pop. "The horrors of being young and creative. About a house full of narcissists trying to free themselves from their imaginations long enough to make human contact. How since World War Three hasn't started yet, we spend our time consumed with inane bullshit." Her gums beat without reserve. "It's called *The Palace of Wisdom*. I'll be there in a couple of hours. I'll bring you a power sandwich and watch while you read. What'll it be? Tuna fish? Egg salad? Tongue?"

The pea-green institutional wall clock informed me that it was twenty-five minutes past the hour of my appointment. (For those of you too old or too young to remember, in the late 1980s our government had become, under the stewardship of the efficient Republicans, positively Balkan.) I was restless. My arse overspilled the plastic seat. I was unable to look at the faces of my fellow supplicants. Did they suspect that my unusual outfit was merely a costume?

I flapped through a fashion magazine full of dead-eyed anorectics wearing cotton briefs. My God, the pansies on Madison Avenue were turning our nation's women into a pack of boys. Not wholly a bad thing, of course, but how dispiriting for women with hips and bosoms. As the delay wore on, my indignation at Uncle Sam's tardiness set my head spinning. I needed someone to blame for my humiliation and, as usual, my adoptive father came to mind. If he had not man-handled me, I would never have come to associate authority with evil. If he had not saved me from killing myself at the age of twelve, I would today be happily horizontal. And if he had not died himself and left me a subsistence trust, I might have been forced into the marketplace after college and grown into a productive citizen.

A vaguely antipodean female voice hollered from the doorway. She was forced to repeat my name three times before I snapped to. I heaved a mighty breath and rose stiffly.

"Are you deaf?" she asked. She was dusky with a nose like that of a luckless prizefighter. I suspected that an aboriginal hung somewhere low off her family tree.

"Why, no," I replied. "Merely insane. Lead the way, mate."

I clomped through a roar of hearty laughter. She led me inside, down a center aisle lined with Formica desks. The desks held a hundred underpaid drudges, each plagued by back pains and hemorrhoids, and typing his soul away. Lucky for them, their computers would give them thyroid cancer long before they realized they had wasted their lives. My inquisitor stood waiting for me at the end of the aisle, his manicured hands clasped in front of his crotch. He was very short, clad in a broad-shouldered yellow blazer and big designer spectacles. He was entirely unintimidating but for one fact: *He was the spitting image of Pip at fifty.*

I trembled.

My scalp crawled.

My stomach kicked.

"This is Mr. Moy," my escort said, gesturing with a callused hand. "He'll be conducting your interview."

Mr. Moy's shake was teensy and cold. His breath was redolent of peppermint and self-righteousness. I fell into the chair opposite him. Morning grape splashed my tonsils.

"Let me tell you right now, Mr. Troop," the Chinaman began, his face turning very nasty. "I expect the truth and nothing but."

As though on cue, I bent at the waist and threw up.

Within minutes of my departure, Adrian had settled back into sleep, but my parting shot had wrecked him. He dreamt of knife-wielding pursuers, nude theatrical debuts, and forgotten math tests. He let out little whimpers and broke wind with reckless abandon. Relief came at last in the form of a shout from outside his door, followed by a series of fleshy thumps. Seconds later, Carl banged in, striding like an old-time tragedian treading the boards. He waved his arms and bugged his eyes to the cheap seats. Adrian was scared out of his wits.

"I have taken my place among the immortals!" Carl declaimed.

"What happened?" Adrian asked, barely awake.

"Guess, boy!"

"You got the part?"

Carl dropped his hands to his thighs and fell into a humble bow. "Verily, I did."

Adrian let out a cry and leapt up to hug him, but he stopped short when he saw his friend's dangling manhood. Carl had gotten the news fresh out of the shower. He punched him on the shoulder instead.

"Congratulations!" Adrian said.

His happiness could not have been more sincere.

Carl turned dramatically to the window, his penis swinging after him like a bit of rope. "Soon I will fly away, young Huck, to that surfboard dealership by the sea!"

"How much— I mean, if you don't mind my asking. How much are they paying you?"

"Twelve thousand a week."

"Holy shit!" Adrian screamed. "What's your part? Who do you play?"

Suddenly Carl was out of character, speaking quickly and frankly. "Adrian it's great. I'm this lawyer, see, but I really want to be an actor. Since I have to make a living, I work at my father-in-law's law firm, but I hate it, so I stir up all kindsa trouble. You know, TV hijinks. I go in and out of funny voices, play practical jokes at big meetings. I'm the office wag!"

"That's perfect for you."

"I know!"

"Are you still gonna speak to me when you're famous?"

"Nope." He darted for the door. "Wait'll my folks hear!"

The downtown avenue was infested with scruffy scullions, sly mal-formations, rude varlets, caterwauling buskers, shuffling weed-heads, saddlebagged cat lovers, and suicidal children. Passing these moral and aesthetic insults, Miranda was utterly oblivious of every-thing but Michael. She had scraped her middle finger on a hook at the gallery and, sucking on it now, she floated along, chattering gaily, fueled by the delight of the first morning she had ever spent with the man she loved. Hanging her paintings together, they had laughed like idiots, especially when he insisted that she was nailing them too low. "No one's gonna see them except your fellow midgets," he said. "Is that what you want? Your work hanging in dollhouses all over the city?"

What a wonderful day.

Abruptly, something troubled her. It had been tugging at her sleeve for weeks. She might as well get it over with. She stopped dead. "I have something to tell you. I did something bad."

Michael doubted it. He smiled indulgently. "What?"

She started walking again.

He followed her.

Again, she stopped. "I stole one of your stories."

She checked his face to see if he was angry. Before she could tell that he was not, she was moving again.

"Hey!" he called, grabbing her by the shoulders. "Stop it! You're wearing me out!"

She turned, her eyes crushed with worry. "I did it because you wouldn't let me read anything. I got frustrated. Do you hate me?"

"It depends," he answered.

"On what?"

"Which story it was."

"'Paint the Town Black.'"

His favorite.

"Oh. What did you think of it?"

"I liked it. It was disturbing and honest. It reminded me of you."

He smiled despite himself. That wasn't so bad. Maybe he ought to show her some of the others.

Miranda brought the wounded fingernail to her mouth. "Anyway, there's more. I sent a copy to my uncle. He's a book editor. He's sorta powerful."

Michael's heart gripped. "What'd he say?"

"Nothing yet. He's been traveling. But he's coming to the opening." She dared a glance at him. "I know it was wrong, but I knew if *I* didn't help you, nobody would. And you'd never help yourself."

Michael felt understood, cared for. Seeing how tormented she was, he laid a rough hand on her soft cheek. With his other hand, he fingered her tiny crucifix. "You're a real Catholic, you know that?"

"What do you mean?"

"Altruism and self-hate."

Also feeling understood, she buried her face in his big chest. "I like you so much. You have no idea how much it hurts."

His arms reflexively encircled her. He stood that way for a long time, during which he grew increasingly uncomfortable. Miranda sensed it, but she couldn't pretend anymore.

"Can I sleep over tonight?" she asked. She felt him start to pull away, so she grabbed him harder. "Please," she whispered. "Nothing has to happen."

But he knew something would. Perhaps nothing sexual, but progress even more intimate. The warmth of her little body was already yanking at the fastenings of his reserve. Even he was unsure what lay beneath his suspicion of love, who he really was, of what he was actually capable, but he knew that for her to accept what was there, she would have to be as free of judgment as nature itself. Could she do it? Could this person, more child than woman, accept in him what he could not even accept in himself? He eased her away. He glanced down and, although his eyes barely grazed hers, he knew that no one would ever try harder.

George Buchner took a messy bite of a sesame bagel, forcing egg salad out the side. A chunk of it plopped onto the wax paper, but he kept reading. Nearby, a red light flashed every time his secretary intercepted a call. Louise sat across from him, sunk deep into the scoop of a Danish chair, hugging herself against the chill of the air-conditioning. She had often dreamt of a turning point like this, one where her career lay in the balance, but now that it was here, it was not at all what she had expected. She had imagined that she would be frightened out of her wits, psychotic, really—clinging to a light fixture, teeth bared, wings flapping— but instead she felt preternaturally calm. It was just life. One more human being reading her work. The fact that this human being had the power to publish her book struck her as negligible. All publishing would mean was that even *more* human beings would read her words, more human beings like herself and like him. It would mean money, too, of course. If she was lucky, enough to give her more time to write. But she would get used to that soon enough, and then she would pass her days and nights as she had since high school: hunched over her typewriter, lonely and lashed, brain boiling. Money wouldn't change that. Neither would fame. Nothing could.

George looked up, wiping his mouth with the linen napkin she had brought him.

"It's good, isn't it?" Louise asked.

He pinned her with a long stare.

"It's not really a novel," he stated, finally.

It was the last thing she had expected to hear. She forced a toddler's sweet smile and said, "It's not?"

"Do you want me to be honest?"

"Yes."

"It's a mess."

Her heart slid, but at the last instant she caught it between her knees.

"Don't get me wrong," he continued. "You're talented. It's full of wonderful language, wonderful surprises. But it's anarchic. It reads like . . . well, like ramblings. Like a diary. As though you were just typing whatever came into your head. Or whatever happened to you and your friends that day."

She nodded solemnly, but the sounds in the room were fading away beneath a roar emanating from her own frantic brain. The roar held words, but they came so quickly she could not make them out. It was the devil's din and it was the buried soundtrack of her life. She wondered if she would cry. She never cried. Next she wondered if maybe it had been a mistake to go off her medication.

Whenever Adrian or any of his school friends had succeeded, it had always been at something academic and local, never creative and national. Yet here was Carl, after a decade of the most abject struggle, about to be rewarded in the most tremendous way imaginable. Anything seemed possible now. Adrian's body relaxed against the stoop and he told himself that enough was enough. He must listen to Louise and write his own poem no matter what, and if he wasn't prepared to sacrifice something in its creation, then it would be no more meaningful than tying his shoes or completing a crossword puzzle. He was ashamed now that he had ever bothered his housemates. He had behaved like a spoiled brat.

He flicked his morning cigarette into the gutter. It was time to grow up. He would push through the pain. Today, no matter what he wrote down, he would not destroy it. Even if it stank, he would finish it. A thought struck him like a slap. Maybe the reason he had been blocked all summer was not that he had no talent or courage.

Maybe it was that he was a liar. Maybe it was impossible for a liar to write a good poem.

A taxi stopped in front.

In my frenzy to pay the nosy Haitian driver, I dropped my macramé. By the time I had recovered it, I was crying again. I crawled out and slammed the door. My revolting costume was damp and wrinkled. Adrian leapt to his feet at the sight of my veiny, empurpled face and asked what had happened.

"Catastrophe!" I cried, as I bolted past him.

Adrian turned and watched as I tumbleweeded up the stairs. When I returned, five minutes later, wearing all white and pressing an ice-cold Bellini to my forehead, Miranda and Michael were just walking up.

"B. K. had his interview," Adrian explained to them gravely.

A silence ensued.

Adrian made an urgent face at Miranda. She, in turn, jabbed her new pal with a sharp elbow.

"Oh! How'd it go?" Michael asked obediently.

"Unspeakably," I quavered. "The worst ordeal of my long life. My interviewer was from Taiwan and he was the spitting image of the evil Pip."

"Who the hell's Pip?" Michael asked.

"Hung Su," Adrian explained, unaware that not all of my lodgers were honored with the details of my personal life.

"And who's that?" Michael asked, grinning now.

"It doesn't matter!" I cried. "The point is that he reminded me of a cold-blooded murderer with whom I once shared my bed. At least Pip had been emotionally accessible. This little horror was absolutely opaque . . . as unreadable as . . . as—"

"A Chinese phone book?" Michael suggested.

I stamped my espadrille and pointed a finger. "Don't you dare mock me!"

Above us, Carl leaned out of my bedroom window. "Did you tell 'em my news?"

"Oh, yeah! Guess what? Carl's got a part on a TV show! He's moving to Hollywood!"

"No!" Miranda screamed happily, clapping her little hands.

"*You?* A bum like *you?*" Michael said, grinning up at him.

Mary and Caroline, their curiosity piqued by the commotion, emerged from downstairs, conjoined.

"What's going on?" Mary asked.

"Carl got an acting job!" Miranda cried. "On a TV show! He's moving to Hollywood!"

As the girls lavished their congratulations upon Carl, my hackles rose.

"*What about me!*" I shrieked, floating a high note only dreamt of by the world's greatest castrati.

"Oh, yeah, your big interview. How'd that go?" Mary asked, smirking unforgivably.

"His interviewer was Chinese," Miranda explained. "A real pip."

I cut the child off: "The very first thing he said to me was, 'You must tell me the truth and nothing but.' His tone was so cold, so full of rancor, that I threw up my breakfast."

"Nooo!" they all moaned together.

"All over his desk. And once his ugly Maori secretary had swabbed it up and I had lain down for a few minutes, I simply could not bring myself to lie. I wanted to, oh, how deperately, but I couldn't! What's wrong with me?"

"You have integrity?" Caroline offered.

"*Who the hell are you?!*" I screamed.

I knew perfectly well who she was, but the rude thing had no way of knowing it.

"Her name's Caroline," Mary snapped. "Be nice to her or I'll kick your ass."

"Well, I *don't* have integrity," I resumed. "I was simply frightened. I was sure if I lied, he'd find out and throw me in jail."

Louise walked up, dressed in a sky-blue cotton frock, with an unopened parasol resting on her shoulder. Her other hand clutched her manuscript. "Hey, guys! Guess what? I just met Miranda's uncle George."

Miranda darted a look at Michael, who was already worried.

"He called when you were out. I invited myself to his office. He read some of my novel."

"Wow." Miranda was annoyed, but she tried to hide it. "What did he say?"

"He thinks I'm weak on structure and story." She set her manuscript and parasol on a step. "He thinks I need lithium."

This came as no surprise to anyone.

"Did he say anything about Michael's story?" Miranda asked.

"No, he said that would be unfair. He can't make it to your opening, by the way. He wants you to call him."

"Well, *I* have news, too," I sniffed at Louise. "Of course, it can't compare with *yours* because—"

"Guess what, Carl got a part," Adrian interjected. "On a TV show. He's moving to Hollywood."

Louise grinned up at the window. "Sell-out!"

"I can't wait!" Carl sang.

"What about me!" I shouted. *"I had a day, too! I had a day!"* Of course, I was behaving like a perfect monster, but I had a perfect right to. I did nothing but give, give, give to these arty ingrates. It was high time they showed me some consideration.

"B. K. had his interview," Miranda explained to Louise. "It went bad."

"Oh, I'm sorry, B. K.," Louise said sincerely, bless her heart. "What happened?"

"My interrogator was a sadist. I wanted to say everything just the way I'd rehearsed it, but I couldn't. I was too afraid, so I told him the truth." I gulped at my Bellini.

"What did you say exactly?" she asked.

"That Dr. Osman was a criminal quack. That I'm as capable of holding down a job as anyone. That I type ninety words a minute. That I'd make a brilliant executive secretary." I let the words sink in. I heroically tossed back my head. "Now, if you'll all excuse me, I must go upstairs and cut my throat."

"So, hotshot," Louise said, looking up at Carl, "when're you taking off for Tinsel Town?"

"That was just a figure of speech!" I bellowed to the heavens. "Let's talk about me! Everything's falling apart! The gyre widens! The center cannot hold! You all have futures! What do I have?!"

"Getting a job isn't so bad," Caroline noted. "You might even enjoy it."

I raised a fist to strike her, but then I remembered Mary's warning and scratched my head instead.

"She's right," Mary said. "It's good to have something to do every day."

I spoke loftily, like an innocent man addressing a mob from whatever you call those things where guillotines sit. "That's easy for you to say. You're all artists. When *you* get a job, you know it won't last forever or at least you have reason to suspect that it won't. Your dreams sustain you. But when *I* get a job, I face an eternity typing under fluorescent lights, growing older and fatter by the minute, while the computer sows tumors in my thyroid!"

"Ah, life," Carl mused from the second floor. "Ain't it grand?"

You'll Be the Waiter

In the words of that great prurient puritan, Mr. D. H. Lawrence, "I shrink from beginning. It is most difficult to begin." Watching the slow, feline stretch of morning light across the ceiling, Mary Pilango, contemplating her own new beginning, also felt afraid, but at the same time more at peace than she had in years. It had been a dark, ugly struggle, but at last she was moving toward the light. And she owed it all to Caroline, she knew that. Divine Caroline, who lay snuggled in the firm valley of her arm and chest. When Mary's friends asked her about this young woman who seemed to have won her heart overnight, Mary described her as "unbelievable," "incredible," "amazing," and, although she knew these weary words conveyed next to nothing, no others came any closer to conveying the perpetual wonder that Caroline inspired in her. Mary smiled down at her sleeping face. She was subtly stirring, as if the movement of Mary's mind had wakened her.

"Morning," Caroline mumbled, eyes still closed.

"Hey, guess what?" Mary whispered. "I've decided to give a concert. Finally. A small one. Right here. In the backyard. What do you think? It's not fair to start playing for the public when I haven't even played for my own housemates yet. What do you think?"

Caroline burrowed an approving smile into a fold in her neck.

Mary gazed at the ceiling with a mystical smile and conjured. "I'm going to call the concert Birth-something. The Shock of Birth. Or the Birth Trial. Birth—I don't know. Something with birth in it. Birth Rites. Birth Trauma. Or Birthday something. The Cracking of the Egg. Or maybe Evolution something. Songs of Evolution. Something like that."

"Mmm," Caroline murmured warmly, because she found all of them good.

Carl Alan Dealey made trip after trip up and down the creaking stairs, lugging in both arms his whole worldly treasure, which included a broken television set, a child's globe, a near-empty bottle of baby oil, 249 headshots and résumés, and various articles of conservative attire. He delivered this fabulous trove to his younger brother, Chad Eric Dealey, who stood at the curb, packing the Dealey family station wagon.

At ten o'clock, there was a knock on Adrian's door.

"I'm off!" Carl said.

Adrian opened the door, his eyes jellied with slumber.

"So early?"

"I rise with the sun now, pal."

"I was up writing all night."

"Good stuff?"

"No, just a bunch of shit."

"Glad to hear you swearin', Huck. Anyway, my steed awaits me. I'm dumpin' everything in my folks' garage. They'll ship it out to the coast once I'm settled." He jammed a paper bag into Adrian's hands. "A little something to remember me by. You can look at the stars with them."

Adrian pulled the binoculars from the bag. He smiled crookedly and made another of his rare jokes. "I can look at *you*."

"I'm not a star yet, but I appreciate the sentiment. Here, take this, too." He pulled his toupee from his back pocket. "I'm gonna buy a bushier one."

Adrian took it and inspected it from every angle. "What am I supposed to do with it?"

"Wait a few years, you'll see."

They shook hands.

"I'll say good-bye to your lesbo-girlfriend if I see her," Adrian muttered dryly.

"Don't bother."

Carl turned away.

Adrian stopped him before he reached the stairs. "Hey, Carl? Thanks. You've been a good friend."

Like a good Protestant, Carl winced at this unseemly display of emotion and escaped.

Adrian stood motionless, listening to the footsteps diminish. He had never met such an odd fellow. He would miss him. Life in the house would never be the same. He remembered the Keats ode, and, thinking of autumn and how it was just around the corner, he felt, carried to his heart, everything kind and cruel about the passage of time. So fast. He wished he were a little boy again, before there were so many decisions to make, before the death of parents.

Meanwhile, Chad, a cocky young salesman built like an automatic dishwasher, rearranged his big brother's life in the back of the wagon. Carl skipped down the front steps but stopped to look at the church across the way. His face gained alertness, as though the crumbling, holy place, now a refuse for recovering addicts, might offer him some last-minute counsel.

"So you're really leaving," Louise said, leaning down from her bedroom window.

Surprised, Carl turned around and looked up. "When you gotta go, you gotta go."

"That was brilliant. Make that up yourself?" She laughed hoarsely and coughed. "So, where're you *really* going?"

"The top, honey." He unwrapped a stick of chewing gum.

"Don't bullshit me. I know you're not going to L.A."

"Oh, yeah?" he said, chewing sloppily. "Is that what a little bird told you?"

"No, common sense. Where're you *really* going?"

"That's for me to know and you to find out." Carl waved over his shoulder as he descended the steps.

"Tell me!" she shouted. "Or in my book I'll have you sleep with Adrian in the last chapter! How would your parents like that? Or I'll turn you into a psycho who shoots up a playground!"

"Use your imagination, baby!"

Suddenly, another voice rang out. *"Wait!"*

Adrian, having come down to watch Carl drive away, had overheard everything. He bounded down the steps, arms flailing. "You're not really going to Hollywood?!"

Carl, full of regret, exhaled hard and looked into his friend's innocent, unhinged face. He could not carry the deception an inch farther. "Nope."

"You mean—"

"Yup, I lied."

Adrian was poleaxed.

Carl slapped a hand on his shoulder. "The world's an ugly place, kid. It sure ain't Iowa. Iowa ain't even Iowa anymore."

"Where're you really going?"

"Dealey's the name, panties the game. I'm joinin' the family empire. I'll crash with my folks at first . . . till I've saved up some dough . . . then I'll set myself up in Jersey somewhere. Off one of the prettier exits."

"You're quitting show business?"

"I'm tradin' it in for a backyard, a picket fence, and a dog. Maybe even a wife."

"And you'll be happy?"

Carl shook his head, disappointed at how little the boy had learned. "Happy's not the issue. How many times has life got to kick you in the nuts before you figure that out? It's about *peace of mind.*"

Chad, impatient with the farewell, muttered for his brother to hurry up.

"But why did you lie to us?" Adrian begged. "We would have understood."

"Tell B. K. I quit acting? Are you nuts? I'd have been his example for the next ten years. 'Poor Carl. A regular Dame Gielgud. But he betrayed his talent and went into the girdle business.' No thanks. This way I go out a legend." He smiled at his brother who was gesturing now. *"Really* gotta run, Huck."

They shook hands again.

When Carl walked away, Adrian called out, "Will I ever see you again?"

Carl turned. "Sure, we'll run into each other at a restaurant someday. I'll be the bald guy with the lobster bib and the gaggle of squawkin' kids."

"And I'll be the poet," Adrian said softly, a tear welling in his eye.

Carl smiled and pointed at him. "You'll be the waiter."

When Adrian came back inside, understandably pensive, he peeked into the front room. All the way in back, I stood in profile at the dining room window, gazing out at the garden, motionless and serene, as though posing for a society portrait. There was poise in my bearing, a noble handsomeness in the relief of my coarse features against the glass.

"You didn't want to say good-bye to Carl?"

I turned slowly and shook my head. My eyes were ennobled by an otherworldly sadness. Adrian suspected at once, quite correctly, that I had, at long last, surrendered to the Fates, resigned myself to the end of life as I knew it. My lofty, yielding mood, and his own dismay at Carl's deceit, helped convince him that the moment had at last arrived for him to come clean. As he moved closer, he wondered what on earth had taken him so long, why it was that the truth, which ought to be the simplest thing on earth to confront, was so often depicted by the mind as a wall of fire.

"I have something to tell you," Adrian said.

When I did not reply or move, he snatched something from the mantel. The springs of the sofa wheezed as he settled in. A faint dust rose. The fretling squirmed in silence for almost a minute, waiting for me to join him. A metallic pop sprang from the kitchen. My toaster waffle was done. I buttered it, folded it, and jammed it into my mouth without syrup. When I returned, I was carrying a tumbler of *Liebfraumilch* (hymen intact, yet brimming with lactose).

"You look positively green," I observed.

"It's about yesterday. Something you said." He looked down at his neat lap. "You said that if you got a job, you'd have no hope of ever leaving it. Well, I just want you to know that it's that way for me, too." He looked up and saw that I was listening intently. "I'm not a poet, B. K. I'm just an astronomy student."

"Duh," I replied quickly.

He was astonished and a bit embarrassed. "You knew? Who told you?"

"I don't need informants. I am exquisitely intuitive. I was on to you from the first minute, but I wanted you to come clean in your own way, in your own time."

This was untrue, of course. I had been fooled entirely. Even now, my brain was toppling. But I couldn't very well let him know that. If I did, word would spread and others would be emboldened to keep secrets.

"Tell me something," I said, advancing the subject. "If you're nothing but a student stargazer, what on earth possessed you to apply to an artists' colony?"

"Well, that's what I want to talk to you about." He chugged a deep, painful breath.

I realized with a shock that he was about to reveal something even more momentous. Because almost every surprise the Fates had dealt me in my earthly tenure was of the excruciating variety, I slammed back a hearty gulp of wine, avalanching ice into my nose. As I pulled the tumbler away, I coughed a mighty splash of grape onto the blossoms and branches of my kimono.

"I came here," Adrian began with difficulty, "because I'd heard about you from my father when I was a kid. He said that you were like family and that if I was ever in New York I should look you up. Well, this was my first visit, so that's what I did. I had no idea you ran an artists' colony."

"What are you talking about? Who's your father?"

A frown appeared on his wide lips. He lifted from his lap a framed photograph and turned it around. It was the shot of my college chums perched on the snowbank. He pointed to the ascetic young man in whom he had for so long shown such a keen interest. For a moment my face was still, then I looked in every direction as though I wanted to run, but did not know where.

"My name isn't Adrian Malloy," he explained. "It's Adrian Daigle. Charles Daigle was my father. I wanted to tell you, but you and my father had lost touch. You hadn't spoken in so long. And I didn't know why. I thought maybe you'd had a fight. I was afraid you wouldn't let me live here."

"How could you think that?" I cried indignantly. "I never treated either one of them badly! I was even kind to your horrid mother! They must know that!"

"But *I* didn't!" he pleaded, matching my passion.

"What? What do you mean?! Why didn't they tell you before you came?"

"Because they're both dead."

Silence.

I could not think or breathe.

Finally, I gasped, "So you *did* arrive here from his funeral?"

"Yeah. My mom died when I was in high school, like I told you."

I lunged toward him with outstretched arms and fell facedown on the carpet, losing my tumbler. I knew it was precisely the sort of reaction the poor thing had hoped to avoid, but I was deeply moved. He helped me to my feet and deposited me back on the leather, where I cried for a long time. Funny, isn't it, how we spend the first half of our lives unable to access our emotions and the second half unable to contain them? I snatched again and again at a box of tissues.

When I finished blubbering, Adrian dropped his head and spoke. He knew that he must remain calm or else he would be forced to feel the heartbreak all over again.

"My mom had cancer in her late twenties," he began. "Hodgkin's disease. She thought it was gone. But one day she had this pain in her jaw. She went to a dentist. He was the one who found the tumor. She died pretty soon after that."

"And your father? He really was a drinker? In college, he never drank. He detested alcohol."

"He changed" was the lad's simple reply. "After he died, I wanted to be alone for a while, but I didn't want to *feel* alone. So I came here. To you." He settled into mute reflection, then leaned forward and slid one leg under the other. "Remember when I arrived, I had that garbage bag with me? It was full of my father's scientific papers. I inherited them. It turned out that one of his lab books was actually a diary. Until I read it, I never even knew he wrote poetry."

"He never told you?"

"I hardly knew him. My parents divorced when I was twelve, and he moved to Maine. I hardly ever saw him after that. There's so much I didn't know. And still don't. Like, why did you guys stop speaking? Did you have a fight? And how come he stopped writing poetry? In his diary it was almost all he cared about."

"Please sit."

"I'm already sitting."

"Oh, right. Hold on a minute."

I charged up the stairs.

Adrian rose and walked to the window. It had begun to rain again. All the summer, the rain had been a welcome break from the heat, but today it brought winds too cold to be of comfort. Yes, autumn was on its way. School would be starting soon. He looked down at the snapshot of his parents, which he still held. The snow-bank rose high out of the frame. A tree, laden with ice, wept its burden to the ground. The winter sun burned in the distance, hazy and small. He looked at his father, skinny, smiling, and tried to imagine the scratchy fit of his woolen trousers against his legs, the shiver of the raw wind against his neck, the rough warmth of his beloved's hand in his. He noticed for the first time that there were dark rings under his father's eyes. There was something forced about his smile, too, as though he were trying to conquer despair with willpower alone.

A slammed door, heavy thumps, and I was back, nose wiped, face washed, wearing a mohair sweater. I banged back in the leather, a hand held against my taxed heart. I reached for a cigarette.

"So many ghosts," I said, fumbling as I lighted it.

I wanted to get this over with as quickly as possible and avert another embarrassing display of grief, so I spoke rapidly without inflection. "Your father and I were pals," I said. "One Saturday we were in the cafeteria, when we noticed a tiny girl hunched over her books, drinking a malted. He liked her face, so we approached. The three of us chatted until the library closed. I found her strikingly ordinary, but he did not. The next day, your father rang her up and asked her to a dance. Very soon after, they were in love."

"My mother," the lad whispered reverently.

"No. Your mother was the girl's roommate. When your father caught the first girl rooting some dreadful greaser in the back of a Packard, he dumped her. *That's* when he began dating Nancy . . . your mother. A year later, they were engaged to be married. They had no choice."

"She was pregnant?"

"Heavens no. She was a prude. He proposed to her so that they *could* have sex. That's how things worked in those days. The well-bred girls were only willing to spread their legs once they had rocks on their fingers. Pardon my French." I nervously flicked my ash. "Anyway, the three of us were inseparable. Your mother studied pre-medicine in the corner while your father and I ignored our studies and recited poetry to each other. Dylan Thomas was all the rage then. I quickly discovered that your father had a gift. It was in the way he recited. A fine ear. I encouraged him to write poetry himself. Your mother found this absurd. He was very unsophisticated, you see. When they first met, he had admired Eisenhower. But soon your father was writing verse like a madman.

"Your mother once upbraided me, saying that she had fallen in love with a scientist and that I had turned him into a poet. But she was wrong. He was born a poet. Your mother thought poetry was like a good meal or a well-made shoe. Your father and I knew better. We knew that it changes forever the way one feels and sees and hears."

I stared off for a moment, toward the sideboard, as though the faces of the mighty dead of English verse flashed on the wall above it.

"I hate to be insensitive," I purred, "but your mother was a philistine." While the boy digested this difficult fact, I squashed out my fag and lighted another. "The day we graduated, your parents got married and moved to Ithaca. New York, not Greece. Where your father pursued his doctorate, studying God knows what.

"Hydra."

"Right. I was lucky enough to have a subsistence trust, left to me by my wicked adoptive father, which allowed me to move to San Francisco. My goal was to elevate the smelly-sweatered ethos of the post-Beats with a dash of panache and classicism. Your father and I promised to correspond, never to lose touch. Someday our children would play together. He still had no idea I liked only boys."

Adrian smiled skeptically.

I let it go.

"We wrote to each other twice a week. Finally, a few years later, after returning to the city and moving in here with Sasha, I hopped a bus to Ithaca. A visit was long overdue. I did not like what I found. Things had turned out badly for your parents. No money. Constant rows. Your mother wasn't pregnant yet, which depressed her to no end. Aside from a few hours of work at the medical library, she had nothing to occupy her. Your father was unhappy, too. Of course he was. An artist must never serve the Fates. He can only obey the Muses. He had no time for poetry anymore. He was stuck in the laboratory. So, I took drastic action. Someone had to."

"What did you do?"

"I told him the truth. I told him that he had made a mistake marrying your mother."

"Wow."

"Wow, indeed. I insisted that she did not really love him, or, if she did, it was not for what was best in him. I urged him to flee the marriage immediately, before children came."

"Did he get mad at you?"

"If he had, it might have blown over. Instead, he agreed. He poured his heart out to me in every direction. He showed me the poems that he'd written since our parting, not very many, but lovely, lyrical things about his growing up in nature . . . about his search for God. One was called 'River Stones,' and I remember lines of it even today. He said how he grieved the fact that he had no one to share them with. He missed me, you see."

"B. K.?" the boy asked. The question was so fraught with peril that it required him to ball his hands into fists. "Were you *in love* with my dad?"

A brave question that deserved a frank reply. I nodded slowly, feeling once again the great wound of my first love. I met his gaze.

"He loved me, too," I said.

I considered telling him the rest, but so little these days is held sacred. Besides, I feared he would be unable to comprehend it. So I added simply, "Otherwise, he never would have agreed to my plan."

"For him to leave my mom?"

"And everything else that thwarted his poetic gift—the charts, the test tubes. I was renting the basement here. All three rooms. What is today Michael's dungeon, I used for my calisthenics. I told your father we would make it his study. We would create a gorgeous but frugal life together, living only for art, supported by my trust. I knew Sasha would adore the plan." I sat up straighter, smiling as I relived the old excitement. "All shackles to the quotidian broken! With one brave cut of the cord!"

"What happened?"

"We synchronized our watches and I left town. He would arrive in Manhattan on a Greyhound bus three days later. I still remember the time—6:48 p.m. I counted the minutes. When the bus pulled in, I was there waiting, bearing gifts, but he did not get off. I slept at the bus station. He did not arrive on the next five buses either. Finally, I crawled home and rang him. Your mother answered and promptly hung up in my face. Clearly, he had told her everything. I wrote him a desperate letter. A plea."

"Did he write back?"

"Months later. He said a baby was on the way, that Nancy was feeling ill but blissful, and that they had never been more in love. I knew he was lying, of course. He was a poor liar. But now he had chosen to *live* a poor lie. Much worse than speaking one. No wonder he hit the sauce."

I looked over and was met by two of the saddest eyes I had ever seen.

"But some good *did* come of his choice," I whispered. "He and Nancy had a child. A boy. You're not too upset about *that,* I hope."

"I don't know," he muttered grimly. "Was it worth it? I've never read any of his poems."

"Trust me, you're every bit as gorgeous a creation."

It was then that we shared our first honest smile of the summer. It should come as no surprise to you that when Adrian returned to his cave that afternoon, relieved of his deceit, he sat down and began to write and did not stop for many days.

It Even Sings a Little

Benjamin whistled merrily, and for good reason. The first harbingers of fall were already tripping down the pavement. Ahead were chilly afternoons and early dusks; no more sweltering days. Eventually, winter would come, of course, and that would bring its own hardships, but he couldn't bother with that now. He parked his cart and mounted the steps of my house. A handcrafted sign in the window read, "ROOM FOR RENT." He gave the bell two sprightly rings, then peeked through the door's porthole window. The wind ruffled my blouse-sleeves as I dashed toward him. Lately, I had been so eager for my mail that he suspected, incorrectly, that I was expecting *good* news.

"Hello, Benjamin," I said as I opened up. I smiled bravely, grabbed my mail and, using a pair of garden shears, snapped the rubber band. I moved through the stack with a grimace. It was the second-to-last letter that stopped me.

"Oh, oh, oh! Here it is! So soon!" I held the letter against my chest. "I can't open it! You do it!" I extended it to him, but then pulled it back. "No, I mustn't be a coward."

"Have you got yourself a lady friend, Mr. Troop?" Ben teased.

Ignoring him, I ripped open the letter with my bare hands. I devoured the text, my eyes streaking down the page.

Embarrassed by the fact that the art gallery that was to launch her career also styled hair and served cocktails, Miranda had asked that we all miss the opening-night reception. Everyone reluctantly agreed, except for Michael. There was no reluctance in *his* agreement; he was overjoyed. But the little scamp had double-crossed him. That morning at dawn, dressed only in a nightshirt, she had appeared at his window and tapped the pane. When he lifted the blind, expecting to find a bird with a broken neck, she told him with supplicating eyes and fluttery hands that he *had* to come, he just *had* to be there.

Now, wearing a too-tight suit jacket and a tie, his chin clean-shaven, he was on his way. Even more embarrassing, he carried a bouquet of flowers wrapped in pastel tissue paper. Why had he agreed to come? He knew all about these sorts of things: crappy wine, putrid cheese, bored fashion models, loud-talking intellectuals, pony-tailed Eurotrash (their watches set to Prague time), hunchbacked homos smoking brown cigarettes—everybody milling from one painting to the next, sharing their opinions as though they actually had value, while the artist stood by, clammy-handed and panting for praise.

Maybe this one would be bearable somehow, he told himself, as he leaned down to a bundle of rags, checking to see whether the creature inside was alive. Miranda was his friend, after all, and he had been invited not for another warm body to fill the room, but because he was actually needed. She *needed* him, that's what she had said through the window. Of course she was wrong, but no one else was laboring under a similar delusion, and for some reason when she said it, he had not recoiled. Seeing that the wretched female inside the rags was, like himself, not dead but merely dying, he considered giving her the flowers, but he gave her five dollars instead. When he reached the gallery, now named The Manhattan Public House, Michael stopped at the storefront window, which was decorated with an antique barber pole, gaudy beer steins, and a poster announcing Miranda's debut. Inside, there was a crowd he did not recognize: no Francophiles dressed in black, no pretentious twits decked out in Soho motley. No, these were the same types that had destroyed the bar where he worked and were now threatening to spoil the entire planet: women with cyclone hair streaked with silvery highlights, men in suits and vests and spotted ties. Potbellies hung over designer belts, beefy grins slurped at imported beer. Everywhere, crispy leather, dark tans, white teeth, and designer watches. And worst of all, not one drop of black or brown or yellow skin tinged the Caucasian sea that flowed from the door all the way to the steps of the haircutting loft.

Fighting an urge to cut and run, Michael heaved a deep breath and squeezed inside. He fought his way to the steel bar. To get the barkeep's attention, he waved a twenty. While he waited for his highball, he remembered with a jolt the reason that he was there. He turned around to look at the paintings, but a wall of loud, oblivious fools blocked his view. They were not looking at the art. Their backs were turned to it. He picked up scraps of their conversations:

"Yeah, yeah, I talked to Stu last week. It rained every day. He was so pissed, he closed the house down and flew to Spain."

"I know! I know! And they weren't even on sale!"

"How am I supposed to get the place clean, when she can't understand me? My Spanish is okay as far as nouns go, but verbs? Forget it."

"Where's Scooter? Have you seen Scooter?"

"Four bedrooms just isn't enough anymore!"

When his drink arrived, Michael held out the twenty to the bartender and told him to hang on to it. When he needed another drink, he'd signal.

A voice rang out: *"Mike!"*

Jerry Sheridan, his head barely swimming above the crowd, was making his way over. "Don't you pay for that! Don't you dare!" Michael jammed the bill in the barkeep's hand. "Aw, why'd you do that?" Jerry moaned when he arrived. "I wanted to spot you one!"

"Not necessary." Michael had met Jerry last week, during the hanging of the paintings, and had hated him at first sight.

Jerry dropped a hand on Michael's big shoulder. "Great turnout, huh? Unbelievable! Hey, Nicole! *Nicole!*"

A woman by the door was being helped on with an admiral's jacket, adorned with gold epaulettes. When she saw Jerry, she pushed a smile, smeared with petulance.

Jerry shouted: "You happy? You *like* the new you?" She ran her painted claws through her freshly cut hair and nodded, showing the same nasty smile. "God, that girl!" Jerry said, turning back to Michael. "Shoulda married her. Smart, cute. But I just wasn't ready to settle down." He flashed a lascivious smile. "I'm still not." He slapped Michael affectionately on the arm, rattling his flowers. "Got a cigarette?" Jerry's eyes darted away and he spoke to someone across the room. "What? Oh, okay, sure, see you next week! You get the court! Yeah, *you* book it, you dick! I'm not your friggin' secretary!"

Michael shook him out a cancer stick.

Jerry took it with a look of good-humored shock. "Whoa, no filters. Tough guy, huh?" He leaned in for a light. "So what do you think of the place? Great concept, right? Although I don't know how Miranda's stuff's gonna do. Her work's a little *out there* for this crowd."

"Out *where?*"

"You know what I mean."

"No, I don't. Where is she?"

"I was just gonna ask you." He turned to look for her, but he spotted someone else. "Phil! Whaddaya think of the art?" Phil could not hear him, so Jerry tugged at the sleeve of a giant standing nearby. "Whaddaya think, Ted? About the paintings? Not bad, huh?"

"Frankly?"

"Sure, why not?"

"Looks like a bunch of pussies."

Two young men nearby broke out laughing.

"Easy now," Jerry warned.

"You asked for my opinion, I gave it to you." Ted shrugged dismissively. "It's one pussy after another. It's not erotic, it's not beautiful. It's just gross."

Michael's spine stiffened. He laid his glass down with a sharp crack.

Jerry whispered. "Relax, Mike—he's a developer. What the hell does he know?"

"He's your friend."

"So?"

"So tell him to *learn some manners!*"

Ted, overhearing, pushed his way over. "What, you got a problem with me, friend?"

"Uh-huh. Why don't you go home and count your money and leave art appreciation to—"

"I've got a right to my opinion! You don't know me!"

"I know a million of you."

"Oh, yeah? Well, if it weren't for Jerry here, I'd tear your goddamn head off!"

"Tear the head off these instead!" Michael smashed the bouquet into the man's mouth.

Customers recoiled and gasped.

Ted stumbled back, spitting, then he charged at Michael.

Jerry lunged, blocking his way. "It's not worth it!"

"You punk!" Ted screamed. There were petals on his face and pollen on the hairs of his chest. "Come on! Outside! I'm gonna teach you a lesson!"

"I don't need an MBA."

There was laughter.

"That's it! Let's go!" Ted grabbed Michael by the jacket. "Come on, *outside!*"

Michael violently jerked free. "Forget it! Someone might see us together. I have a reputation to uphold."

"Motherfucker!" Ted lunged with new strength, but Jerry stopped him and shoved him toward the door, pouring into his ear a steady stream of mollifying talk.

Ted protested. "Look what he did to my shirt! You're gonna let him get away with that? You're gonna let scum like that—"

The door closed and they were gone.

Michael shook his head, trying not to smile. It might be time to go. He turned and saw Miranda at the end of the bar, working her way toward him, looking frightened. He felt a surge of affection for her. She was right. She *did* need him. It struck him hard. He had a choice to make.

"Miranda!" Jerry shouted as he reentered. "Come here! *Now!*"

Michael did not like his tone. He turned around and told him so. Jerry's little eyes bugged and there was spit at the corners of his mouth.

"Go!" Jerry barked. "Now or I'll call the cops!"

"What happened?" Miranda asked, reaching them.

"Nothing," Michael said. "A minor mêlée. Here—" He picked the bouquet off the floor. "These are for you. Congratulations."

She accepted the gift happily, as though it were not squashed and mangled.

Michael grabbed her other hand and turned to Jerry. "We'll be back for her paintings tomorrow."

Minutes later, walking backward, swinging her flowers, Miranda, beside herself with happiness, asked him how he knew that that was exactly what she wanted, to cancel her show and never come back.

"Misogynist's intuition," Michael replied. He stopped short and smiled. "What did you do to your hair?"

"Yvonne Metz cut it. For free. What, you don't like it?"

When he saw how much it mattered to her what he thought, he stepped close and, unable to stop himself, kissed her on the mouth. She dropped her flowers and slapped her hands across his broad chest and kissed him back, open-mouthed, with surprising strength. (There was an ox in the girl; her hungers were limitless.)

When she pulled away, she cried, "When I saw you come in, I died of embarrassment! I hid in the bathroom! But you didn't leave! I can't believe you didn't leave!"

"I *did* leave," he said softly.

"But you took me with you. Why, Michael? Is it because you care about me? Is that why?"

He pulled her close and looked over her head at the green streetlights and bleeding neon. He ran his hands through her short, silky hair. Mere words could not answer her question, or any other question, for that matter. Answers lived in action. But sometimes people needed words, anyway.

"Sure, I care about you," he said. "I might even love you a little."

She gasped and pulled away with suspended joy. She wanted his face to show the same look of rapture as hers. When it did not, she shook him by the lapels. "Don't look sad! Why do you look so sad all the time?"

He felt his eyes grow even heavier.

She hurled herself back into his arms. "God, I love you so much I'm going to explode!"

An hour later, the two lovers, still strangers to each other, lay side by side in his narrow bed. With her head on his shoulder, she wrote the word "mine" over and over again with a fingernail on the muscles of his bare chest.

She spoke cutely: "All right, so today wasn't very good for my career, but it was *very* good for me personally, right?" He nodded, his eyes shut. "And your day was very good personally, too, but it was nothing professionally, right?" Again, he nodded. "Well, that's not fair, is it? I mean, a good relationship should be equal, right? So, I think I should tell you what my uncle said." Michael's breathing stopped. "Remember what *you* said about your work? That it was depressing and narcissistic?"

"I just said it was depressing."

"Oh. Well, he agrees with you. Only he thinks it's narcissistic, too." She slapped a hand over his mouth. "*But.* He said you have tons of talent. A gift for language. And he said you'd do better if you wrote about other people, not just yourself. I defended you. I said, 'But he doesn't *know* any other people.'"

He sputtered a laugh beneath her hand.

"But you will. You're going to know me now."

She removed her hand and replaced it with a kiss.

My joy upon learning that my monthly disability checks would not only continue but be generously increased was immense, but it gave way in no time to the most abject melancholy. To aggravate matters, my wine rack was empty and I was too inert to restock it. As the sun fell, I sat motionless at the patio table, sober as a judge, bathed in the amber glow of a security bulb. The night was made menacing by an eerie gibbous moon, veined with shadow. The future had never looked so grim to me. I sat with a protective hand across my midriff. The other held a cigarette. In front of me the *Times* lay open.

"B. K.?" a voice said, from the shadows.

I gasped and turned. "What? Who is it?"

"Just me. Mind if I join you?"

I nodded Adrian closer.

"What's wrong?" he asked worriedly.

"Everything. Come. Sit. Allow me to bore you to ribbons."

He took the wicker next to mine. I torched a fag for him. For a minute we said nothing, mingling smoke.

"Tell me," he said finally.

"The feds," I answered.

"What about them? You got what you wanted."

"Yes, but you see, I told them the truth. The whole truth and nothing but." I turned to him with an imploring look. "And yet they still declared me mentally ill."

"Maybe it was your clothes."

"Or because I *am* ill."

I left a silence for him to disagree.

He did not.

I shook my head, rattling the newspaper. "I don't understand how ordinary people do it. Look at these jobs! Systems Analyst. Marketing Consultant. Key Punch Operator. I don't even know what these mean! If I had been denied my benefits and forced into the market-place, I'd have been lost. There's no place for me in this society."

"There's a place for you *here.*"

"Yes, to let out absurdly inexpensive rooms to young artists who avoid me like the plague."

"I don't avoid you."

"The others do. They deem me a cumber and a nuisance at best. At worst, they despise me."

"That's not true. And even if it was, where would they be without you?"

"Elsewhere. Less bothered."

"They'd be working day and night to pay their rents. At jobs just as gross as the ones in that paper. And I'd be in graduate school."

"Perish the thought."

"Miranda's got her show. Louise is on the last chapter of her novel. Mary's gonna give us a concert. Miranda's uncle's gonna keep reading Michael's short stories. Carl's gonna . . . be on TV. All these exciting things and none of it could have happened without you. You should be really proud."

"You're very kind," I whispered.

"*Also.* Drum roll, please." He put out his cigarette and reached into his back pocket. "I've written something."

"What?" I asked, suddenly alert.

"Nothing. A poem, but it's bad."

I lunged for the page, then froze. "No. You recite it. Whenever possible, one's introduction to a poem should begin with the poet's own voice."

"Really?"

I nodded. He nervously smoothed the paper. I sat back and closed my eyes.

"Read slowly," I instructed. "Very slowly. One word at a time."

He cleared his throat, then began, his voice shaky:

Youth

I've yet to place my morning star
Amidst the dark and numbered sky.
And yet it will, as all things must,
Achieve its apogee in time.

My soul is untried power,
My heart an unspent trust;
But neither knows the chill
Of death's encroaching touch.

I pass these days in constant bloom,
Oblivious, in steady climb.
The oldest truth revealed to Man:
Youth—a bold and blinded time.

We exhaled together.

"It's bad, isn't it?" he whispered, looking at the page.

"Yes."

"Shit!" He threw it down with disgust.

"But it's also good."

His uncomprehending eyes slowly lifted to meet my wise and worldly ones.

"Because it's sincere," I said. "It even sings a little."

"Really?"

"Really."

"But . . . then . . . what's bad about it?"

"Everything else."

"Oh."

"But it doesn't matter." My mood was lifting. I was gaining energy. "It's just a beginning. A first step in a long journey."

"Oh. Okay. So what do I do next?"

"Learn your tradition. Fill your soul with images of magnificence. Gorge on wonders. Pan your native tongue for gold." He tried to speak, but I gestured him silent. I felt a surge of happiness and hope, as though *I* were the one with the talent. I leaned forward and took his hands in both of mine. "But it's so much more than the work, boy. It's a way of life. Poetry is a balm to the soul's care. And the pursuit of it is unlike anything else. No one lives as the artist does. The burden is terrible, but so is the freedom. Most people *think* they're free, but in fact they're just caged birds, hopping from perch to perch until they're dead. But the artist is *truly* free! He knows it every time he sets pen to paper, experiencing what the Gods felt on the first day of creation. Even if you give up one day, go back and pursue your studies, what a marvelous adventure you'll have had!"

Adrian bit his lip with fear, but at the same time lightning flashed in his eye. I knew at this moment that there was something in the boy that his father, for all of his gifts, had lacked. Christopher had lacked it, too. For lack of a better term, I will call it *the hunger for an alternative universe.* Yes, it was true. Adrian loved his dreams more than he did life.

"Will you stay?" I pleaded. "Stay so I can be of help to you? If you do, I promise to be happy."

The lad broke into a smile and, without the slightest warning, embraced me. I was so surprised it took my breath away, but, once I had recovered, I hugged him back. I tell you, Cynical Reader, with all the honesty of which I am capable, I felt not even a hint of impure longing. I felt as though I were holding *my son*.

One story above, dear, lunatic Louise watched us from the bathroom window. Her magical eyes spun and her electric hair danced like happy snakes. It was the ending of her novel, the ending she had been searching for on her long, unpremeditated search: a cold, black sky dotted with a sprinkling of stars, a lover's moon with a bite taken out of it, and down below the sweeping away of ghosts.

Adieu

Since that summer there have been many more summers, but few quite so charmed. Lodgers have come and gone, some heading off toward lives of artistic fulfillment, others toward madness and marriage or, worse, mediocrity. I am reluctant to share with you what happened to the six lodgers who have filled these pages and in whom you have invested your hearts and time. I am loath to dash, or even to confirm, whatever fond or foolish hopes you hold for their futures. I am a novelist, however, which means I am, at the marrow, merciless.

Miranda Buchner and Michael Shannon were wed. Not to each other, but to partners less damaged, to whom they were, therefore, far better matched, but less passionately. Michael was first. One fine spring morning, I subwayed off to a Catholic church in Queens and watched as he pledged undying fidelity to a young Nicaraguan named Alma something. They live today in Poughkeepsie, New York, where Alma raises their two hairy children and Michael teaches English at a local junior college, toiling all the while on a gargantuan novel brimming with characters who bear little resemblance to himself. He has refused to show me any pages until it is complete, which I have a hunch will be never, but he seems to thrive on the process.

A year later, Miranda, by now a successful society portrait painter specializing in dogs, followed him down the aisle, hitching her wagon to a duck-footed, sway-backed financial analyst named Daniel something who bears the slick, unpleasant patina of a retired jewel thief. For some reason, she adores him. I know this only by way of hearsay. I did not attend the ceremony or the reception, because it was lavish, repulsive, and I was not invited.

I am happy to report that Mary Pilango and Caroline Lang are still together, having settled into the sort of domestic contentment so prevalent among their kind. I believe the mental health care professionals call it "lesbian bed-death." There are lots of cuddles and kisses, but very few shared orgasms. Yet their love is deep. Mary has forged a fine career for herself, not as a singer-songwriter, but as a songwriter. She is quite wealthy and last year the pair moved to Vermont, where they live in bucolic splendor. Mary composes out back, while Caroline runs a health-food restaurant on Main Street (carob milk and almond steak a specialty).

Carl Alan Dealey is also a success, not only as a peddler of panties but as an actor. A few summers ago, I and one of my newest charges, a gifted saxophonist (à la Sonny Rollins, but of Danish extraction), boarded a bus and arrived at the Jersey shore just in time to see Carl play Levin in a dinner-theater adaptation of *Anna Karenina*. Sadly, the great work had been set to music by a local singing teacher and Carl has a bad voice. Still, the audience seemed to enjoy his game performance, as did he. Having grown quite fat and sporting a bald spot the size of a yarmulke, he now bears slight resemblance to Franchot Tone. He is married to a once-slender schoolteacher and is the proud father of five gorgeous little girls.

Poor Louise D'Aprix. Nothing would please me more than to report that she managed to control the conflagration of her four-alarm blood, but, even when she returned to her lithium, her mania progressed unabated. She stopped writing and began to shop instead, indulging in furious spending sprees financed with kited checks. Just when it appeared that the parade of debt collectors and policemen at my doorstep was going to force me to kick her out, she disappeared. A few years later, I thought I spotted her, filthy and scabby, staggering up the steep decline of the Guggenheim Museum, but I could not be sure. Because no one ever came to claim her belongings, after a few years I sold them on the sidewalk in lieu of back rent. All that remains in my possession today is her tattered parasol and the big manuscript of her formless but brilliant novel, from whose pages I have liberally borrowed to write this one. If she ever reappears, I will share my royalties with her, but I am almost certain that they won't amount to much and that she is dead.

As for Adrian Daigle, our hero, *my* hero, I swell with pride to tell you that he has devoted his life to art. Oddly, he and Carl were both right, for he works as both a poet and a waiter. There are no riches to be won as a poet, but if there were, he would be wealthy, indeed. His quill is nimble. His work is lyrical, learned, and sometimes even a touch sublime. He consecrates whatever he looks upon. One day the world will know it. Until then, he will live, as he does today, in The House Beautiful, where in his cozy garret he passes his free hours reading and writing, sometimes smoking and at other times resolutely not smoking. Except for occasional bouts of rage and self-pity, born mostly of his inability to secure a life partner, or even a temporary bedmate, he is at one with himself. Our friendship is the finest thing I have ever known.

Now for our supporting players: Yung Su rots behind bars. (I have not had a steady boyfriend since.) The mystery of what happened to the mortal coil of Dr. Gary Marker remains unsolved. Cassandra married Emiliano and moved to Arizona. Appearances often deceive, but from the looks of the pair in their photo-Christmas cards, they seem to grow happier and more in love with each passing year, even as they wrinkle and bake, hurtling toward melanoma under the bland Tucson sun. Toby Twain died of an accidental overdose. The jealous Tanya Hill is fat and the star of a soap opera. Benjamin still delivers my mail.

Which brings me to myself—a wonderful terminus.

All things considered, I am not half-bad, having somehow dodged the dire fate of many, if not all, male homosexuals over sixty. (Loneliness, depression, plastic surgery, public spectacle, suicide.) My hair is nearly gone, yes, but I wear a russet beard flaked with snow that almost compensates. My health is less than perfect, I am sorry to report—my cheek is loose, my belly big, my memory poor, my wind short, and my heart failing—but I do not let it bring me down. If the weather is pleasant, I perambulate the city with enormous pride in my position. I wear a well-brimmed felt hat, strung with plastic laurel. The effect is staggering. When I return from my walks, I have my lodgers, my books, my smokes, my wines, my Adrian, and my unexpected career as a novelist.

Whatever the future holds, no one and nothing can rob me of the wonderful years I have spent surrounded by so much youth and genius. Certain of nothing but the holiness of the heart's affections and the truth of the imagination, I am continually inspired by these brave young souls, who spend their days and nights attempting to express the inexpressible, to lend form and beauty to what is and what must always remain random and hideous. Failure is their very medium. They are born to it, live in it, breathe it, and, in the end, die of it. If an autopsy is performed, traces of failure are found in the marrow of their bones. And they wouldn't have it any other way. They know that failure is what makes their calling tragic and singular. And, through it all, they never stop seeking companions with whom to share their lives.

Their example has been a gift, a grand consolation to me. Over the years, it has been my one indissoluble tie to the universe, to the eternal cycle of life that runs from conception to abundance to decay. I have been brought closer to it by every work of art, every season of love, that over the years I have seen them step into, inhabit, and leave behind.